**Their pursuers
were relentless . . .**

Amanda sat in the cab of the old school bus, terrified. The Mercedes had been on their trail ever since Mexico City. Now it was approaching the barbwire fence that the bus had just driven through.

"Go!" Brad shouted to Enrique, who was hunched over the wheel.

The bus, its engine straining, jerked and bumped, then slowly began to gain speed. It had traveled almost fifty yards when the Mercedes hit the fence head on. The barbwire snapped with explosive reports.

Amanda knew that the car would be upon them in seconds—and they would be at the mercy of killers. . . .

## ABOUT THE AUTHOR

Rianna Craig is the pseudonym of a married couple who are a team in all endeavors—as authors, film producers and directors, and maritime historians. Residents of Houston and the parents of five children, they once spent three years aboard an old schooner and now own a small, private maritime museum. Their love of Mexico has provided the setting for *On Executive Orders*, their first Intrigue.

## Books by Rianna Craig

HARLEQUIN AMERICAN ROMANCE
56–LOVE MATCH

These books may be available at your local bookseller.

Don't miss any of our special offers. Write to us at the following address for information on our newest releases.

Harlequin Reader Service
901 Fuhrmann Blvd., P.O. Box 1397, Buffalo, NY   14240
Canadian address: P.O. Box 2800, Postal Station A,
5170 Yonge St., Willowdale, Ont.   M2N 6J3

# ON EXECUTIVE ORDERS

## ORDERS

### RIANNA CRAIG

# *Harlequin Books*

TORONTO • NEW YORK • LONDON
AMSTERDAM • PARIS • SYDNEY • HAMBURG
STOCKHOLM • ATHENS • TOKYO • MILAN

To the warm and loving people
of Mexico

Harlequin Intrigue edition published April 1986

ISBN 0-373-22039-1

# Chapter One

Amanda knew it was going to be one of those days. Everything had been fouled up since dawn. First her early-morning workout had gone wrong. Her company car wouldn't start. Then came a mechanical breakdown at the bottling plant, followed by some office problems an hour ago. That was when she'd kissed it all off and gone to lunch early. Not the best way for the regional manager to react, she knew, but the deed was done.

The air was already fiercely hot. Mexico City's traffic was at its worst—and this was only May. What would August be like? Amanda paid the taxi driver and dismissed him in the crush of cars half a block from her destination even though her ankle was tender and she wore three-inch heels. Taking a deep breath, she imagined herself safely across the wide avenue, then clutched her shoulder bag and made a dash for it. She was doing fine until a streak of gold honked so near that she jumped back, scared to death. As the grinning driver whipped the Jaguar around, he cut much too close for safety and zoomed away.

"Fool! Crazy fool!" she gasped, then continued across the street. Her mood was blackened further at the thought of tourists who endangered lives merely to get a woman's attention.

When she arrived at the entrance to the Palacio del Sol, one of the city's exclusive hotels, she couldn't help but notice the long black limousine. Its darkened windows reflected the sun into her eyes as it eased around the stalled traffic and came to a stop three cars away from her. American flags fluttered from its front fenders. Amanda wrinkled her upturned nose in disapproval. As Harvey would say, this was just one more example of a diplomat's throwing his weight around and flaunting his position.

Across the wide avenue, seated in a low-slung black Porsche, a thin, hard-faced man and his squat companion also took note of the scene. The man at the wheel switched on his two-way radio as he watched the crush of people being swallowed by the huge brass doors of the magnificent hotel.

The moment Amanda disappeared inside, a uniformed driver opened the back door of the diplomatic-corps limousine. A pair of long, shapely legs emerged. They belonged to a tall, striking blonde, middle-aged, ramrod erect and exuding power. The woman said something to her driver while carefully smoothing the slim skirt of her cream linen suit; a few moments later she, too, entered the hotel.

The sinister stick of a man sitting in the Porsche held a microphone to his mouth. "Information correct," he said in Spanish. "Subject has arrived at destination—as you predicted. What do you wish us to do?" Although his tone was grudging, it bore a calculated measure of respect.

"Patience, Guando! Watch the street and await my orders." The voice coming over the radio responded decisively against a background of noisy static and the muffled sounds of other voices. "I'll handle this my way."

"Yes, El Tigre," he said, then replaced the microphone and snapped off the radio with a vicious flick of his fingers. The long knife scar on the left side of his face darkened. He closed his fists over the steering wheel and squeezed tightly, trying to keep a rein on his anger. "Patience, Guando!" he echoed with a snarl at his heavyset, swarthy companion. This business of waiting grated on Guando's nerves. "In minutes I could have more information than we will ever get by doing things in a—civilized manner. Why not move in now and take what we want from that woman?" But he would wait as instructed. He quaked involuntarily at the thought of El Tigre's wrath if he disobeyed.

Guando hated women, and vice versa, especially those he subjected to his carnal demands. An idea occurred to him and provoked a hideous smile. Perhaps this woman didn't have the answers with her; she might resist.

Inside the building, Amanda savored the cooling effects of the air conditioning as she crossed the spacious lobby to the restaurant. The plush room hummed with the energy of the luncheon crowd and the clink of silverware on china.

Where was the maître d'? Not even a waiter was in sight. Amanda sighed and seated herself at a table near the entry that gave her a view of the lobby. She glanced at her delicate diamond wristwatch, her engagement gift from Harvey. He was late. That was odd. Late for the first time in his life.

Good old dull Harvey. What a terrible way to think of one's fiancé, she mused. He was attentive, dependable, a good businessman...and dull. She felt a familiar stab of guilt and that indecisive, trapped feeling she always got whenever thoughts of her wedding day loomed too close. Amanda wondered if she was unconsciously causing her own problems, trying once more to escape the encroaching reality of a boring future with Harvey.

A busboy appeared with a crystal glass of water. She sipped it and let her attention circle to the bar.

Several people noted the half smile that hovered on Amanda's lips as her alert, intelligent gray eyes took a quick inventory of the frenetic action. She caught sight of a few celebrities among the tourists and local businessmen who jockeyed for space along the ornate, heavily carved wood-and-brass bar. Its overstated elegance, which she considered typical architecture for tourists, had no appeal for her.

Then she saw her young friend, Enrique, neatly groomed in his black-and-gold bellboy uniform, cross to the bar and call out, "Paging Mr. George D. Slater." He stopped in front of an aging, publicity-hungry American congressman who was busy introducing himself to a beautiful, flame-haired female.

Amanda recognized the woman as the internationally famous newspaper publisher Zena Ballanger. Her face often appeared on the front page of various weekly tabloids; her controversial use of the press made headlines. But the lovely, soft-spoken Ballanger also had monumental achievements to her credit in the world of journalism.

Enrique, the self-professed sharpest bellboy at the Palacio del Sol, suddenly sported a wide grin as he accepted what must have been a large tip from the congressman. He pivoted on his heel and with great

Latin dignity, threaded his undersized, wiry body through the crowd. Enrique was fifteen years old but looked about twelve. Amanda smiled to herself. What he lacked in stature, he made up for in moxie. Enrique was truly a treasure. Only she seemed out of step with the world, unable to find a hint of happiness anywhere in her future.

She tried not to stare, but her table was situated so that she could watch unobtrusively. As one woman judging another, Amanda had to admire not only Zena's Dresden-doll-perfect complexion but also the graceful flourish with which the woman made the most ordinary movements. She'd just snapped her handbag closed—a good-looking buttery leather one. Tucking the slim rectangle ever so gracefully under her arm, she dazzled the leering congressman with a cool smile, the kind that did not cause even one crinkle in the corners of her eyes.

A neat trick, but Amanda could never master it. She took a sip of water and watched Zena's hand float upward like a feather to accept a note Slater was handing her. He paid her homage with a heavy mustachioed kiss on her delicate fingers. The woman reacted with perfect aplomb; her radiance seemed to capture everyone around her.

Amanda's musings were cut off by the virile arrogance of a dark-eyed devil who was smiling directly at her from the bar. Shocked, she slashed him with a look of haughty disapproval and hoped it censored his smile, then cut her eyes away to gaze indifferently at the crowded tables beside her.

Still her mind's eye retained an image of the man— medium height, broad shoulders, white knit shirt over a tight, flat stomach, white tennis shorts. Something about him was vaguely familiar. She turned slightly. The movement of his tanned hand raking through smooth, dark blond hair hooked her attention again. He proceeded to stare her down, then had the gall to wink knowingly, insinuating a dream of possession.

She turned her back to him. Just another Yankee bastard on the make. She could do without this irritation.

Obviously, the man was everything Harvey wasn't—in looks, anyway. Harvey wasn't very exciting, but he was reliable—until today, of course.

She adjusted the skirt of her entirely correct, conservatively tailored navy blue suit. Remembering her new straw hat, wide brimmed and high crowned to make her appear taller, she removed it. It wasn't fashionable, just necessary in this climate. She had a few too many freckles spattering her nose as it was.

Automatically, she sifted her fingers through her short brown hair, pressed flat by the hat. She envied women with long hair, straight and soft, but kept her natural curls extremely short to withstand her daily gymnastic workouts. Suddenly self-conscious, she dropped her hand, afraid that the man at the bar might mistake her gesture for flirtation.

Amanda focused her attention on the ankle she'd twisted that morning. She crossed her legs and slowly pointed her toe, then made small circles with the stiff ankle to test the injury. *Should have put ice on it. Must exercise more carefully. Warm up longer and don't get sloppy. Give it a few days' rest.*

Abruptly, she stifled a bored yawn. Where was Harvey? Had Mexico City's infamous snarled traffic claimed his perfect record at last?

El Tigre's eyes narrowed at the sight of Amanda's feigned yawn. This woman was easy to read, even when reflected in the dim shadows of the oversized mirror behind the bar. The time spent waiting at this vantage point had been worthwhile.

Imperiously, El Tigre scanned the mirrored reflection of the entire decadent scene—the loud-mouthed tourists, the leering business people, the opportunistic congressman, George Slater, attempting to gain either publicity or an afternoon of sexual entertainment from a newspaperwoman. Such futile, petty goals. Terrible waste of precious time. And time was all anyone ever really had. Ah, there now! Exactly on schedule. So predictable. Amanda Perry was the chosen one. Why?

"Ms. Perry?" a woman's incisive, clear voice inquired just over Amanda's shoulder.

Amanda turned, still recovering from her yawn. "Excuse me." Her hand covered her lips and muffled her husky voice. "Yes, I'm Amanda Perry." A message from Harvey, no doubt, expressing his regret for being late. Good old thoughtful Harvey.

She looked up to see a stiffly coiffured but smartly attired middle-aged blonde extending her gloved hand. Amanda grasped the smooth kidskin and noted the woman's firm grip.

Dark eyes zeroed in. "Hello, I'm Margaret Cullen, officer in charge of the Economic Section, United States Embassy. May I join you?"

Amanda blinked at her tone, more like a command than a request, and replied with trepidation, "Certainly."

Nearly all American residents in Mexico City had heard of the politically powerful Ms. Margaret Cullen from the embassy. She was always bad news. Was something wrong with Amanda's passport, or worse yet, her import license? That was all she needed. All the biggies would eat her alive. The soft-drink business had to be one of the most cutthroat in the world.

With intimidating confidence, the older woman placed herself in the chair next to Amanda. "Thank you," Margaret Cullen said as she perused the crowded dining room. "Perfect," she murmured, then nodded almost imperceptibly at a man standing at the bar. Amanda caught the movement, however, and realized that he was the same man who had winked at her moments ago. His grin seemed rakish, brash, and Amanda thought it killed his appeal. But not to Ms. Cullen, who apparently had a friend several years her junior at best.

Unable to wait for the bad news, Amanda asked, "What have I done wrong now?" She sounded peevish but didn't care. Doing business internationally was always difficult, but lately it had become nearly impossible, or so it seemed. Always more and more regulations.

"Done wrong?" Margaret Cullen echoed. "Oh, my, you've done nothing wrong. It's the State Department that has the problem. I need your help, Ms. Perry."

"My help?" Amanda became alert.

"Yes."

"Hmm. That's a switch."

Ms. Cullen spoke softly. "I suppose so, but it happens. You were specifically chosen."

"Me? Why? How do you know me?"

"We didn't exactly know you at first. But we had heard of you because of your father."

"Oh, I see." Amanda felt glum again and shrank back into her chair. "I'm afraid I'm nothing like him."

"Very few people are. Medal of Honor winner, colonel in the Army Rangers, commando raider. A loyal American with nerves of steel. He was quite a man." Her sigh held a wistful strain. "Quite a man. However, that is not the reason I'm here to talk to you. It's true that we keep dossiers on Americans who could help us. They are handy things to have when the State Department finds itself in a wringer and has to ask for help from a patriotic American citizen."

Amanda felt this woman's forceful dark-eyed scrutiny and tried to modify her reaction. "Well, I'm flattered, of course, but I'm merely the regional manager of Tri-Cola, and our bottling works is just coming out of the red. We're not even really on our feet yet. I couldn't be of any use to the government."

"Oh, not true at all. You are perhaps the only person in Mexico City who can help us."

Amanda was dubious. "Me! How?"

The State Department representative shifted in her chair and began to remove her gloves, pulling slowly at each fingertip as she proceeded to explain. "Diplomacy on an international level is the art of never appearing to be in trouble, even if you're up to your neck in piranhas."

"I see," Amanda lied.

"Yes, of course you do," Margaret Cullen agreed, implying they were equals. "The State Department is in a bubbling stew as of this moment. Washington has dumped the mess into the capable hands of our U.S. ambassador here in Mexico City."

"And he's tossed the ball to you," Amanda said, glancing about for Harvey, or a waiter.

"Perceptive of you. Yes, it's an explosive situation that must be defused before it blows up in Uncle Sam's face—to be frank about it."

Amanda had heard enough. "Pardon me, Ms. Cullen, but you have the wrong Perry. My father would have jumped at the opportunity to grab a bomb and run with it, but he's dead!" That word resounded in her head. She felt the bile of guilt well up, and then a need to soften her statement. She cleared her throat and said slowly, "I'm as loyal as the next person, but I'm neither interested nor qualified. I adored my father. I probably even learned a few things from him, but I'm just a company manager, not a commando."

Margaret Cullen suppressed a smile. The spirited, straightforward young woman before her was truly perfect for the task. "Oh, you're qualified." She was irritatingly matter-of-fact. "But I'm not talking about physical fitness and self-defense and commando tactics. That was the old days. Today we need a person of exceptional ability and resourcefulness—and your business qualifications." She hurried on to enrich the prospect. "Your country's economic security is at stake. There's an old saying: when the U.S. sneezes, Europe gets a cold, Japan already has pneumonia and the rest of the world markets are ready to expire."

Amanda's gray eyes narrowed. "I suppose that's a veiled threat to Tri-Cola and Company."

"My dear! Never! I'm appealing to your—" she paused for emphasis "—sense of duty."

The woman had hit a nerve. Amanda was ambivalent. It seemed America was always doing something that made her extremely proud or extremely embarrassed. For a moment she contemplated the gold linen tablecloth, debating her response. Reluctantly, she sighed. "Well, I guess you can tell me about it."

Margaret Cullen needlessly folded her gloves in her lap and allowed no triumph in her voice. "You're not expected to make a decision at this moment. Just give me your answer after you've heard what it's all about. I assure you, it can be a simple yes or no. Only I will know that you've been approached on the matter, and I'll respect your wishes. But I must have your answer this afternoon." Her eyes swept the room. "We can't talk here, of course. Do you see that man at the bar?"

Amanda followed the woman's gaze. "That one? How could I miss him?" She didn't try to hide her scorn. "He winked at me, ogling like some overage jock playboy. You'd better tell him to get his act together if he's some kind of agent."

A stern look crossed Margaret Cullen's features, then disappeared. "Oh, good heavens, I was afraid of that. His hormones are a little active." Her voice hardened. "Don't worry; I'll attend to him."

"Thank you."

"Anyway, I'd like you to wait for about ten minutes after I leave, then go out the front door and meet him."

"Meet him? Of all people—" Amanda stole a glance at the man. Disbelief flooded her features. That did it! She'd cancel now and have nothing more to do with Ms. Cullen's project. But while she stared at the man, she couldn't deny that he was an attractive person. Suddenly, a very unexpected—and disconcerting—tingle began somewhere in her body. She could see he'd finished his drink and was paying the bartender in preparation to leave.

Ms. Cullen continued her instructions. "He'll be in a gold Jaguar sports car, waiting at the curb." She started to rise from her chair. "You couldn't miss it if you tried."

Gold Jaguar! That was why he looked familiar. "Wait a minute," Amanda hissed, suddenly aware of what she had agreed to. "Your agent nearly ran me down earlier as I left my taxi. I can't leave here with him. No—I must get back to my office. And I'm waiting for my—"

"Yes, yes, I know." Margaret Cullen didn't give an inch. Her forceful will encased her voice. "You're waiting for Mr. Harvey Bannon, your fiancé. You're to be married next week, having prolonged the inevitable for two years. You've had a terrible morning at your office. The intermittent gear on the bottle indexing machine has broken down. To be exact, it's the Geneva star drive that advances the bottles with perfect accuracy for filling, capping and packaging. You must order a new gear from LaCross Machine Works in Illinois. You're bored with Harvey. You're an excellent company manager. And you are the only person who can help your government—" the lady chose her words carefully "—out of a hell of a jam."

"How do you know all that?" Amanda demanded, her voice hoarse, her mouth desert dry. At least the woman hadn't mentioned her fall from the balance beam that morning. Small comfort.

"I told you, my job. I learn as much as possible about every American in Mexico City."

"Is that legal?"

"Look, Ms. Perry, we're wasting valuable time. Just meet me and I'll explain it all." Margaret Cullen smiled, but without warmth. Then she patted Amanda's arm. "Please?"

Amanda still searched for an out. "But what about Harvey?"

"Oh, yes. Harvey has been detained. We took the liberty of sending him to the airport to pick up a new indexing mechanism for you. It arrived this morning. He should be here shortly with the part."

"You did that?" Amanda choked. "But the machine didn't break down till an hour ago."

"Yes." Margaret Cullen slapped her gloves into her left hand. "Foresight is priceless, isn't it?" She certainly looked pleased as she extended her right hand. Amanda shook it numbly. "I'll see you shortly. Oh, and be careful of that ankle. It's probably quite tender."

Amanda felt a shiver. Big Brother knows all, sees all. "How could I disappoint my dear benevolent Uncle Sam?" she asked the erect departing figure.

Her mind rioted with questions. She knew she was being drawn into a situation she had no business touching. There was an unpleasant ring of danger to it. It was just the sort of thing her father had loved to tackle in the old days.

Ms. Cullen's request released a flood of memories. When she was a child, Amanda had worshiped Nathan Perry. She thought his way was the only way. She had tried to do everything he asked of her, from gymnastics to combat and weapons training. Then, through a stupid accident when she was only fifteen, he had sacrificed his life.

Amanda's mother had pined away and died three years later of what they called a broken heart. There was no one else Nathan Perry's only child could turn to. She learned to fend for herself in a world that had suddenly seemed cold and hostile.

Since those dark days Amanda had resisted even a kind remembrance of her father. She detested the thought of the weapons training, the military mind, the entire quasi-samurai code by which Nathan Perry had lived.

The part of him she had retained was her love of fitness and gymnastics. It had helped her through the roughest times and still did to this day. The rigorous physical workouts sharpened her perceptions and focused her concentration. At Tri-Cola she was known as tough and all business.

She was proud of that reputation and intended to maintain it. But her work had nothing to do with a patriotic gesture such as Ms. Cullen had suggested.

Still, it was flattering to have such an expert as the officer in charge of the powerful Economic Section of the U.S. embassy regard one as a resourceful person who had exceptional abilities.

Amanda checked her watch again. It was just as well no waiter had taken her order. She had no time for lunch now. A skipped meal would help her hips, anyway.

That thought reminded her to call her overweight young assistant, Chris Hubbard.

She hastily donned her straw hat and hurried from the dining room to a phone booth in the lobby.

Chris, as efficient as always, answered on the second ring. Without a college degree, he could not expect any further advancement in the company, but he liked his boss and the responsibility she gave him.

"Chris," Amanda said, "I only have a minute. Any new problems?"

Hubbard caught the urgency in her voice. "Several. The French representative is scheduled to meet with you and is going to be late."

"Good. You talk to him. Give him a great tour. Show him the secrets of doing business in Latin America."

"Sure will. Also, the Merida distributor called. Needs twenty thousand extra cases of Tri-Cola for the fiesta. Twelve-ounce cans. Can we supply? I couldn't give him a firm answer."

"Yes, we can." She calculated quickly. This was her world of expertise. She loved competing. "Bring it in from our city warehouse and add another five thousand cases of eight-ounce cans from the Monterrey warehouse."

"Great! Can we unload that much on him?"

"Certainly. He'll expect us to send extra. Plus I'll double his discount. Tell him I said I'd take back what he can't peddle."

Chris loved the challenging smile in Amanda's husky voice. He laughed. "Are you kidding? He'd never admit to a woman that he couldn't sell everything she sent him."

"Exactly. He'll hate me for a while, but he'll make more money. Oh, and Chris, make sure all our drivers deliver before seven A.M. I want to beat the other bottlers to the space."

"Oh," he groaned. "Coke and Pepsi will hate us."

"Better hate than death in the marketplace. They may not know we're alive yet, but they will soon. Anything else you can't handle?"

"No, ma'am."

"Okay. Are you at your computer?"

"Yes."

"Good. Punch up LaCross and find out who ordered the intermittent gear."

"Okay. Have we ordered one already?" Chris asked as he punched keys. "Uh, that's strange; I'm locked out."

"Use my access code." She gave him the number.

"It's coming up. Hey, you ordered it, boss—last week. How come you didn't tell us that when it broke down this morning?"

"Foresight is priceless," she said grimly. "Just read me the requisition."

"Uh, okay. Ordered April 27 to clear import May 1. Routed through U.S. embassy?" Chris sounded bewildered. "And you sent an Inter-network computer message to Mr. Bannon at nine this morning. How come you didn't tell me to arrange pickup?"

"Just read the rest."

"Authorized Mr. H. Bannon to accept delivery 10:30 A.M. today. That's wild—the other one broke down about then."

"I know, Chris. Also, I want to review the files of everyone on the production line and in the front office. And I want you to find out the names of everyone who was in the health club this morning while I was working out. Be discreet."

He hesitated. "What am I, your James Bond?" he joked, his tone uneasy. "Anything else?"

"Yes, send someone to Palacio del Sol to pick up the intermittent gear at the front desk. And take care of the operation this afternoon. I won't be in for the rest of the day."

Amanda flung the receiver down. She felt an uneasy flutter in her stomach and closed her eyes for a second, irritated. Why was she rushing? To please that cool embassy woman who was trying to manage her life? How dare Ms. Cullen make it seem as though she would send poor Harvey an impersonal computer message and have him running to the airport for her.

She felt a rush of affection. Harvey was a real dear. She stopped at the front desk to pen a brief note to him.

Dearest: Thank you so much for getting the package for me. Please leave it at the front desk. Unexpected business has come up. See you tonight for a special candlelight supper.

Love,
Amanda

That should do it. Harvey loved candlelight. It saved on the electricity bill. "Waste not, want not," he always cautioned her. Caution Bannon should have been the name on his birth certificate. Better not let him find out about this meeting with Margaret Cullen.

Amanda caught Enrique's eye and beckoned him over. Enrique knew Harvey well. He prided himself on knowing the name of everyone with whom he came in contact; he had a photographic memory. Everyone owed him favors, and he was always helping some unfortunate tourist solve a delicate problem.

She knew he was a born linguist and politician. He spoke English like a Texan, for he had grown up in Austin, Texas, where he had hung over the rail at the capitol, listening to the debates. When he was twelve, his family, illegal aliens for ten years, had been deported. He was always bemoaning Mother Nature's decision to push him into this world in Mexico a month in advance of the night his parents had planned to walk across the river to the United States. Each summer he spent as much time as he could visiting relatives in San Antonio and making friends. Amanda was sure that someday he'd be president of Mexico or at least mayor of Mexico City.

She entrusted him with the note for Harvey, pressing a hundred-peso note into his hand. "Be sure you tell him I waited as long as I possibly could," she instructed him emphatically.

"Hey, Señorita Perry!" Enrique shook his head in refusal. "You don't have to lay money on me. We're friends." His black eyes flashed, and he snapped his fingers. "Just let me take you dancing sometime." He held his shoulders high and swayed his hips in a wicked rumba, half serious, half in jest.

Amanda had to laugh. "I'm sorry, Enrique, but you're too fast for me. Besides, I don't date fifteen-year-olds. Mr. Bannon would disapprove."

"Yeah, Mr. Bannon wouldn't go for that, I suppose. I saw that guy at the bar give you the eye a little while ago. Take it from me. He looks like bad news."

Amanda stiffened. "You'd better forget that."

"Forget what?" Enrique shrugged innocently. "How about I become your houseboy? Everybody needs a houseboy. I'm the perfect age. You know, train me, bring me up right. He couldn't complain about that. Okay?''

"Don't count on it." Amanda could just see herself living with prim-and-proper Harvey Bannon on one side and outrageous young Enrique on the other. She closed his hand over the money and the note. "Take the money, Enrique. To keep things even."

"Okay," he acquiesced. "But I already owe you a few favors. Thanks again for getting your company to sponsor my uncle for that job up in San Antonio. He loves Texas."

"No problem. We needed a man with his qualifications in that bottling plant. Now, just make sure Mr. Bannon gets that note."

*"Sí, señorita."* Enrique gave her his best smile and came to attention with a flourish and a click of his heels.

Amanda stepped from the ice-cool Palacio del Sol into the blazing silvery glare of high-altitude sunshine. For a moment her eyes rebelled, and she wished she'd remembered her dark glasses. At the curb she looked up and down Calle de las Americas for the car Margaret Cullen had said would be waiting. A buoyant sensation filled her breasts again, a small thrill she hadn't felt in a long time, certainly not since she'd met Harvey. Her self-esteem was elevated in spite of her innate disapproval of brashness and arrogance.

A split second later the gleaming gold Jaguar zoomed out of the flow of traffic and angled to the curb beside her. The man she had last seen at the bar leaned toward her from behind the wheel, his deep blue eyes hard and intense and darting glances at the surrounding area as he released the door and indicated she was to get in.

"Where were you? I had to circle the block twice!" he snapped.

She didn't need his reprimands. After all, she was doing a favor for his boss. She knew nothing about this man. Why was she even thinking of getting into his car? She started to turn away.

He must have read her thoughts. His look softened considerably, and so did his voice. "Look, lady... Sorry if I scared you. All I want to do is take you to this meeting with Ms. Cullen. Now, will you please get in? We're late."

Traffic had begun to stack up behind him. The staccato blast of a horn and a stream of vitriolic Spanish that erupted from the taxi directly behind propelled Amanda into motion. What the hell! He looked harmless enough, and she could take care of herself. She slipped in beside her chauffeur, who was engaged in a shouting match with the irate taxi driver. Abruptly, the sleek car responded with a muffled roar from its pipes and neck-snapping acceleration.

"Was that necessary?" Amanda sputtered, scrambling to retrieve her seat belt. "Are you from Chicago?"

"Nope, Washington, D.C., but the traffic's worse here."

Had Amanda not been hurled roughly back in her seat, she would have seen Harvey Bannon step from the cab that had pulled up directly behind the departing Jaguar. Harvey paid the driver and stared in disbelief as the sports car made a U-turn, zipped around the plaza and disappeared. He straightened his immaculate Brooks Brothers three-piece suit, which would have been more appropriate in New York City, and briefly considered the situation. His face was a perfectly controlled mask.

There was no mistaking the fact that he had seen Amanda leave with a rather dashing, ruthless-looking character. Might she have been kidnapped? The thought pricked at Harvey's conservative, banker's mind. No—no, of course not, he decided. Mere conjecture. Time-wasting conjecture.

He peered in the direction that the sports car had driven. There had better be a very good explanation for Amanda's behavior. Harvey's smoothly shaven cheeks sagged a bit, as they did whenever his mouth tightened into a thin line of disapproval—a frequent occurrence.

Although he was twelve years older than Amanda's twenty-nine years, Harvey Bannon was a very attractive man in his own right. He stood still for a moment, not sure of what to do next, then stalked angrily into the hotel. There was no reason to miss lunch.

"Pardon me, Señor Bannon." Enrique affected humility as he interrupted Harvey's black thoughts. "Señorita Perry left this for you."

"What? Oh, yes. Thank you, uh—"

"Enrique."

"Uh, yes, Ricky." Harvey quickly unfolded the note and read it, then looked up, his face questioning. "Uh, Ricky, my good man. With whom did Miss Perry just leave?"

Enrique smiled broadly and decided to play it safe. "Oh, yes, I think her father, maybe."

"I see." Harvey nodded, though his jaw had tightened. "Strange, but I thought he was dead."

# Chapter Two

Guando scowled, and the jagged scar on his tanbark face twisted. He slammed the gearshift into second and swerved around another corner in time to see the gold car streak through traffic a block ahead, then turn. The driver was speeding recklessly and soon would come to grief. The car might crash at any moment. Guando's upper lip twitched; he would be on the scene.

Abruptly, his two-way radio demanded, "Guando! Terminate pursuit. Do you hear me?"

"I am not pursuing; I am merely following at a prudent distance." After a moment's indecision, he floored the accelerator and pushed the Porsche harder. His breathing quickened. The phantom taste of blood flooded his senses. He would deal with these Americans his way now.

"There is no need to follow," the harsh, fading voice on the radio insisted. "Do you hear me, Guando? Report!"

Guando switched off the set; it weakened his resolve and distracted him from the job at hand. He turned to his companion, a heavyset man in a dark suit. "You understand, we are not following the

Americans.'' The man smiled and pulled a .45 pistol from his coat. ''No gun!'' Guando ordered, his voice hard. ''Just help me keep them in sight. With any luck we can pressure them and they will crash.'' He shrugged. ''Then we'll have all the time we need.'' Recklessly, he stomped on the accelerator, taxing the Porsche to the limit, gripped by blood lust. He would prove his worth; he would do this job in his own way.

The streamlined Jaguar, with Amanda hanging on to precious little, snaked smoothly through the mid-day traffic of a main thoroughfare, turned abruptly onto a smaller side street, then immediately drove back through an evil-looking alley to a wide boulevard. Amanda glanced at her driver—square-jawed, un-deniably attractive, and now wearing a worried frown. The way he studied the rearview mirror so intently frightened her even more.

He tightened his grip on the wheel. ''Damn!'' For the fourth time, a low-slung black Porsche turned into view behind them, closing the distance relentlessly. His muscular, tanned leg flexed; his foot arched on the accelerator.

''Hang on, lady,'' he growled. ''Got to lose our friends back there.''

Amanda's new hat swirled up through the open sunroof and away into the distance; her hair twisted into stiff spikes. She gritted her teeth. The man was insane. The situation was entirely out of her control. ''Stop! Stop this car,'' she ordered. ''I quit!''

''You can't quit now,'' he shouted back. ''Wait till we get there.''

The Jaguar whined and picked up speed as though up to that moment its powerful engine had been only idling. Amanda squeezed her eyes closed. How could

he endanger lives so recklessly? Why had she gone
against her better judgment and gotten into the car?
What right did Ms. Cullen have to force an American
business person to do her bidding? And for that matter, who was Ms. Cullen, after all? Was she really with
the embassy? Fear prickled through Amanda as she
realized that the woman had shown her no identification.

Involuntarily opening her eyes, she immediately regretted it. Accelerating and braking at the same time,
tires smoking, the driver slammed the machine around
a blind corner and into a maze of narrow back streets.
Dodging the foot traffic, plus many horse and don-
key carts, he seemed to be enjoying the chase now,
though avoiding collisions and side-swipes by scant
centimeters. Where were the *policía* when you really
needed them?

The Jaguar burst from the winding tangle of back
streets into the great square of the Plaza de la Consti-
tución, known as the Zócalo. How much more pun-
ishment could it take? The whine of the engine reached
its red-line limit of revolutions. Would it explode?
What a haunting thought—to die here and become a
meager, gory footnote to the monuments of Aztec and
Spanish history.

Its engine up to the maximum, like a lethal blur, the
golden car circled the majestic baroque cathedral,
wheeled dangerously around toward Calle Tacuba,
then roared west past the Palacio de Bellas Artes. The
Alameda whizzed by, then the Paseo de la Reforma.
The finely tuned machine weaved its way with preci-
sion through mounting traffic around the splendid
equestrian statue of El Caballito. A series of dizzying
turns brought it onto the broad Avenida de los Insur-

gentes and down to the Juarez section. Quickly cutting to the east, the Jaguar sped across the city onto the narrow and dangerous Calle de los Estados, then headed north again. At last, there was no sign of the Porsche.

Amanda regained her senses and orientation. She was now, miraculously, near the Plaza de Santa Caterina and the spot where the Thieves' Market began. The rich aroma of a hundred spicy foods filled the air. The traffic on the crowded thoroughfare was brutal and increasing as they passed the well-known Lagunilla Market.

"Hang on, lady. I'm doubling back." The car whipped around with a squeal of tortured rubber on a dead-end street two miles beyond the marketplace.

The smell of smoking tires, the ear-shattering clamor and the driver's pleasure in the reckless adventure all sickened Amanda. From the depths of her fear, she screamed, "I don't give a damn what you do. Just stop this car and let me out."

Miraculously, the Jaguar plunged through a minuscule opening in an alley, and Amanda, rigid with fright, realized they were at the edge of the city. Suddenly they were driving as though making a leisurely Sunday foray through the thinning suburbs and eventually onto a winding country road.

"Forget it!" she grumbled, then added to herself, *Nearly twenty million people in Mexico City and I draw a madman for a chauffeur.* Her lips were parched; her pulse jerkily slowed to normal. She paused, then drew a deep breath. Somewhere a bird was singing. She wished she had not begged to be let out. As Harvey maintained, one should keep one's dignity at all costs.

She sighed and turned to her companion. "Was that a test? Or is that how the embassy teaches you to soften up people?"

"Embassy? Ha!" He smoothed his wind-whipped hair.

She mirrored his action. Her hair felt dry and stiff. "What's that supposed to mean?"

"Nothing!" He checked the rearview mirror. "I have no official connection with the State Department. Nor do I want any."

"No connection?" New waves of panic assaulted her. Why was he driving her? Where was he really taking her? Who was he? She gulped and swallowed for courage while debating how quickly she could escape. "You certainly sound cynical."

"Cynical, hell! It's a simple fact."

*Keep him talking.* "Then why do you do this sort of—outrageous thing? For money or just for kicks? Or are you some race driver on vacation?"

"Can the abuse, lady. I don't need it. I don't approve of any of this. I want nothing to do with either you or the State Department. I said I'd deliver you— that's it. Done! End of involvement."

*Keep him talking.* "If you hate your work so much, why do you do it?"

His scalding gaze traveled the length of Amanda's fashionably but properly clad body as he considered her question. It seemed as though he was going to defend his driving; instead, he scowled impatiently. "Apparently you didn't hear what I said. But aside from that, why does anyone work, Ms. Perry? Why did you choose the soft-drink business?"

Still shaken and confused, unprepared for his antagonism, Amanda stared straight ahead at the lush countryside and lifted her chin indignantly. "Because I didn't have the proper credentials to become the president of the United States, I suppose."

"Oh, sarcasm," he mocked. She could feel his eyes again. "Your credentials look all right to me. I think you could wangle your way into the hearts of the public. Other women have, you know."

Her eyes flashed, and her husky voice bit at him. "What *is* your problem, mister?" How easily he provoked her. She was known in management as rock steady, pleasant, controlled. He brought out the worst in her. "Look, I was just minding my own business when that woman approached me, said she was from the embassy, and—" She felt tears crowd her throat. "Hell, I don't know what I'm doing here." She wanted to cry, but crying was beneath her. Nathan Perry wouldn't have approved of it. Hadn't he named her A-*man*-da just to make up for the fact that she was a girl and not a boy. No one could cause Amanda Perry to feel inferior. Except herself.

He glimpsed her glistening eyes and backed off unexpectedly. "I—I'm sorry. Shouldn't have said that. We all have our problems. I'm the worst of the lot."

"Okay, Mr. Worst of the Lot," she said shakily, "what do I call you? Or is your name a secret, too?" She wished she hadn't been so flippant, since he'd just apologized, but he grinned, and some of the tension vanished from his face. Perhaps he wasn't as tough as he wanted people to think. In fact, his smile was awfully nice. She realized she was smiling back and looked away.

His personality was now warm as sunshine. "No problem. No secret. My name is Bradford. Forrest

Bradford, but my friends call me Brad. I dislike my first name.''

She moistened her dry lips and said his name, her eyes straight ahead, her voice, husky, solemn. "Okay, Brad. Now would you please answer a couple of questions?''

He shook his head. "No! Ms. Cullen will explain everything. I'm only the chauffeur.''

Her head snapped around, and she glared at him. "Well—'' She was exasperated. "What the—?'' *Just reason with him,* Amanda cautioned herself, *and try to keep calm.* "Look, I only want to know what's going on. Why were we being chased by that car?''

"I have no idea, but I sure as hell didn't want to stay around and find out.''

"But you took a lot of unnecessary chances. There are better ways to get rid of pursuers.''

"Oh, certainly. I was sure you'd say that.'' He smirked. "I imagine you'd rather I'd pulled a pistol and shot it out with them.''

Amanda bit her tongue. The very thought offended her. That was precisely the way her dad would have handled the pursuit. Or he'd have spun the car around and rammed the Porsche. "Don't be absurd.'' She ground her teeth. "I only meant that *I* have nothing to run from. What kind of dirty dealings are you people up to, anyway?''

He crooked his head and studied her with somber blue eyes. "I wondered when you'd finally ask that question.'' He looked back at the road. "I will tell you this before you talk to Ms. Cullen. You'd better turn down this—'' he paused ''—opportunity.'' He spat the word out bitterly.

"And why do you say that?" Amanda was put off again by his know-it-all attitude.

"Because, young lady, I think you could get your pretty little ass blown off." He smiled sweetly, then continued. "Now, you certainly wouldn't want that to happen, would you, Miss Perry?"

"You arrogant bastard!"

Instantly she regretted her words. She'd stepped down to his level. This had never happened with Harvey. Around him she'd easily maintained her executive dignity, her level judgment. "That kind of talk is uncalled for," she corrected. He looked unimpressed.

"You'll hear worse than that before they let you out of their clutches. You're like a chicken waiting to be plucked, a patriotic sitting duck gobbling the bait."

"Don't count on it." She crossed her arms on her chest and settled back in disgust. How much longer before this would end?

He continued against her silence. "Lady, that persuasive Margaret Cullen is no fool. She's run you through every psychological profile those fancy government computers can come up with. You're as good as hooked."

"Why are you so negative?"

"I'm trying to warn you, you naive goose."

Her anger erupted like a volcano. "Goose? If I were a man, would you talk to me that way?"

His smile twisted ruefully. "If you were a man, you could have delivered yourself."

She was speechless with anger. A few minutes passed before she was under control enough to enunciate crisply, "Just deliver me. No more warnings. No conversation. Nothing."

"Hey, I could care less. I'm only the messenger boy. Once you're delivered safely, my job is over."

The pair drove in silence. Their heated arguments echoed in their thoughts. Amanda considered all Bradford had said. He did have a point. But whose side was he on? Obviously he was retained by the government to do a job, but not the job of recruiting Amanda. He seemed sincere in his discouraging remarks. No doubt he was right. Whatever it was, this was not a job for her. Some man could do it better. However, the very thought galled her.

She had fought hard to enter the male arena in the business world. She was a good businesswoman. The very thought that she couldn't do everything a man could do disgusted her.

She was patriotic but not foolhardy. She would do what she had trained herself to do—manage her company in a profitable and ethical manner. Not her government, not her superiors, not even the ghost of Nathan Perry, war hero, could ask for more than that.

Instinctively, Amanda turned and checked the road behind them. She half expected to see the black car looming behind them again, but it wasn't there. She made up her mind. Once she got to this meeting place, she would ascertain the validity of Cullen's credentials, then tactfully turn down the opportunity, no matter what it was. So what if refusing was unpatriotic. It was simply a matter of not being able to take time away from business.

TEN MILES AWAY, still smarting from the dishonor of losing face, and losing to an American, Guando reported in. He had stopped at a public phone booth and was reluctantly dialing the number. The phone rang once; then a stern voice spoke a single Spanish word. Guando feared that tone. "I await your orders," he said simply, trying to keep anxiety out of his voice.

"You will return to the meeting place to receive new instructions. Use the tunnel entrance. There must be no visible connection between us."

"Understood," Guando said, his interest picking up. Perhaps there would be some positive action soon. "When will we raid them?"

"When we have sufficient data. There must be no mistakes on our part," El Tigre warned. "This opportunity is nearly a perfect setup. It must not be compromised."

"Then the rumor is true? The blunder was planned?" Guando couldn't hide his elation. Thank the heavens that the ill-fated chase had not been mentioned. Perhaps he could prove himself with action soon.

"You will be informed."

"Good! I wish to lead the attack."

There was a pause. Then the voice took on a flat, deathlike tone. "There will be no gratuitous violence. Your frustration is understood, but in the future you will do exactly as told. Or you will answer with your life."

"Yes! Yes! Of course, as you command," he agreed, mopping sweat from his brow. He could see the vast sum of money he would garner if this operation was successful. He, Tomás Guando, always an outcast but a person well trained in the ways of death, would at last become wealthy. He would buy this cursed Porsche, the one with the crumpled fender that might have to be humbly explained away when he reached his destination. "I will be there immediately," he assured the telephone, and severed the connection with a twisted smile.

# Chapter Three

"Hang on," Bradford warned as he downshifted and took a sharp turn into a lane that led to a private estate a mile away.

The immaculately maintained grounds stretched into infinity on either side of them. Amanda snapped out of her reverie. Having never before been near this secluded area, she observed everything with interest. The green smell of freshly mown grass made her recall exciting summers in the Midwest, when she was a teenager discovering life. The world seemed peaceful from here.

A sumptuous white hacienda sprawled in the distance. Beside it, in a cobblestoned courtyard, were a couple of long limousines crouched like black beetles, flags fluttering on their fenders. Verdant lawns rolled expansively, bathed in lazily spiraling sprays from unseen sprinklers. Sunlight glittered on the mist, creating an illusion of rainbows dancing and weaving like pastel fans.

Amanda watched a small stream bubble through the grounds like a twisting silver thread. It meandered down the slope to where Brad stopped the dusty Jaguar. Near them was Margaret Cullen, her blond hair unmussed, as perfect as her cream linen suit. She was walking along the bank of the stream, her shoulder bag in place. Carrying herself erect, she looked completely at ease. Yet there was something ludicrous about the scene. Then Amanda caught a flick of movement. Ms. Cullen was fishing. Occasionally, she stopped and cast a dry fly from a fishing rod.

Without a word to Brad, Amanda left the car as efficiently as she could, ignoring her tender ankle, determined to face her meeting and be done with all this. She ran her fingers through her hair and straightened her skirt and jacket. The thought of her missing new hat made her turn from Brad with an abruptness that relegated his importance to zero.

He did not appear to notice. Displaying an order of importance of his own, he unlatched the hood of the Jaguar and stuck his nose under it.

"Thank you, Bradford," Margaret Cullen said perfunctorily. Brad grunted an acknowledgement. Apparently Ms. Cullen was not considered a friend of his. That made sense in light of his tirade against her earlier.

"There's another rod on the bank over there," Ms. Cullen said. "If you like, we can fish while we talk."

"Fish?" Amanda repeated. "I don't fish, Ms. Cullen," she said acridly. "I'd like to know if you always go to such extremes. I find this situation highly theatrical."

"A-men!" came a muffled voice from under the hood of the Jaguar.

Margaret Cullen gave the ghost of a frown, then recovered. "Now, now, not to worry." She took the time to cast her fly ahead of a large brown trout suspended as if layered in green glass, motionless in the shimmering liquid shadows except for the sinuous undulations of its tail.

Brad dropped the car's hood with a bang, causing Amanda to jump. He came up behind her and said contritely, "Sorry." He pointed out the pole. "Go ahead, try it. It'll relax you." He picked up the rod and handed it to her.

"Thank you," she said curtly.

"In my work," Ms. Cullen continued serenely, either unaware of the tension surrounding her or ignoring it, "the trick is to never break pattern if it's at all avoidable. I fish here whenever I get a chance. At times like this I'd prefer to be back home at Lake Texoma, on the Texas-Oklahoma border, tending lines from my own pier." Her voice was misty with nostalgia. "My mother—she's eighty years old—is there fishing right now." She sighed and cast again. "So goes the world today." The fish ignored her fly.

Impressed by the homey quality of the thought, Amanda gave fly fishing a try. Her imitation of Ms. Cullen's swift, smooth, arching line, which merely landed her fly on the opposite shore, drew no comment.

She sorted out the line, then made another sloppy beginner's cast for a fair-sized trout shimmering in the water over a bed of smooth white stones. "Look, Ms. Cullen—"

"Please, think of me as Margaret."

"Okay—Margaret," Amanda continued awkwardly. "I've come along this far and I've risked my neck to get here." She glanced venomously at Brad, standing discreetly in the background. "Suppose you prove to me now that you are Margaret Cullen, officer in charge of the Economic Section of the U.S. Embassy in Mexico City.''

Ms. Cullen smiled benevolently. She handed her casting rod to Brad, then produced a card from her shoulder bag.

Amanda almost got a strike just as she finished reading the very convincing, official U.S. identification card. It was genuine, but that was no reason to do anything foolish. "I'm like that fish," she noted. "I'm curious, but I'm not buying this yet."

Margaret Cullen began softly, underscoring the seriousness of her statement. "Amanda, when the State Department goofs, it's never a minor matter. We're not infallible. We make mistakes. But on the international scene there is no such thing as a mere error. By the time our loyal opposition party or American television or any one of a hundred foreign propagandists gets hold of it, the small error becomes the raw meat for another world crisis. Each is worse than the last. We really can't afford many more of those."

Perhaps she should decline right now, but Amanda didn't know yet what she would be declining. "I agree," she said slowly. "But we shouldn't be meddling in so many countries' affairs." No harm in speaking your mind. She cast again, better this time.

"Well said," Brad interrupted, lining up with the opposition.

"I can speak for myself!" Amanda glared at him, then turned back. "I know what you mean, Ms. Cullen—Margaret." Again, Amanda's trout had risen to investigate the carefully cast fly.

"I'll come to the point. Somebody back along the line in the State Department has committed a terrible error. A cargo that was supposed to have been flown from New York City to Padre Island, Texas, has wound up in the customs shed at Benito Juarez International Airport just outside Mexico City. It's a disastrous blunder."

"What type of cargo?" Even as Amanda asked the question, she knew she shouldn't, nor should she linger a moment longer.

"Fifty metal cylinders, each containing two liters of a highly secret catalyst for a new synthetic fuel for automobiles."

That didn't sound like a tremendous problem. Though relieved, Amanda was still cautious. Margaret Cullen's face was terribly somber. "Is it dangerous in some way?"

"Yes, it is explosive under certain circumstances, but I assure you it's not very dangerous as long as it remains in the cylinders under pressure."

"I see. Is this some kind of military project?"

"No, no, not in the slightest. That's part of our problem. This is strictly a civilian product; it has nothing whatsoever to do with the military. They are not involved in this at all," Ms. Cullen said, her tone final.

"Good." Another scary thought struck. "Is this some kind of nuclear fuel?"

"Oh, heavens, no! This has nothing to do with nuclear anything. But it is explosive politically and economically, and it could cause a furor throughout the world."

"How so?"

"What I am going to tell you is top secret. We've found a way to produce a fuel that will produce synthetic gasoline for pennies when mixed with desalinated seawater. If news of this discovery leaks out prematurely, it could cause heaven knows what repercussions in the world economic markets. It could cause a financial panic and drastically alter the balance of power.''

''I think the world would welcome cheaper fuel.''

''Ah, but Mexico wouldn't, or the Middle East or Russia, or even Texas for that matter. There is enough trouble with fuel pricing already. Improperly handled, the gasoline could be devastating, perhaps even economically fatal.''

''I see,'' she murmured thoughtfully, thinking, *Run, Amanda. Time to bid adiós.*

''There are many problems yet to be worked out. But one large problem is that this product hasn't been thoroughly tested yet. That's why the government was sending the stuff to our new desalination plant in Texas. It's to be tested there.''

''And,'' Brad injected with bitter irony, ''predictably, through some typical bureaucratic bungling, it wound up accidentally exported to Mexico.''

''Precisely,'' Ms. Cullen continued stoically, ignoring the chastising tone.

Amanda frowned. Brad could hardly be just an errand boy if he was allowed in on this top-secret information. So if he wasn't just a chauffeur, what was he? Realizing that what was being said concerned her specifically, she hastily turned her attention back to Margaret Cullen.

''We had a cover story for the cylinders, bad as it is.'' With a tinge of embarrassment, she continued, ''They were labeled soft-drink syrup. That's where error number two was made. At the moment, there's no licensing for that type of syrup to be shipped out of Mexico.''

"Oh, don't I know!" Amanda laughed in spite of herself. "That caused me many a problem whenever a batch of spoiled syrup came in. I'd have to dump it rather than send it back to the States for credit. All the pesticide laws and such."

"Correct. Due to fears of EDB pesticide contamination and food poisoning, U.S. laws forbid all import of raw syrup back to the States."

"It would seem to me that one phone call to the right authority on either side of the border would take care of that for you. I mean, you are the U.S. government, aren't you?"

"Ah, the visions of youth! I wish that it could be that easily solved!"

Brad interjected, "That's where error number three came into play."

"Sounds like a necklace of pearls falling from a broken strand."

"Oh, lady, you haven't heard anything yet. It gets worse."

"Please!" Ms. Cullen said, her voice taking on an edge. "If I may..." She paused. "We have a U.S. congressman on a junket."

"George D. Slater?"

"The same." Margaret Cullen rolled her eyes in disapproval. "A publicity-hungry politician is the worst. Here we have a man on a junket, stirring up trouble. It's worrisome. He's a board member of several influential corporations, and he's attending the Organization of International Bankers conference in Mexico City, courtesy of the U.S. taxpayers." She nodded her blond head and ignored her fishing rod. "Ostensibly, Slater is here to find out if friendly Latin American countries are reselling U.S. products at a profit to unfriendly Cuba, sitting in the gulf ninety miles off Florida.''

"Cuba? That's paranoid and ridiculous," Amanda blurted. "Mexico isn't going to do that."

"Certainly not. But the congressman is a self-styled watchdog and an atrocious busybody. In fact, if the truth were known, it's nearly a toss-up between the propagandist's exposé and a congressional investigation at this point in time."

"What's wrong with a congressional investigation—to prove the point?" Amanda asked.

"Nothing is wrong with it. Except that every time anything in the civilian sector is stalled for a few months—"

"Or years," Brad said.

"Or years," Margaret agreed, "more billions are added unnecessarily to the national debt. That money would be better spent improving the standard of life everywhere."

"I agree."

"Yes, of course. But that's not all, unfortunately." Ms. Cullen sighed and flicked her fishing line. "Gross error number four." Brad glanced at Margaret, who nodded slightly, then he continued. "Even though the military has nothing to do with this project, the catalyst was flown aboard a military plane to Mexico."

"So?"

"The plane was leased by the government. Therefore, it could be claimed that the catalyst was misdirected here to scuttle the project or that it is intended for use in some conspiracy against Mexico."

Amanda eyed them both. "Is it?"

"Absolutely not," Margaret hastened to reassure her. "But the misapprehensions this single factor might give rise to are endless."

"There you have it." Brad smiled sourly. "Your highly trained, efficient government. Up the creek by its own hand."

Amanda detested his unpatriotic gibes, but Ms. Cullen showed astonishing forbearance. She smiled enigmatically. "Though he's a little outspoken and critical, I'm sure you're aware that Bradford is a loyal American citizen."

"I'm afraid I don't know anything about him," Amanda answered truthfully. "Nor do I expect I shall have to learn."

"Quite true," he agreed quickly.

"That will do, Bradford!"

*How utterly unprofessional he is,* Amanda told herself. *How insecure he must be. He must feel incompetent, hopeless, a mere tool of the government, even though he denies association.*

"You see, Amanda," Margaret Cullen resumed, "this is a relatively small problem on the surface—"

"I'm sorry? Oh, you mean the cylinders, of course. My mind wandered for a moment."

"Yes, the cylinders. A small problem, but there could be serious consequences if relations with Mexico and Latin America are damaged at this time. And beyond that, relations with the rest of the Third World, as well. This has become a delicate repair job for the State Department. We must, so to speak, carry water in both hands and never spill a drop."

Her thoughts collected, Amanda was ready to get on with the business at hand. "The destination of this misdirected fuel catalyst is supposed to be Padre Island, Texas. Do you want me to take it there?''

"Actually, all we need is for you to get it to the harbor in Tampico, Mexico. But it must be taken in such a manner that no one knows about it."

"You want me to—" she lowered her voice "—smuggle it out of the airport?"

Ms. Cullen looked pained. "I dislike using that term, but in essence that's the ticket. I don't need to mention that there are plenty of persons, some right here in the city, who would pay any price to get hold of a sample of that catalyst."

"Now do you understand why I dodged that tail somebody had on us?" Brad said.

Amanda's mind was trying to sort out the information. She had forgotten to fish, but Margaret Cullen began to angle for her neglected trout.

"Okay," Amanda declared. "I suppose you have a plan."

"Yes. Simple, foolproof."

"Famous last words," Brad added.

"Enough, Bradford! Now, you will arrange to release those fifty cylinders from the customs shed without an inspection and without stirring up too much attention. An American businesswoman can make deals with the *aduaneros*, the customs officials, that are impossible for us to undertake without alerting every espionage agent within two thousand miles. After all, unfortunately, the shipment has your Tri-Cola label on every cylinder. You are the only person who can do it without causing suspicion."

Amanda was too taken aback by this disclosure to do more than nod agreement.

"Once the cargo's in your possession, you get it as far as Tampico. A fishing boat will be waiting there to take the stuff to the proper destination."

"When does my responsibility end?"

"When you give the cylinders to our agent at Tampico harbor."

Amanda calculated the time involved. Not bad. She traveled to her bottling works in Tampico and Monterrey regularly. No wonder they had chosen her to rectify this error. It really wouldn't be difficult. "I could be through with the whole assignment in two or three days."

"With luck," Ms. Cullen added casually.

Amanda felt a need to clarify her position. "You do understand that I'm, uh, getting married next week. I have a million things to take care of."

"My compliments to the lucky groom. Mr. Bannon is a fine person."

"Thank you," Amanda said joylessly.

"Let me warn you. This won't be easy. We'll do everything we can from behind the scenes, but if there's trouble, you'll be on your own. There has been a tiny leak of information from somewhere. We cannot admit the U.S. government is involved."

Blessedly, Brad kept his own counsel, but Amanda recalled his earlier words on the subject. He had figured it all out correctly. She masked her thoughts carefully and kept her voice low. "Why not?"

Ms. Cullen shrugged. "Because the people who followed you might be anyone. We cannot trust even our own people on this. We simply have to get the catalyst back to the States with as few complications as possible. To fail will be a huge setback, but if you are apprehended—by anyone—everything will fall apart.

We'll be forced to deny all association with you. You'll be treated as an alien agent.''

How disillusioning to be told that service to one's country was a one-way street, that she could rot in jail if things went wrong.

Amanda's heart pounded. No wonder Brad had fled from the Porsche with such dedication. He'd been right to do so. She swallowed. "Just fill me in on the details,'' she heard her voice say casually, like the voice of some stranger.

"Then you'll do it for us?''

Amanda raised her eyebrows in disbelief. "Don't kid me now, Ms. Cullen. You knew I'd accept the challenge or you'd never have put it to me.''

Brad stood in the background, unsmiling, unemotional. He had known it, too. After all was said and done, Amanda was an adventurer, whether she was able to admit it or not. She probably had no more sense than her father, Nathan Perry, who had charged the enemy with a machine gun and captured a regiment single-handed. Heroic? Yes! But he could have killed himself and all his men, as well.

Ms. Cullen smiled with unabashed glee as she reeled in her line. She had caught Amanda's trout—female, sleek, in perfect condition, in the prime of her life, ready for mating. The swirled spots on her sides glowed against the dark browns and deep butter-yellows. A very prime catch indeed.

## Chapter Four

Guando shielded his eyes as he and Paco stepped from the dimly lit interior of the small elevator. He shrank from the brilliant glare of sunshine and the scorching blast of hot wind that greeted him on the rooftop of the fifteen-floor parking building, but there was no escape from the afternoon taste of hell.

He cursed silently as he glanced around. The rooftop was deserted. How long was he expected to wait? He knew the answer. Forever if need be. He had been summoned. He dared not protest.

"Guando," Paco grunted. "Someone comes." A heavy automobile was climbing the spiral slope, its engine purring with a soft growl. A large slate-gray limo hove into view, then turned and approached the two men. It moved abreast of them and stopped.

The distorted image of Guando's own grim face was reflected in the black mirrors of the windows. He knew that he must appear to be a subservient, squinting fool, but what else could he be in this situation? He could only stand and wait until asked to enter the vehicle.

The summons didn't come. A moment later, one of the rear windows slithered downward; it stopped a third of the way. From the dark interior of the car a breath of cool air escaped and taunted his forehead. It brought no comfort. He could see no one. A gun could be trained on him. He could only steel his nerves and wait.

"Guando. I have reason to believe that you came close to compromising the operation earlier today. Had you done so—" the crisp sound of an automatic pistol chambering a round punctuated the voice "—you would be dead by now, a corpse where you stand." The unseen voice of El Tigre spoke slowly, making the point painfully clear. "Do you understand?"

Guando managed a brief nod. He tried not to move. Honor required it. "*Sí*, El Tig—" He caught the word and smothered it. Curse all blunders! He'd doom himself yet. Never mention that name where anyone could hear. "*¡Sí!* No mistakes."

Seemingly satisfied, El Tigre continued. "In the trunk of this car you will find an attaché case that contains a listening device. You will take it and go directly to Amanda Perry's building. Paco will accompany you and wait in the car while you install the device in her apartment. You will tape every word you hear and bring the information to me immediately for analysis."

A small sound came from the rear of the limousine. Guando whirled toward it. The trunk had been unlatched. "Get the device, Paco," he ordered roughly, trying to steady himself.

"I must have as much information as possible tonight," El Tigre added. "Take no unnecessary chances, but be certain you do not fail to bring what I'm looking for."

Guando nodded. Afraid El Tigre could read his mind, he kept his face slightly averted from the gloomy interior of the car. He was hot and nervous. Sweat trickled down his hair, temples and neck, to his tight collar. His eyes burned from the afternoon smog.

"Well? Speak!" El Tigre ordered. Time was short. Few were to be trusted. If one was lucky, one could turn a series of blunders made by a great power into the stuff upon which new empires are built. What would the U.S. pay to buy back this secret? What would the Soviets pay? Or even certain Third World countries? El Tigre would reap dazzling benefits should all go well.

"No mistakes—I will succeed." Though humiliated, Guando would not allow his voice to betray him.

"Good! Tomorrow I must coordinate a large number of people and schedule the submarine to be at the rendezvous in the Gulf of Mexico, or have an alternative plan—unless this is some trick being perpetrated by the Americans. But even at that, perhaps we may use it to further discredit the American government."

"I will bring you positive proof of what they are doing," Guando promised, his black eyes glinting in the light.

"I'm counting on that." El Tigre's voice was heavy with unspoken menace. "You had better hurry. There is little time. Report as soon as possible."

"¡Sí! Do not worry. I will not return empty-handed. This I guarantee upon my honor!" Guando backed away, grateful to escape. He rushed to the elevator, Paco following close at hand.

His spirits began to rise once he was safely on the elevator and plummeting to the lowest depths of the underground parking lot. He feared these meetings with his leader. Always the threats. He hated all international people. He hated their power. He could never understand their complicated intrigues. But as long as he was paid well, he would work for them. He wanted only money. Money was power.

Guando turned and smiled at his squat friend. "Do you realize what this means?" He didn't wait for an answer. "We are trusted. We will succeed, Paco. We will have riches beyond our greatest dreams. El Tigre must pay us well to keep secrets, eh, partner? No matter what happens next."

Paco grinned toothily and shoved a cigar into his mouth. "Eh, Guando, got a match?"

"Don't light that thing around me, you greasy pig. I don't want the stink of your cigar smoke on my body when I visit the lady's apartment."

"Ha, ha," Paco growled. "Visit, eh? What you gonna do with the lady? Maybe you should wait for her to come home and have fun with her instead of just listening to what she says." He raised his brows. "More fun, maybe? Maybe not. I know what kind of woman excites you, eh? One that fights you."

The elevator doors hissed open. Before them was the tunnel that led to another building, where the Porsche was parked.

"Perhaps I need none of them!" Guando grunted as he plunged from the confining elevator. "I doubt that such a fragile person has anything to give a man like me. She would faint away, if I looked at her." He glanced at his watch. "Quickly, Paco, we must hurry. It is late." In a way, he almost hoped they were too late to plant the bug. He had a new idea.

BRAD BROUGHT THE JAGUAR to an abrupt halt in front of the apartment building. "So this is where you live." His tone was derisive, the words a challenge demanding an answer.

Amanda intended to create no further opening for his ridicule. She felt gored by his incessant "I told you so's" throughout the long ride to her apartment. Before today he had been nothing to her; tomorrow he would be out of her life. Good riddance.

Knowing that he had been right was all the more galling. She had found herself unable to resist Margaret Cullen's persuasive patriotic rhetoric. *Say nothing further,* she cautioned herself. *Bite your tongue.* "Yes, this is where I live," she repeated flatly.

She reached for the door handle, unfulfilled in some way, uneasy, as though she needed to lash out at him or at least have the last word to shake his superior attitude. His job was done, he'd said. Now he could just stand back and watch her mistakes. She would have to do all the illegal and clandestine work. *Say nothing further,* she told herself once more.

"Humph!" A grunt of disapproval.

Good intentions be damned. "What is it now?" she inquired crisply.

He eyed the big ornate double doors of iron grillwork that stood imposingly in front of the entryway where the concierge had his quarters. "Nothing. It's fine with me."

She cocked her head. "No, don't back off now. Go ahead; say your piece. Why stop now? You've been throwing little barbs at me from the first minute we met. No—even before that, when you gave me that drunken leer at the Palacio del Sol. Are you some kind of sadist who loves to bait people? Or are you just trying to drain my blood with a thousand little cuts to test my mortality?''

Apparently bewildered by the ferocity of her attack, Brad glanced around to see if they were being observed. ''Wait a minute, Miss Perry,'' he said gently. ''I'm certainly not trying to upset you. I was just concerned about the security of this place.'' He gestured at the building. ''Anybody could break in and walk right past the concierge's rooms. Who'd see them? I'll bet you're the only gringo in the building.''

''So what? I don't have anything to fear. I've never had any trouble here.'' Amanda's voice surged up a decibel. ''I'm a legitimate businesswoman, not a spy. I'm not involved in any espionage or international skullduggery.''

''How do you know that, lady? How do you know what you're doing? You bought the story at the first telling.''

''I—I—''

''Took everything at face value.'' He was unbearably smug again.

''What else could I do?'' The words were more a challenge than an admission of naiveté.

Brad surprised himself by gripping the wheel tight enough to turn his knuckles white. Why was he so angry? ''I don't know.'' His eyes swept the area. ''But I do know this isn't the place to discuss it.''

That made sense. Amanda sighed wearily. Perhaps he really did have her best interest at heart. What would be lost by listening to him? ''Okay,'' she said, ''perhaps you'd like to come up to my apartment and enlighten me.'' No, that didn't sound right at all. Her ears burned; a wave of heat flushed her cheeks.

''I thought you'd never ask.''

"Don't push it, Bradford. I'm not being social. Things at work have probably gone to hell. There'll be at least a hundred messages on my machine that I'll have to answer. I should have my head examined, discussing anything with you. After all, you told me you were only the errand boy, with no connection to the embassy."

"Not exactly the entire truth but close enough," he hedged.

"I thought as much."

"It's not like you think."

"You have no idea what I think!"

"I hope I'm wrong," Brad said, leaning over to open her door, "but I think you're just like your illustrious father."

"And what do you mean by that?" Amanda snapped.

"Ready to charge in and save the day, not knowing what the hell you're doing."

Amanda blanched. He had no right to point out what she already suspected. He had no right to say anything about her father. What did he know of Nathan Perry? Nothing! She took a deep breath, exhausted from a day-long roller-coaster ride, cursing the emotion that choked her. "You have no right to bring my father into this. I may very well be a woman who doesn't know what she's doing all the time, but—"

"Oh, Amanda, I didn't mean it that way. Let's get off this street."

"No, just hear me out. I let you speak; now listen to me for a moment. I think I understand. You harbor some feeling of masculine superiority probably inherited from your own father and not even your fault.

But that's no excuse. I don't give a damn if you're some kind of hired mercenary—you probably feel you should have been chosen for this mission. Maybe—just maybe—you have some misguided credo that tells you to protect women like me from the world—from myself—from failure, perhaps.''

Brad shook his head and squirmed in his seat. Amanda railed on, her voice decibels higher than the rising concert of evening crickets. ''But I reserve the right to fail on my own. And you're wrong. I'm not the strong, go-in-with-machine-gun-blazing person that my dad was. He was a great man who could do anything. But I'll damn well do exactly as I promised I would do or die trying. Do you understand, Mr. Bradford?''

He took a long moment to answer. ''Yes,'' he said, ''I understand. And I envy your wanting to defend your father, right or wrong.''

''Why envy that? You're so critical.''

''I don't know.'' He frowned. ''Maybe because I can't praise my father like that. Blame it on my bum childhood.'' He seemed to regret his answer.

''Why do you say that?'' she persisted.

His eyes became veiled. He debated with himself for a moment before he answered. ''Because...if you must know, I was the result of a—a union between two very irresponsible people. I didn't feel wanted. I was shunted off to relatives and barely knew my parents. I formed my own defenses against the world. I suppose it confirmed me as a cynical bastard.''

''I'm sorry to hear that. But I meant what I said. My success or failure will be mine and mine alone, not my father's. Is that clear?''

"Yes, ma'am!" Brad grinned crookedly. "Perfectly clear—just took a little 'attitude adjustment,' that's all."

Amanda retained her solemn gaze for a moment, then smiled. His reaction was not what she had expected. He had revealed a small part of himself, and he had taken her seriously. Her speech was a little melodramatic, but he had been closer to the truth about her motivations than she cared to admit. For years she had tried to bury the similarities between herself and her father.

"Now, since we understand our respective positions, would you care to come up for a drink?"

"Okay, a truce." He held up the packet of papers that Margaret Cullen had handed him when they left the country estate. "I still have to go over all these documents with you, since we're still on speaking terms."

As they entered the building, a black Porsche cruised by slowly. Guando had arrived too late. The woman and the American agent had already returned, and he had not yet placed the listening device in her apartment.

"Drive around the block, Paco." His long face was pinched; his eyes squinted and shifted with his thoughts. "I must consider our next move."

"We call El Tigre for instructions?" Paco offered.

"That's unnecessary!" Guando assured him darkly. His hand automatically caressed the heavy pistol beneath his coat. "This turn of events is exactly what I needed. I have a viable alternative. One that El Tigre will have to accept."

"You gonna kill 'em?"

# Chapter Five

Brad paced restlessly through Amanda's third-floor apartment, the clink of scotch on the rocks in his glass only mildly placating him. When would she get off the phone? A brilliant fuchsia wall hanging above the fireplace caught his eye. It was handwoven and he liked it. A massive teak dining set, ornately carved, captured his attention. A nice change from his traditional town house in D.C. An area rug set off a floor of terra-cotta tiles. The lady must like the local crafts. He crossed the living room, and at the open terrace door, cast an anxious glance down at the street.

Impatiently, he turned toward the sound of Amanda's voice coming from the bedroom, where she was disposing of her messages.

Amanda kicked off her shoes. One foot massaged the top of the other. Elbows braced on the desk, she rubbed her temples. She had to handle the business messages. *Let him wait.*

Chris Hubbard had followed through on everything she had asked, and she was sure he'd be able to deal with any crisis that might confront him while she was out of town. He always handled the office when she was on business trips.

The last call on her list was to Harvey. Her tone changed from efficient crispness to a husky, conciliatory murmur. "Yes, Harvey. I appreciate it. And I'll make it up to you, I promise. I—I love you, too, dear. Yes, meet me here in—" Amanda held up her wrist to read her diamond watch and caught sight of Brad grinning from the doorway.

He was enjoying the sight. She'd removed her tailored suit jacket, and the silky beige blouse seemed much more friendly, revealing curvy attributes a man could love.

She wondered how long he'd been there. When she spoke again, her tone was harsher than she had intended. "At nine. Oh, no, Harvey—" with a touch of impatience, she brushed him off "—just bring a light supper. Let's eat in tonight. No, like shrimp salad. Yes, I'm fine. See you shortly, dear." She hung up the phone, then gave Brad her full attention. "Do you always eavesdrop when you're a guest in someone's home?"

"Sorry, but you are the most fascinating liar. Perhaps I've misjudged you." He lounged against the doorway, his strong arms crossed over his broad chest. His hair, now combed, shone a smooth dark blond in the waning light.

"I thought we had a truce," she said haltingly.

"We have. But the bit about my being the French representative of your company in town for a training seminar was too good—"

"It just so happens the French representative is in town."

"I gathered that when you described him as nothing to worry about, overweight and fifty. Do I look like that?"

The direction of this conversation was too personal. "That's irrelevant. Besides, what was I supposed to say?—that I'm entertaining a spy, a chauffeur or a hired mercenary—" she slipped her shoes on "—who is in my apartment at this very moment?"

"Is he the jealous type? From what I heard, he sounded pretty reasonable."

"No, he's not jealous. He's infinitely reasonable. And he's a gentleman." She stood up and sighed to herself. "It's just that I feel so damn guilty. I always feel guilty."

"Why?"

"You'd feel guilty, too, if you'd postponed a wedding six times because of business."

"Oh, I see."

"I doubt that."

"How long have you been engaged?" He edged into the bedroom.

She turned and looked up. "Two years and a month, not that it's any of your business."

"That long."

"So?"

"Nothing." His deep blue eyes held her suspended, it seemed, in order to probe the truth he sought in hers. She felt her heart begin to beat erratically but couldn't look away. He kept his gaze steady. "I just know I'd never let you postpone our wedding if you were marrying me."

Even more flustered, she swallowed and tried to cover her reaction with a flippant "Oh, really? Talk is cheap. Just what would you do?" The words echoed in her head. Why had she said that?

Smiling enigmatically, Brad took a deliberate sip of his drink and debated this lady's surprising challenge. She blushed; her arms dropped to her sides. He took a step closer and set his glass on the bureau. "I might just toss you into bed and—"

She held her ground and even managed a devastating glare in spite of her heart thundering against her breasts. He was much too near, too appealing, too— basic! "That wouldn't be wise. It could get you some very painful bruises." She took an erratic breath. "You really make me appreciate Harvey."

Brad stopped, tilted his head and lifted one eyebrow, moderately impressed. His expression changed. "Don't worry; I'm not going to attack you."

"Do I look worried?"

His voice was so deep and resonant. If only she could stop her body tingling.

"Not at all. You are too confident. A trick or two up your sleeve?"

"Perhaps, or maybe I'm a good judge of character. The move wasn't your style. I think you fancy yourself a charmer, a lover—although I can't imagine why."

Brad threw back his head and laughed heartily, clearing away the residual tension. "You're right, Amanda, absolutely right. You've frustrated my record as a—what was it?—a charmer, a lover." His laugh subsided, and he asked softly, "What does it take to get to you, to love you? Am I out of line again?"

"How did we get on this? Back to business." Amanda brushed past him into the infinitely safer territory of her living room. "Just get to the business at hand. I've returned all my calls. I'm meeting my fiancé in exactly three hours, at nine. Now show me the papers and the plan and let's get it over with." Too nervous to take a seat, she went to the terrace door to stare at the panoramic view of the city beyond. Distant traffic noises mixed with the quickening sounds of the exhausted day.

"As you command, my lady." Brad left his drink and followed. For a moment, he stood beside her and checked the street far below. Then, frowning, he walked back to the coffee table in front of the sofa. Wordlessly, she joined him and flicked on the lamp beside them.

"Let's see," he said as he tore open the packet, "some of this stuff isn't pertinent." She sat down on the edge of the sofa as he began to separate the numerous papers into two groups. Laying aside several pages bound with a rubber band, he gave her a wicked smile and sat down much too close to her. "Private stuff." He leaned in more intimately. "Incidentally, I'm thirty-six, not fifty."

"Really." Amanda projected indifference and edged away.

"And you?"

She answered automatically. "Twenty-nine."

"Ahh." He nodded. "First marriage?"

"Yes," she breathed, impatient with him, impatient with the silken threads of desire tightening about them again. Why didn't she feel like this with Harvey? Why was she feeling like this with a man she didn't even much like?

To get his attention away from herself, she asked, "Where does your wife live?"

"Wife!" He seemed surprised at the query. "I was married briefly ten years ago, but my wife divorced me after a year. Didn't care for my life-style."

"I can only guess. Too dangerous?"

"I'm glad you're interested." He tipped his head and leaned back. "No, that wasn't the reason at all. As a matter of fact, she was bored by it. Too many meetings and luncheons."

Amanda stifled a grin. "Never took her for a ride, huh?"

"No!" He chuckled and relaxed even more. "You may find this hard to believe, but I usually don't drive as I did today. Today I wasn't working." He straightened up and picked up a slip of paper.

"Heaven help us all should you ever go back to work."

"Yeah." He handed her the paper and smoothly moved the subject back to business. "Here's the name of the fisherman you're to contact in Tampico. He'll be aboard a chartered vessel called the *Grand Finale*. If everything is go, he'll be flying a red telltale flag. If there are problems, there'll be a blue one up."

Amanda nodded. Her mission sounded real suddenly, yet new and mysterious—certainly nothing like industrial espionage in the bottling industry. She wished she felt less nervous.

Her insecurity must have shown, because Brad handed her another paper. "Here's an emergency telephone number. If you panic or need anything night or day for the next few days, call. I'll be standing by. And here's my home address while I'm in the city. But just keep all this to yourself. If you talk to Margaret again, don't tell her I gave it to you."

"Why?" Amanda asked, a sinking feeling in the pit of her stomach.

"I'm afraid she'd disapprove," he said simply, hurrying on. "And here are the documents you'll need for the customs officials at the airport."

As Amanda studied the myriad documents, Brad leaned close again, his voice conspiratorial. "How are you going to get customs to release the cylinders without opening them? If they do, you know, the whole ball game is over. There are people in this city who would kill to analyze a sample of this stuff. And that worries me."

He was so near that she could feel his body heat. Concentrating on the papers was hard until the word "kill" focused her attention sharply. She blinked. "Well, no one knows it's not Tri-Cola syrup."

"Somebody was suspicious of your connection with Margaret or we wouldn't have picked up that tail this afternoon."

"True." Ms. Cullen's first name came easily to him. Perhaps her earlier suspicion that he was romantically involved with the woman was justified.

"Look, I'm just grasping at straws, but could a rival soft-drink company be after your formula? Perhaps that car following us had nothing to do with the cylinders."

She shook her head. "No, that's ridiculous. I'm afraid we were followed by people other than Tri-Cola's rivals. They all have our formula. Our formula is their formula. We doped that out years ago. No, our business is cutthroat, but only in the market place."

"Yeah, I was afraid of that. Then the tail is the fault of the State Department and all their foul-ups. Damn! Lady, I hate to say this, but this job is too dangerous for a woman."

"You can sound intelligent, logical and even human until you start that old chauvinist routine again. Look, I don't think I'll have any trouble. Is this everything?" Amanda indicated the mass of papers he had handed her.

He nodded. "Yes, ridiculous, isn't it? Put 'em in a safe place." He squared the papers up and slid a rubber band over them, then stood up and stretched, as if to leave.

"Don't worry, I will. To set your mind at rest, I've had dealings with customs before on emergency airfreight shipments of syrup to replace products that've gone bad for one reason or another. It won't be a problem. I'll simply have one of my drivers bring a company truck to the customs shed. I'll fill out the necessary documents, pay the duty and take the cargo north to Tampico. Simple. If it came to it, I could even drive the truck myself."

"Would it be better if I came with you?"

She walked him to the front door. His suggestion, strangely enough, had a lot of appeal, but she knew that having him along would invite new problems and would be taken as a sign of weakness.

"Certainly not. A mercenary in a Tri-Cola truck would most assuredly cause attention."

"I suppose you're right," he agreed, so easily as to cause Amanda a small prick of jealousy.

"I'm sure, Ms. Cullen can find more interesting things for you to do than nursemaid me."

"No doubt!" He hesitated at the door. "I guess that's it, then. I've done all the damage I can do. I can't talk you out of it, can I?"

"No, and you'll have to leave now. I have to change for Harvey."

"Oh, yes." He offered his hand. "Well, good luck."

"Thanks." Amanda looked at his hand, hesitated, then extended her own for a brief, businesslike shake.

Solemnly, he took her small hand in his. The heat of his palm jolted her wonderfully. The room seemed bathed in warm darkness. She looked up, and their eyes locked. Amanda swallowed nervously. Neither released the other's hand. He leaned closer. His aftershave was faint but very pleasant; his skin, tan, flawless.

He tilted his head, fascinated, confused, obviously reluctant to leave. When she spoke again, forcing herself to form coherent sentences, he was only half listening.

"Don't worry. I, uh, listened to you. I agree; things aren't always what they seem. But I—I said I'd do this. Ms. Cullen and the State Department expect it. I can handle it." If only he would let her hand go. She kept talking. "I just wish they'd never put Tri-Cola labels on it in the first place. Why not Coca Cola or Pepsi? Why me?"

He blinked and cleared his throat. "Because your company's smaller, and—you're a fantastic woman, Amanda." Brad's voice was unsteady. She thought he was going to kiss her, and she knew she was going to let him. But he pulled away, shaken.

She stood breathless, terribly aware how much she had wanted that kiss. She was disappointed in herself.

He seemed equally remorseful. "I—I—" he stammered. "You're right, you know. You're able to take care of yourself. I, ah, guess you know—" his baritone deepened "—I find you very attractive. That can only make for trouble. Good night." He turned to open the door, then stopped and returned to the coffee table in three long strides. He angrily snatched at his packet of personal papers and knocked all the papers onto the floor, then he scooped the packet up and bolted out the door, a portrait of masculine anguish.

Amanda closed the apartment door and leaned against the cold varnished wood for support. She felt drained of emotion, exhausted. What had affected him so strongly? What had she done? What had she said? Had she used some unconscious sexual attraction in order to bring him under her control? Or had she simply lost control of herself?

She pushed herself away from the door and stood staring into space.

Harvey had never excited her. Business was their common denominator, not sex, and she had never really missed it—but perhaps she had never let herself think about what she was missing. Maybe marriage to Harvey would be intolerable to bear because of its lack of zest, its lack of primal attraction, its predictability.

No! Harvey was a good man, steady, an established international banker who would do anything for her and make no demands; he had no demands to make. He was just what she wanted.

Thank goodness Bradford had left before the scene had gotten out of hand. Harvey would be here soon. She had to hurry to be ready in time.

She started for the bedroom, but a discreet knock on the door stopped her.

Brad!

No, Harvey. The discreet knock was typically Harvey. He was early.

"You're early, Harvey," she said, throwing open the door. "I'm not even dressed yet."

"Forgive me, *señorita*, for intruding on you. I am Detective Guando from the neighborhood police substation."

The oily voice came from a tall, threatening man who was touching his black fedora and holding a badge too far away for her to inspect.

Amanda shrank back. The man wore civilian clothes: a light blue sport coat, blue T-shirt and beige linen slacks. He might have been a detective, but it wasn't likely. He was too intimidating even without the jagged scar that ran from the corner of his left eye to his chin.

He moved into the room quickly, his black eyes darted about, then settled on the packet of papers lying on the floor by the coffee table.

"I will take only a moment of your time," he promised, cataloging her fear. He pocketed the badge and advanced on her slowly. "A criminal known to us was seen leaving this building. What was he doing here?"

Amanda hoped she looked calm, though her heart was trying to leap from her chest and her breath was in short supply. Instinctively, she knew what this man Guando was after.

"No one has been here all evening, Señor Guando." She edged away slowly. "But my fiancé will arrive at any moment." Her voice cracked as she found herself backed against an end table.

"Why are you frightened, *señorita*?" Guando's sleazy sincerity was all the more menacing as his black eyes narrowed and slithered over her body. He loved to deal with frightened females. His interest quickened. First he would caress her entire softness while she tried to fight him. Her clothes would accidentally tear. He could feel the sensation already. "You are in no danger under my protection. Have you something to hide?'' Guando moved forward with the swiftness of a striking cobra.

Amanda's mind was a step ahead. "No, *señor*. Please leave." She inched to the side with slow deliberation, even though she was desperately frightened. She avoided his reaching hands by twisting away with a gymnast's speed and strength. She needed some distance from him. Her breathing was ragged, her throat tight. *Don't panic,* she cautioned herself.

Guando's hands grasped thin air, and he turned rapidly. The woman wanted to prolong the inevitable; so be it. "I will leave in a moment," he said. Then he blocked her way to the door and fixed her with a baleful stare that was always effective.

Amanda cleared her throat, but it still seemed filled with cotton. "Please," she murmured, hoping she had not shown him that she could defend herself. Her knees shook. Did she really have a chance to stop him? She didn't know for sure. She was moving on instinct and training now. Her skin crawled with sensations. One last try. "Take the papers and leave."

Guando looked pointedly beyond her at the bedroom. "In a few moments."

Amanda prepared for the final moves that could bring either a quick victory or her death. She tensed, remembering her father's advice, every muscle in her body prepared.

A slight sound came from behind the apartment door. Guando turned like a snake, dropping on one knee, and pulled out his pistol.

"Harvey," Amanda screamed. "Run, there's a madman here." In the same instant, galvanized by a new fear for Harvey's life, Amanda changed her mind and grabbed a heavy brass lamp from the end table.

She followed through with a perfect golf swing that slammed the base into Guando's back.

Brad burst through the door and dove for Guando, wresting the gun from him before it barked its single lethal word. The two men rolled across the carpet in silent deadly combat.

Fully charged with adrenaline, Amanda leaped forward with a guttural howl and swung the lamp at Guando's horrified face. He ducked, and it grazed Brad's temple. For a moment Brad seemed stunned by the impact. Appalled by the enormity of her mistake, Amanda stood frozen. Then, groggy and bleeding slightly, he tried to get up, only to be thrown down by Guando, who freed himself and scooped up the packet of papers.

"Oh, no," Amanda cried, her face screwed up in a painful grimace at the sight of blood on Brad's face.

Guando hesitated for a moment, deliberating, then snarled, "Thank you so very much, señorita. You will entertain me another time."

She threw the lamp at him as he scrambled out the door, unhampered. She ran to the door and locked it, then turned to Brad. He lay barely moving. "What have I done?" she wailed as she sank to her knees beside him. "Are you all right?"

He groaned and tried to get his bearings. "Yeah! Yeah! I'm fine. Damn! That guy throws a hell of a punch. I thought I had him just before he hit me. You all right?"

At least he was alive. "Yes, I'm fine—but he didn't hit you," she mumbled, overtaken with self-reproach.

Brad was too confused to understand her. "Where'd he go?"

"He got away with the packet." She sniffed the acrid smell of defeat.

"Oh! Thank goodness for small favors."

"What's that supposed to mean? I'd better put some ice on that nasty lump on your head."

"No, I'm fine." Brad swayed to his feet, Amanda's surprisingly strong arm firmly supporting him around his waist.

"Why 'thank goodness'? Everything's ruined, blown."

"Nothing's blown. He got the wrong packet. Bait and switch." Brad pulled the duplicate package from the back of his tennis shorts.

"You left the wrong papers on purpose?" Amanda's eyes burned.

"Now don't go bananas on me. I'd have handed the real packet back in the morning. I was prepared to wait out there all night if I had to for them to make a move. I just didn't want to take any chances on a foul-up."

"Out front? What do you mean? Did your friend Margaret Cullen tell you to do that?"

"Well—it was left to my discretion, depending on how things looked when I got here."

"I'll bet! You could have gotten me killed—for nothing. Why didn't you tell me you didn't trust me?"

"It's not that I didn't trust you. You're just not used to this racket."

"Oh, sure, big deal. And you are! What are you, some kind of CIA man?" She glared at him defiantly her hands on her hips. "When do I find out who you are, Mr. Bradford?"

"Wait a minute. I came back, didn't I? I brought the real packet back."

"And just why did you do that? Remorse?"

"No," he admitted. "I caught sight of the Porsche when we came into the building earlier. I had a feeling they'd wait around until I left and then come after you. So I took a chance, switched the papers and pretended to leave."

"Of all the harebrained—"

"I felt it was the only way to get those people to make their move."

"Why didn't you tell me that?"

"I didn't want to scare you. And I had no intention of leaving a woman here alone while they were out there."

"Thanks a lot." She gave him her back before he read her mind. *You really misjudged him, Amanda.*

"Okay, I'm sorry. I apologize. I'll wait until Harvey gets here."

"No, thanks, Bradford. I'll alert the concierge to deal with any intruders." She pointed toward the door. "You may leave now."

He looked skeptical, but Amanda's determined look finally seemed to convince him. He nodded his head painfully. "Okay, we smoked out that slime and sent him off with phony information. We won't have any more trouble with him. They won't be back, anyway."

He sounded so sure of himself. He had handled himself well—until she had hit him. But of course agents were thoroughly trained for combat. "How do you know they won't be back? I thought you were just the errand boy. No connection with the embassy, remember?"

He sighed. "I know. Because that's the way it works. And I told you the truth. I don't work for the government."

"Certainly. You're just doing this out of the goodness of your heart—out of love for a friend."

"You're right. That's very perceptive of you."

"I thought as much." Her voice betrayed a little too much emotion. "We both know who she is, don't we."

He grinned, then groaned. "Oh, my head. Yes, we do. What is this? The future Mrs. Harvey what's his name jealous of my contact at the embassy?"

"I don't think I'd call it jealousy, more like getting my perspective straightened out. You're right; the future Mrs. Harvey Bannon was a bit confused."

Brad started toward her, more amused by the moment.

She backed away. "Just leave; now, before he gets here."

"Okay, okay, I'm gone. But do me a favor; when I get out of here, lock your door until Harvey arrives and don't let that packet out of your sight. Okay?"

"Out!"

"I'm leaving," he said reasonably, closing the door behind him.

Amanda threw the dead bolts and hooked the burglar chain, then sighed with relief. Her stomach was in knots from hunger and of extreme emotion. She flattened her hands against her waist and took a deep breath.

"Good night, Amanda." Brad's voice filtered softly through the door.

"Good night!" she barked.

Once in the shower, she relaxed a bit. Yes indeed, it had been one of those days. Odd, though—she felt more alive than she had for a long, long time.

# Chapter Six

The special candlelight supper with Harvey was anything but the delight Amanda had promised in her note to him. It was utter disaster. He arrived precisely on schedule, his arms filled to overflowing. She took his bouquet in her arms. "These are delightful. Thank you." He'd remembered how she loved the rare red ranunculus.

He pecked her cheek, pleased with himself. "Nothing but the best for Amanda Perry." With a flourish he set the bags and boxes on her kitchen counter and proudly unloaded from them cartons of gourmet food, at last presenting her favorite wine.

Under normal circumstances, it would have been a very romantic evening, perhaps the most romantic of their smooth-running relationship.

"Amanda, sweet, we must discuss today's events," he began as he removed his suit coat to put on his checked oilcloth apron, which guaranteed that his impeccable white dress shirt and conservative burgundy tie would remain spotless. He thrust a stemmed glass of Riesling into her hand and waved her out of the tiny kitchen.

Numbly, she sampled the chilled wine and over the thin crystal rim smiled agreement with him. Walking aimlessly back to the living room to place the flowers on the table, she tried to think pleasant, contented thoughts. Harvey wasn't a bad sort.

He interrupted her efforts by bustling into the dining area with a tray of place settings and remarking approvingly, "I'm so glad these linen place mats are properly ironed. They're my favorites." After lighting the candles, he noticed the broken lamp and crumpled end table. "Bit of a mess here. You could do with a change in housekeepers, sweet. There's no excuse for this."

"Yes, dear," she said meekly. Why tell him anything of what really happened? It would just worry him unnecessarily. "I'll finish the table."

"Very good." He went back to the kitchen and started to remove the food from its cartons.

With the first whiff of the fresh hot bread, Amanda realized she was famished. She hadn't eaten since early morning.

She attacked the meal. Not until Harvey cleared his throat did she lift her eyes from her plate. Glass raised, he was preparing to make several witty toasts, a long-standing tradition. She made apologies with her eyes and agreeable sounds through a bread-filled mouth; then, in one swallow, she downed the wine left in her glass just to get the ritual over. She rose from her chair, kissed him on the cheek—another ritual—then returned to her seat and dug into the veal ragout.

Harvey watched. Amanda was behaving in a most uncharacteristic way. She never made a single comment. She didn't mention the crispness of the lettuce under the shrimp salad or even ask which of his favorite chefs had prepared the meal. Flabbergasted, he was thrown off his normal routine. Instead of eating, he delicately, if not cunningly, questioned her further about the man in the Jaguar. By the time Amanda had finished and laid her silver to rest on her plate, Harvey had eaten little but had consumed a second bottle of wine.

Perhaps the unaccustomed amount of alcohol was influencing him, but Amanda seemed different to Harvey tonight, more alive. The change in her so excited him that he made an uncharacteristic move himself.

Of all the times to become amorous, this was not it. For the first time in their courtship he was keyed up and ready for romance, but Amanda was both surprised and turned off by his advances. She had never had to fight Harvey off, even though there had been occasions when she would have welcomed a well-planned campaign. But she had no time for nonsense now.

"It's too late," she said prophetically, pushing him away.

"Too late?" he grinned sheepishly. "It's not even eleven yet."

"Well, I have a headache, and I'm not feeling well at all."

"I can imagine," he agreed reasonably. "I've never known you to, uh, pounce on your dinner."

"I had a bad day. That meeting with that terrible French representative, the trouble at the plant, and my car has died on me. I'll make it all up to you after we're married."

Harvey patted her arm discreetly and rose to leave. "I understand completely, dear." His lips touched her cheek.

He was so understanding. He really was too good for her.

"I mean it, Harvey," Amanda said fiercely, almost angrily. "I just have to straighten out a few business problems over the next few days."

"I understand. How about lunch tomorrow?" he suggested as she began to close the door.

She could think of no reason why she couldn't at least do that for him. He had endured her on-again, off-again wedding plans for so long. "Okay, meet me at the University Club tomorrow at twelve-thirty," she said hurriedly as she closed the door. "Good night, dearest."

She stood with her back against the locked door. Thank heavens that was over. Why on earth had she agreed to lunch? Why, indeed. It was the only decent thing to do. Now that he was gone, reality began to intrude. She pushed a heavy chair against the door, although she was relatively certain no one would come back. Uneasily, she fell into bed, listening for an hour to any sound out of the ordinary, then finally fell into a fitful slumber, only to awaken time after time through the endless night. She would turn over, plump her pillows under her head and blame overeating for her restlessness.

THE HATEFUL MORNING SUN assaulted Amanda's eyes. Today she would have welcomed rain, and where was it? All the way to the airport she failed to appreciate the clear, deep blue sky and the cabdriver's attempts to practice his English. She paid him, pulled her weary body from the seat and fled toward the cool interior of the customs building. Airport traffic was already at its peak, with thousands of world-hopping tourists arriving and departing on endless flights. Oblivious to it all, she plodded forward through the sea of bodies. She was bone tired from a sleepless night. She clutched her briefcase as though it would be ripped from her hands at any moment. Every car she passed looked suspicious. Unusually cautious, she crossed the street to avoid walking close to a black Porsche parked near her destination.

Amanda walked into the *aduana*, the customs duty office, regretting she had ever undertaken this job. She feared everyone could see through her cheerful facade and strained to look casual. She rubbed her moist palms against her white linen skirt, then casually shoved her sunglasses up to sit atop her curly head.

*"Buenos días, señorita,"* the cheerful *aduanero* greeted.

What did he mean? Was it really a "good day"? What did he know? Amanda asked herself. Trying to sound normal, she said, *"Buenos días, señor."* She spread out her papers and gave her story, filled with apologies for any inconvenience caused by the lack of the proper papers. Miraculously, the customs man was understanding and cooperative. Amanda paid the fees and additional paperwork fines and was on her way to the customs shed ten minutes later. As previously arranged, her driver and Tri-Cola van were waiting. Her spirits soared. Bradford be damned, she'd pulled it off.

She had felt a momentary pang of fear when she arrived at the shed. Parked just around the corner from her van was a Porsche. There was no one near it, and business was brisk at the shed. *There are thousands of Porsches in Mexico,* she chided herself.

Still, she had to be sure. She entered the shed, actually a huge bustling warehouse, and after a short conference with her driver, Luis Garcia, she phoned the bellboys' desk at the Palacio del Sol.

Amanda replaced the receiver nervously and waited a few minutes. Luis had backed the Tri-Cola van into position at the loading dock at the far end of the warehouse. The Porsche had not moved from its position. Amanda began to feel foolish. Perhaps she'd wasted both time and money. The agonizing minutes ticked by as trucks came and went with regularity.

Forty minutes later, right on schedule, Luis's Tri-Cola van eased away from the docks. Tensely, Amanda stepped back into the building's cool shadows. An ancient, gaily decorated, school bus was blocking her view of both the van and the Porsche. The strange vehicle backfired noisily, then lethargically pulled up to the loading dock. Amanda's ears rang from the din.

Now that the bus was out of the way, she could see the sleek, low-slung Porsche again as it cruised slowly after the distant Tri-Cola van, keeping it in view. Amanda swallowed nervously; her heart was pumping adrenaline faster than her body could handle it. She had to get back to that phone quickly and call Brad. This was an emergency. Where was that number—the panic number—he'd given her?

She had tried to dial it four times before her hands stopped shaking long enough to hit the correct numbers. The phone rang.

"Yes," Brad answered immediately.

"Oh, Brad," her whisper cracked.

"Amanda! What's wrong?"

Thank God he was there. She tried to whisper, but her words tumbled forth in a husky torrent. "I'm at the airport—customs' shed. The Porsche was following me, but I got rid of it. I sent the van—"

"Damn! Forget the catalyst. Are you all right?" His voice sounded tight. His worry had a wonderfully calming effect on her.

"Of course. I'm trying to tell you, the catalyst is okay. It's not on the van. I had my driver take the van to Mazatlán. They'll be driving for a week if they follow him there. I hired a truck from Enrique, and he'll be here soon."

"Wait a minute," Brad interrupted gruffly. "Who the hell's Enrique?"

"He's a bellboy at the Palacio del Sol."

"A bellboy? Are you crazy?" he hissed. "What's going on. Why not broadcast it on Radio Mexicale?"

Amanda's fear was turning to a slow-burning anger. "He's not just a bellboy; he's a young man with connections and—" Oh, why explain? Why had she called this man in the first place? Who needed a lecture? Who needed anything? The deed was done! She had it made. In actuality, she was just reporting in, even though she knew she shouldn't have called.

"I called to tell you—" She took a deep breath. "Everything is fine. I'm leaving for Tampico now."

A hand touched her arm. Amanda's tense nerves reacted with a shudder. She twisted away sharply, dropping the phone receiver and screamed involuntarily.

"*Señorita*, it's only me—Enrique." The little bellboy ducked, nearly as frightened as Amanda.

The phone receiver continued to swing and bounce against the wall.

Several workers in the distance picked up on the action and watched curiously. "Enrique," Amanda said with a gulp, barely able to appreciate his natty attire. "Thank goodness you're here. Did you find a truck?"

"*¡Sí!* It's already at the loading dock."

Amanda grabbed the phone receiver and handed the customs papers, all stamped and cleared, to Enrique. "I'll be there in a minute. Could you have them load the Tri-Cola cylinders, please, Enrique?"

He grinned widely, glad to oblige. "You got it, Señorita Perry." He touched the brim of his cap and winked.

Amanda smiled, comforted by his friendly gamin face. Then she remembered Brad was still on the line. "Brad," she said with an obvious note of relief in her voice, "everything is okay. They're loading the cylinders now."

"Good, Amanda, you're doing well," came a chill voice over the line—not Brad's voice. It was Margaret Cullen. Amanda flushed with embarrassment. She hadn't suspected that the emergency number wasn't at Brad's home.

"Oh, Ms. Cullen," Amanda stammered. "I—I'm sorry to bother you. I didn't realize this was the embassy. I really didn't need to call. I won't call again."

"That's quite all right," Ms. Cullen said with a trace of sternness in her voice.

"Uh, I was talking to Mr. Bradford. May I say another word to him."

"I'm afraid not, Amanda. He's not here."

"Not there?" Amanda's heart jolted, she felt alone again. "But I just spoke—"

"Amanda—" Ms. Cullen scolded. "Get hold of yourself. You're doing fine. Bradford was here, but he has just run from the house, shouting at me like a maniac. When he arrives there to save you, please send him home."

"He's coming here, to the airport?"

"I believe so."

"But I don't need him. Everything is under control," Amanda said without confidence.

"I hope so; I expect so; I told him so. He left against my wishes, and his interference might endanger your mission."

"Why?"

"Because of his unofficial connection to the embassy."

"You mean to you," Amanda said, bitterness in her voice.

Margaret Cullen sighed audibly. "Yes, Amanda, that's what I mean."

At least that little deception was out in the open now. "He told me he didn't work for the embassy."

"That's true; he doesn't."

Home. The word suddenly struck Amanda with obvious meaning. Ms. Cullen was at Brad's home. It all added up. He was living with the woman. "This is Brad's house? This is his home phone number?"

"Yes," Margaret Cullen replied easily. "Amanda," she said, changing the subject smoothly, "take care. I know you can do this. You're a very remarkable young woman. Just take everything one step at a time."

"Yes, ma'am," Amanda agreed, her voice flat. She hung up the phone. Everything just seemed to go from bad to worse.

So what was she going to do about it? First, send Brad back to his highly placed, influential lover. Second, go make amends with Harvey at lunch. Third, deliver this cargo to Tampico.

Filled with resolve, Amanda checked in with Chris Hubbard. All was under control, and that made life easier. Chris had put all the information she'd requested on her desk, and it would be waiting there for her when she returned. Perfect! One more call confirmed her luncheon date with Harvey. He was in high spirits. He had just met a most fascinating newspaper reporter who wished to do a story on Amanda and Tri-Cola. He seemed to want to talk forever. Nearly half an hour later, Amanda walked out to the loading dock.

"All loaded up," Enrique said proudly as he delivered the signed papers back to her. "Fifty two-liter containers of Tri-Cola syrup."

"Thank you, Enrique." Amanda patted his shoulder warmly. "Which truck is it?"

"I couldn't get a truck," he admitted, "but I got something better." He pointed proudly to the ancient dinosaur of a school bus.

Never had Amanda seen a more unlikely prospect for a hard journey overland. "No, no." She sighed. "That won't do at all." From the corner of her eye she noticed a streak of gold closing in on the customs area. The distant pavement was already shimmering with heat. "We'll have another visitor in about two minutes; then we'll get going back to the city. We'll rent another van there."

"No, *señorita*," Enrique said, surreptitiously glancing at the fast-approaching Jaguar. "It's old, but with a little help, it'll be tough enough to make it."

"AMANDA, you've got to be kidding," Brad protested. "You can't drive that thing back to the middle of Mexico City. It'll never make it."

"Not true at all," she disagreed. "It may be old, but it's reliable. It'll never break down. Right, Enrique? I'm sure we can make it to Tampico easily."

"*Sí,*" Enrique agreed solemnly, assessing Brad carefully. The man had class. His idea of casual attire suited Enrique just fine. He'd like a shirt like that, one with wide blue-and-gray stripes, and the gray chinos, too. He liked Brad much more than Harvey, even though he could see Ms. Perry had a problem with the man.

"I don't dispute the reliability," Brad said, "or that it's got one of the finest engines Detroit ever produced, but this is a tough job. We'd never make it."

"We? You're not going. I have orders to send you home to Mama."

Brad gave Amanda a thunderous glare. "She told you that?"

"In so many words." Amanda readjusted her sunglasses on top of her head.

"*Señor,*" Enrique intervened, "this bus is in excellent condition, and no one would believe we'd take a vehicle like this all the way to Tampico on a secret mission."

"That's true."

"And Señorita Perry will rent a van in the city. The people who are trying to follow her will pick that up from the computers in a minute. They'll watch for her to collect the rental van and never see the bus pass by."

Brad looked at Amanda with renewed respect. "That's a hell of a plan. Why didn't you say so? I thought you were just going to go off half-cocked."

"You didn't ask me." Amanda cast a quick smile of thanks at Enrique. She had only planned to rent a van; she had never realized that the rental could be traced.

"Well, let's get going." Brad glanced around. "Who's driving?"

"My cousin." Enrique indicated a middle-aged man in the front seat. "It's his bus."

"Okay. We're going to the city." Amanda led the way. "I have a luncheon engagement with my fiancé before I leave town."

"You mean this whole operation is on hold until then?" Brad demanded, incredulous.

"That's right. You've been dismissed."

"No way, lady. I'll follow you into town and wait until you get under way. Then I'll fold my tent. That's the way it's going to be."

Amanda couldn't have been happier.

Several minutes later the exotically painted bus, a '37 Ford with extras, cousin Carlos at the wheel, rumbled back toward Mexico City, past the satellite towns and villages, through the heavily traveled interchanges. Enrique was perched atop one of the fifty cylinders in the compartment behind the driver. Even in the front seat next to Carlos, Amanda found the ride hard and bumpy. She clung to the dashboard with one hand and the armrest with the other, uncomfortable in her tight linen suit. Every jolt and wobble made her wonder and worry more about the stability of their cargo.

After a few minutes more, she grew more confident in the bus. Braced for the ride, Amanda surveyed her surroundings. Yes, the vehicle was quite a unique creation. It must have been a truck of some kind years before in another life. Even though it was now a very old bus, it was a little roomier than a large, modern van. The front compartment had a padded seat, comfortable enough for two. There were two doors. Behind an opening covered with a handwoven curtain was the rear compartment, from which several seats had been removed. The cylinders were there. The whole arrangement was actually quite cozy.

Getting accustomed to the jolting ride as the vehicle proceeded along back streets toward the center of the city, Amanda calmly began to sort out her situation. She didn't feel she had events under control, functioning smoothly, moving forward in a business-like manner. She wasn't leading yet. Brad, unlike Harvey and Chris Hubbard, questioned her competence. That she was not experienced in this area of skullduggery was immaterial. She had been forced to let Brad monitor her progress. He had refused to allow her to leave the airport without him. And she was saddled with Enrique, and his cousin Carlos, as well, plus a strange bus, not to mention an unprofessionally loaded cargo. Much had to be done before setting off for Tampico.

She still intended to meet Harvey for lunch, but she could picture the ludicrous effect of her arrival at the restaurant with this colorful entourage. What would the newspaper reporter think of her professionalism? What would it do to her relationship with Harvey? She would never find another man as understanding as

Harvey. Better not bring the old school bus and its cargo into Mexico City.

Amanda looked back at Enrique on the other side of the curtain, bouncing along without a care in the world. She got his attention and explained she wanted to stop a moment. He relayed the order to Carlos. Immediately, the bus began to slow and pull over. Behind, Brad's Jaguar pulled over on the narrow shoulder. Carlos and Enrique came around the front of the bus to stand by her door. She stepped out into the intense glare and immediately mourned the loss of her hat. The sun was ferocious. The traffic whizzed by, depositing a whirl of dust and grit in the air.

Brad came forward and joined them. "What's the problem now?"

"I want to change my plan," Amanda said quickly, brooking no opposition. "I want to hide the bus until after dark. It'll have to be completely safe and out of sight. And I want this load repacked. Any suggestions?"

Brad shook his head and laughed. "You'll need a blimp hangar or a very large haystack to hide it. Beats me."

"Haystack!" Enrique said. "How about a bull ranch? My uncle works on a bull ranch not ten kilometers from here." He asked Carlos if they could hide the bus at the ranch.

"*¡Sí!*" His cousin nodded lethargically.

Before they went one foot farther, however, Amanda felt she had to buy the bus from Carlos. After all, something could happen to the venerable old vehicle in the long journey to the north.

Amanda smiled and tackled Carlos in Spanish. "Would you consider selling your bus to me? I think that would be the best way to proceed."

Enrique added a few comments as Amanda explained her reasons for buying the bus.

"Oh, my Lord," Brad muttered under his breath. "An antique freak." He leaned against the bus, crossed his ankles and listened in silence to the roadside negotiation. It wasn't going very well; that was plain to see. Even though Amanda could be very persuasive at times, she obviously wasn't going to have the time to make any kind of deal with Carlos, who wasn't taking the *señorita* very seriously. Even Enrique couldn't come up with anything that would make the deal work. Carlos could not be swayed by mere pesos or dollars.

Frustrated, Amanda turned to Brad. "Instead of just standing there, Mr. Bradford, you could help me. Where are all your many ready answers today? I've got to meet Harvey in thirty minutes or my marriage is dead."

"Sounds good to me." Brad had an egotistical grin on his handsome face.

She was hot and under pressure, and he infuriated her too easily. "That's it, huh?" She drummed her fingers on her briefcase. "I'll remember you as a nothing who came up with nothing." Scowling, Amanda stalked away to lean on the Jaguar, leaving Enrique to argue her cause with Carlos.

Brad ambled up. "You really want help?"

She gave him a disgusted look. "You also owe me a new hat! Of all the ridiculous questions. Of course I want help."

"Will you admit that this is one situation that a man might just possibly handle better than you?"

"Look, wise guy," Amanda growled under her breath, "I've offered him everything except my body, and to tell you the truth, I don't think he'd go for that, either."

"Hmm, we might work something out."

"No deal." Amanda glanced at her watch furtively.

"Okay! Okay!" Brad threw up his hands. He opened the driver's door to the Jaguar. "Hop in. I'll go talk to Carlos. You wait here."

"Good luck."

At least it was out of the sun. Discouraged, she watched from the car, feeling inadequate and deserted as Brad gestured and talked animatedly with Carlos and Enrique. Then, abruptly, the three shook hands. Apparently a deal had been struck. Brad walked back to the Jaguar, his face noncommittal.

He opened the door and leaned in. "For better or worse," he said quietly, "you're the proud owner of the bus." He didn't look very happy, however.

"What on earth did you say?"

"I'll tell you later. Right now you'd better hurry." He picked up his sport jacket from the seat and gave her the car keys. "You drive this to your date with Harvey, and we'll take the cargo to the bull ranch, Hacienda Rolaca. Meet us there when you finish." He gave her the directions to the place.

"Well done!" She grinned. "Thanks. And—drive carefully." A small measure of confidence returned.

He nodded, his face solemn. "Right."

"And see if you can get some rope and cross-lash those cylinders a little better."

"Sure." He sighed and backed away to shut the door.

"And Brad," she added, feeling a swell of gratitude, "I take back all those things I said." She bestowed a beneficent smile. "You've saved my life."

"I probably have," he agreed with a touch of irony. "Take care of this baby." He patted the car roof and shut the door.

"I will," she promised as the engine roared to life. She waved goodbye to Enrique and Carlos and sped away from her benefactor toward the man who loved her.

At last she had begun to make progress. Government agents like Bradford were interesting people, she had to admit, but they were dangerous to associate with. Nothing at all like the reliable banker she was on her way to see. Now that he'd assisted her this one last time, she'd be free of Bradford. That was as it should be. Why didn't the thought bring some feeling of joy?

Brad nodded sadly as he watched the gold Jaguar disappear toward the smog-drenched horizon that was the interior of the city. Amanda Perry was a determined person, he mused. More vulnerable here in Mexico because she was a woman, and a beautiful one at that. She was her own worst enemy, driven by demons to push herself and not even realizing she was doing it. One thing was clear—she didn't love Harvey.

He walked back to the bus. "Okay, guys, let's go to the ranch. I hope to hell we make it."

## Chapter Seven

Amanda rushed into the University Club, slightly late for lunch. The hushed, elegant atmosphere calmed her as she wound her way through the profusion of palms and tables to the smiling Harvey, who stood to greet her. His appearance was faultless—conservative dark gray pinstripe suit, burgundy silk tie, immaculate white shirt, solid gray vest, black wing tip shoes. Not one gray hair was out of place. Before she could offer an excuse, he seated her. He seemed troubled.

A thread of fear coursed through her. Had he seen through her explanation of the events of the previous day? Perhaps she should just confess everything and forget her mission. "Harvey, I want to clear the air. I've not been—"

He held up his hand and shook his head to silence her confession before it started. "Yes, yes, but first I must talk to you about something urgent. And we may not have time later. The reporter will be here to interview you right after lunch." He glanced around nervously, then leaned close and murmured so that only she could hear, "I must apologize for my unseemly behavior last night."

"*Your* behavior?"

His face looked stricken with remorse. He moved his chair closer, then thought better of it and eased the chair back again. "I didn't sleep all night," he confessed.

"I had a terrible night, too."

"I knew it!" he murmured. "I mean, I'm sorry! I'm not an animal with no control over my— My advances toward you were untimely. Please forgive me."

"Harvey, I—"

He put his hand on hers. "I know that you can't respect a man who forces his will upon you. I've been very civilized and reserved in the past, but last night—" He hesitated and shook his head. "I was peeved with you. No, jealous! Maybe a bit angry. But never again. I want you, but not in that manner."

Dear Harvey. Amanda sighed.

"I know, and I do appreciate that. But to tell the truth, I was flattered by your attentions."

His milk-blue eyes widened. He cleared his throat and straightened his already-perfect tie. "You're being very kind, Amanda, but you rightly stopped me before I made a mess of it. My attempt to—ravage you was unforgivable."

She reached over and patted the top of his hand. What to say? His shamefaced apologies had altered their usually rigid relationship and lulled her into a warm brown haze. She felt wonderfully cared for. "Harvey," she said, her voice low and husky, "it's mandatory that I take this business trip, but I'll terminate it quickly and hurry back. Then I think we may consider resuming our number-one priority." He seemed taken aback by her frankness. She looked into his eyes and tried to feel something electric. He was about to return her look, but a hovering waiter caused him to redden.

Harvey retreated behind the menu. Amanda could have kicked herself. She had offended him. As soon as the waiter departed with their orders, Harvey leaned across the china and crystal and whispered surreptitiously behind his stiff linen napkin, "I assure you that is not at all necessary. I don't want you ever to consider giving your career the short end of things because of our relationship."

"I'm sorry; I didn't mean that."

"No, no," Harvey hastened onward. "Don't apologize. Dear, I know how hard you've worked to make a go of it here in Latin America."

"Yes, I have."

"I also know that marriage is secondary in your scheme of things. I support that. Marriage is quite an emotional burden for anyone who is a truly dedicated executive. One must accommodate that type of person."

"Yes," Amanda agreed, falling into the routine.

"We see eye to eye. Amanda, I knew you were an excellent corporate person three years ago, when I approved the bank's first million-dollar expansion loan to your company."

She stiffened. The loan. He had to mention it. In a way, she wished she'd never accepted it or gotten involved with Harvey the next year, when he had approved three more loans and they'd begun dating, which had led to their engagement. "And I appreciate that."

"It was long before I had any personal interest in you. I admired the way you had set up the various bottling and wholesale operations so that you had a smooth-running, taut organization.''

She nodded, knowing he was about to make a point that he'd made before.

''Thus,'' Harvey concluded, ''business and bed are horses of a different color. One has no need to prove oneself like barnyard animals. Especially when one is mature and not planning a family.''

Harvey was so wise. Amanda retreated even more. He was always right.

Over their luncheon of white wing dove on wild rice, Harvey discussed Pemex, Amex, Filmaxx, Banco Americanos and his excellent loans for mergers soon to be approved by the Mexican and U.S. governments. ''And,'' he added smugly, ''I have some further news. Representatives of the Organization of International Bankers are meeting here for the next thirty days. I intend to hammer home some of my ideas to those sharks in world banking.''

Amanda changed the subject. ''Harvey, about that man you saw me with yesterday—''

He waved his hand expansively. ''The French representative?'' He chuckled. ''More momentary jealousy. Dismiss it from your mind. That's settled.''

''No,'' Amanda insisted, ''I want to explain.''

Harvey pinned her with his most earnest expression. ''Please, no. The representative was a business contact. I had no right to question it. Business is business. Missing lunch was no problem; in fact, that's when I met the reporter who's interviewing you today. I assure you, I do not feel threatened. Whatever you're obliged to do to make the business run smoothly is mandatory.''

"Yes," she agreed absently. Perhaps it was best to leave the matter alone. But what would a marriage be like in which both of them were slaves to their respective businesses, intertwined and dependent on each other through multiple loans, investments, mergers and expansions?

At 1:30 P.M. the newspaper reporter arrived. Harvey smiled broadly and stood, triumph glazing his eyes. Amanda turned and was shocked to realize she was about to be interviewed by the internationally famous Zena Ballanger.

Nearly everyone in the club, male and female, turned and watched Zena Ballanger glide across the room and down the steps into the glass atrium to Amanda and Harvey's table.

Harvey handled the introductions with aplomb, but Amanda stammered and hesitated when Zena held out her hand. Zena was far more than a reporter. At thirty-six, she was the toast of three continents and owned one of Mexico City's English-language newspapers, along with a dozen other papers around the globe.

"I—I had no idea I'd be talking to you," Amanda apologized. "I—I'm not prepared; I thought I was to meet a reporter. I mean, you own the paper! And I usually read your columns. I saw you yesterday when that man tried to pick you—" Amanda stopped in mid-sentence.

"Oh, my. You were at the Palacio when that man Slater started coming on to me? I didn't think I'd ever get rid of him."

Amanda had said everything wrong. All she wanted to do was leave. Her white linen suit seemed tasteless next to Zena's coral silk tunic and long, tight straw-colored pants. Zena's makeup was fresh and exquisite, hers nonexistent. Her mind was still filled with the cylinders and the bus. She was not prepared for a big interview.

Amanda sank back into her chair. Harvey held a chair for Zena Ballanger, then returned to his.

Zena strove to put Amanda at ease. "Amanda, I am a reporter. It's what I enjoy most, and I've looked forward to this interview with you." She glanced at Harvey and pursed her lips with a smile. "I have an idea Mr. Bannon wanted to surprise you. And I think he's succeeded. He's probably ruined my chances with you."

"Oh, I hope not." Harvey looked charmingly abashed. "I know how much Amanda admires your work."

While Harvey ordered a Campari for Zena and fresh coffee, Zena focused on Amanda. "Actually, the idea of interviewing you has come up rather quickly. But please forgive Harvey. He's the one who came to my rescue in the Palacio bar. He sat down next to me and gave me a chance to get away from that dreadful congressman, who was trying to impress me with the fact that he was here to speak at the O.I.B. Conference."

"Yes." Harvey looked pleased with himself. "He's on the board of a Beverly Hills bank and thinks he can rule the world, at the expense of the taxpayers. I told him a thing or two."

"Yes, you did," Zena agreed, jade-green eyes shining admiringly.

Harvey sobered and turned to Amanda. "Truthfully, I went in to drown my sorrows in a gin martini after you stood me up for lunch."

"I'm sorry, Harvey."

"No problem. I met Zena and told her about you and your fantastic career in the soft-drink business— a woman managing a booming young U.S. company in Mexico. And she took it from there and called me back this morning to set up this interview."

Zena gently placed her graceful hand on Harvey's arm. "You have a gem of a man here."

He and Zena looked perfectly matched sitting beside each other. A flawless pair. Much more suited than she and Harvey. "Are you married, Zena?" Amanda asked.

Zena lifted her hand from Harvey's arm. "Divorced, I'm afraid," she said wistfully. "I don't have anyone I care for at the moment. It takes a rather special man to put up with the likes of me. I'm always on the go. But enough of my woes.

"This morning, Amanda, after Harvey told me all about you and your dedication to business, having to rush off with your French representative and all, I knew I had to talk to you right away. You've evidently trained your fiancé perfectly for a happy future."

Harvey smiled. Zena Ballanger was remarkably charming. He liked her modest reserve especially. No wonder she always drew wonderful portraits of people she interviewed. Everyone must succumb to her spell.

Amanda was no exception. Zena even had Amanda talking about her past without her usual diffidence.

"Yes, I won a partial scholarship in gymnastics," Amanda was saying readily. "With that and a part-time job on campus, I got through the toughest business school I could find. It was a struggle, but I got my degree, and even graduated with honors.''

She grew reluctant to answer questions only when her father was mentioned, but made a point of saying, "One thing I will tell you, my father taught me that anything worth doing is worth doing well. To this day, it doesn't matter how insignificant or important a task is; if I choose to accomplish something, I give it my best."

Zena wisely didn't press for more about Nathan Perry. "No doubt that has enabled you to forge ahead in your company. I understand you started in the shipping department in Tri-Cola's Chicago office and moved steadily into management. Is that correct?"

Amanda nodded. "When an international market became a reality, I asked to be assigned to the Mexico City branch. Some people scoffed, I remember. They didn't think a woman could handle Mexico."

Zena leaned toward her encouragingly. "Obviously, you could and did. You manage all Tri-Cola's Latin American branch bottlers, right?"

The interview continued and eventually even embraced her views of world politics. At one point, she volunteered abruptly, "I hate guns! Any kind of violent action. I can't stand violence."

"I understand," Zena murmured, "and I agree. It's only too bad that everyone in the world doesn't hate guns. We can only keep trying. If only we women could discourage all the militarism, the macho strutting around with guns and bombs. It's just sheer luck that this planet hasn't been blown up already."

Amanda agreed fervently. Those were her sentiments exactly. She liked Zena. The interview wound down, and Zena made preliminary arrangements to have an elaborate set of pictures taken when Amanda returned from her business trip.

At three o'clock, Amanda said regretfully, "I really must leave now."

"I wish you didn't have to leave, but I understand," Zena said sympathetically. "I have really enjoyed talking to you. I've been so depressed lately. It seems so many women are always on the short end of things. I'm so happy for you, for your career—and for you, Harvey."

"What did I tell you, Zena? Isn't Amanda interesting?" Harvey beamed with pride.

Zena sighed enviously. "Yes, she certainly is. Thank you for talking to me, Amanda. Don't forget—I want to do a complete picture story, too. Your work, your gymnastics, your hobbies. Everything upbeat. This has been great fun. You've made my day." Zena checked her wristwatch. "I had better be thinking about my next appointment, and I'm sure you two have a few things you wish to say in private, with the wedding coming up next week and all."

She gathered her notes, shook hands with Harvey and hugged Amanda. "Goodbye. I truly admire you two." Her exit garnered as many admiring glances as her entrance.

Amanda felt ten feet tall. No wonder everyone was dazzled by Zena Ballanger. The glamour and brains were impressive enough, but her charm was in her warmth and candor. "Well, what do you think?" she said to Harvey.

"Think?" Harvey enthused. "My God, Amanda, she loved you. You'll probably get an entire section. *Time* magazine may want a story next. You're in."

"No, I mean what do you think of Zena? I'm impressed that she'd take the time to talk to me. She's quite a woman, don't you think?"

"Yes, I think she's an excellent interviewer. You'd better get going, love. It's after three." He leaned over and kissed her cheek discreetly. "Besides I have a meeting here in the banquet hall in half an hour."

"Oh, who with?"

"No one you'd care to associate with. Just some stodgy old O.I.B. members, including George D. Slater."

"That disgusting congressman who was after Zena?"

"The same." Harvey chuckled. "He's going to present the Beverly Hills plan for world conquest. Take care on the road."

"Oh, I will," she said. Good old Harvey. Her lips touched his cheek.

As she walked away between the crowded tables, she didn't notice heads turning, but she did feel rather regal, her self-esteem momentarily raised by Zena's admiration. But she came down to earth the moment she went through the front door. She paused to put on her sunglasses and was struck with her dilemma. Ahead was no simple picnic in Tampico. She was on her way to a situation that was more complex and difficult than anything Zena or Harvey had ever faced.

## Chapter Eight

From a vantage point two floors up in the University Club building, El Tigre watched Amanda tip the efficient young parking attendant, then climb gracefully into the Jaguar, adjusting her skirt as it rode high on her thighs, revealing shapely legs. Hard, calculating eyes held a fleeting appreciation of her trim body, but it passed quickly. Amanda was a devious woman. She had tricked Guando into following a Tri-Cola van for hours. But once the vehicle was far outside the city, a traffic accident had occurred. A timely happening, even though a perfectly good Porsche had been sacrificed.

The van was empty. Very clever. The Tiger knew how to deal with very clever women, and Amanda would be dealt with soon. Even now she was being followed, although she would never know it. Guando had wisely assigned the driving to one of his men, a former race-car driver who would not be tricked by an amateur driver. Amanda would lead them to the catalyst eventually—of that El Tigre was sure—and Guando would not fail this time. His instructions were precise. "Do nothing rash. When you actually see the cylinders, contact me and we'll arrange to transport them into international waters. Then we'll take them to Cuba and make our announcement to the world.''

Amanda arrived at her apartment without incident. No one had followed her. Of that she was positive. Taking no chances, she parked the Jaguar directly in front of her building and asked the concierge to keep an eye on it and ring her if anything at all suspicious happened. He promised, and she rushed upstairs to pack for her journey.

How should she dress for a secret mission? Brad would know. She hurried out of her suit, showered quickly and slipped into jeans. Knowing the extremes of heat and cold she would face in the bus, she layered a yellow blouse over a snug cotton knit shirt and pushed the long sleeves to her elbows. Into the overnight case she slung a couple of warm-ups, lacy underwear, a minimum of toiletries and makeup basics. As she tied her jogging shoes and fingered her ankle, which was better today, she was reminded to call Chris in case he had found out who was spying on her.

He answered on the second ring.

"What's happening?" she said.

Chris launched into his report, accustomed to her quick calls. "We're at full production. I need clearance to order half a dozen carloads of the old standard labels."

"What was the survey result?"

"The public loves the old-time red-and-white logo. Reminiscent of the good old days."

"Double the order but get maximum discount first. Tell them you want only three carloads unless they'll cut the price on paper and glue. But do it quickly before they up the price. Anything on who used my computer access code or the names of people who could have seen my workout?"

Chris hesitated a moment too long before he answered. "Uh, I hate to say this, but no."

He was a bad liar. "Who, Chris?"

"Okay, I'm not positive, but there seems to be some connection between—well, between our bank, your code, Mr. Bannon and—"

"Certainly there is," Amanda interrupted. "Harvey knows the access codes of all of our officers and the corporate access code, as well. We have to trust our banker. He has charge of all of our accounts."

"I know, but if he didn't send himself the message, somebody in the Inter-net Banking System must have tapped in. Anyway, I traced it to a bank computer and found a blind federal override code, access denied. As I said before, the embassy approved the import."

So that's how Ms. Cullen had done it. She had tapped the Inter-net Banking System and used Amanda's code.

Time was flying. "Did you find out anything on the people at the gym yesterday?"

Again, that hesitation. What was it with Chris? Or was she just feeling suspicious of everyone? "Uh, other than your gym coach, old Mrs. Salcedo, the only other people at the club that early yesterday morning were Mr. Bannon, a couple of his banking friends..." He faded away mumbling.

Chris sighed and reluctantly concluded, "And me."

Amanda choked. Chris hated exercise. Thirty pounds overweight, he avoided all exercise, moved heavily and slouched. "You? What were you doing there?"

A devastating silence hung on the line. Had Chris, her faithful assistant, who was like a younger brother to her, betrayed her?

"It's really important that you know?"

"Yes!"

"I was watching you work out."

"Why? What on earth for?"

"Well, to tell you the truth, I like the way you do all that stuff. I'd give anything if I could just do one back flip. You look like a champion; you defy gravity out there. If I could move like that, I'd think I had died and gone to heaven. It's—anyway, I'm sorry. I should have told you."

Amanda was touched. "Oh, Chris, I had no idea. When I get back, I'll work with you and teach you a few basic moves."

"Ah, no, no. That's all right. But I assure you, I didn't tell a soul you slipped and fell."

"You saw me fall?" Now she was embarrassed. "Okay. Thanks, Chris. Just keep the shop rolling. I'll be back in a couple of days."

She severed the connection. What next? Lock up and leave. She glanced around the room, hating to go but exhilarated and ready to get on with the job. But first she had one more thing to do. She found the slip of paper on which Brad had written the emergency phone number and his Mexico City address and tucked it into her purse. On her way out, she grabbed her favorite jacket, a lightweight cranberry-colored blazer, a well-worn old friend.

The Jaguar downshifted smoothly and whipped onto the Chapultepec Park freeway interchange. No wonder Brad drove this car so fast. It was a driver's dream—nothing like her staid company car, a four-door sedan that ran erratically. Traffic was light as Amanda whirled around the confusing multitude of circles, then out and around into the wealthy and exclusive Polanco section of the city.

Was it curiosity that led her past Brad's address? Like all the houses on this wide, tree-lined boulevard, his was a huge hacienda-style affair, immaculately maintained. He must be very rich.

She floored Brad's accelerator, then felt a twinge of shame, slammed on the brakes, cut the wheels around and whipped around a corner. A brown Mercedes sedan loomed directly in her path. Its driver braked hard to miss the Jaguar, which had appeared out of nowhere in his way. He swerved to avoid Amanda, who simultaneously turned to avoid him in the same direction. The cars seemed doomed to crash.

Her fast reflexes spurred by panic, Amanda whipped the Jaguar away, but again the other driver chose the same side. At the very last second the Mercedes managed to skid out of Amanda's path and up and over the esplanade, bouncing and crashing through to the other side. The driver leaned on his horn and honked raucously and righteously. He was extremely angry; Amanda had very nearly caused a serious accident.

Amanda skidded the Jaguar to a heart-pounding stop. A miracle, indeed. The cars had not touched each other. Either the other driver was very good, or Amanda had been extremely lucky. The heavy European monster made a U-turn and zipped back down the street. Amanda fearfully watched it recede into the distance.

She realized she was holding her breath and exhaled. She flexed her shaking foot. Her legs had turned to water. The Mercedes didn't reappear. The driver wasn't going to scold her or cause an incident. Thank God! Luck! What a wonderful commodity. Brad would have killed her if she'd wrecked the Jaguar.

Back to business. She started out again and checked the rearview mirror to make doubly sure no one was on her tail. Nothing behind now, nothing ahead. She maneuvered onto the expressway and around another series of turns.

She had taken a suitably complicated route but had seen nothing suspicious since leaving Harvey. He was undoubtedly deeply involved in his meeting with the congressman.

As she drove, Amanda pondered Harvey's future. She was beginning to wonder whether she and Harvey were well matched, after all. Perhaps Zena Ballanger was better suited to him. But no. Zena was not after a man. She was dedicated to the welfare of the world.

Amanda left the side streets and began to angle toward her true target, the Consulado Alemán. From there a circuitous journey would lead to a country road and eventually to Hacienda Rolaca. Brad wasn't the only one who could elude the enemy—whoever they were.

AT DUSK, Amanda brought the Jaguar to a stop outside the courtyard of the Hacienda Rolaca. Brad was pacing restlessly in front of the courtyard gate. Behind him, a fiesta was in full swing. Mariachis strummed guitars and strolled about singing while ranch's cowboys flirted with dark-eyed *señoritas*.

Stationed by the gate, Enrique saw her and signaled to his numerous relatives—his cousins, his aunts and his uncle, the foreman of the ranch. They began to gather in a lively group by the gate.

Brad flung open the door of the Jaguar. The crowd quieted and hung back shyly.

"Thank goodness you're back. I was getting worried. Any problems? Any Porsches?" Concern etched his brow; his voice was sharp as he leaned into the car. Amanda was more than glad to see him.

"None," she said easily. Why tell him she'd nearly wrecked his baby through her own fault? "I took a very devious route. Now, what's happening?" She looked about expectantly. "A party?"

"Sort of," he murmured in her ear as he helped her from the car. "I'm going to need a little cooperation from you."

"What kind of cooperation? Is everything set?"

"Of course. Just remember, I got the bus for you."

"I remember. But you didn't exactly say what kind of a deal you made."

"Yeah. Well, you were in a hell of a hurry, so I had to improvise. Just act thrilled and giddy when you see the bus and don't blow the whistle on me."

Cousin Carlos had left the throng and was walking toward them, his grin widening with each step.

"Enrique got carried away." Brad took Amanda's luggage out of the car.

"What on earth are you raving about?"

"You'll see. Do you have my keys?"

"They're in the car."

*"Buenas tardes, señorita,"* said the jovial Carlos. "May you have a most happy future and have many boy children."

"Thank you, Carlos; she will," Brad answered for Amanda, who started to smile back at Carlos but couldn't find a suitable reply. While she struggled with Carlos's confusing good wishes, Brad gestured toward the golden Jaguar. "Here. The keys are in your car, Carlos. Have fun."

"What?" Amanda stared at Brad, dumbfounded.

Immediately, Enrique's uncle, aunt and a dozen cousins surrounded her, all of them talking at once, surpassing one another with complimentary exclamations on her making such a fine and beautiful bride. Bride? She blushed furiously. Why had Brad told them about her marrying Harvey? And why was Carlos driving away with Brad's Jaguar? And where had Enrique disappeared to?

The crowd, excitedly chattering all the way, drew Amanda toward a huge canvas tent that had been set up at the edge of the cavernous courtyard. Brad, who was now wearing a magnificent serape, seemed to bask in the compliments when he joined Amanda before the tent. He took her hand. She tried to snatch it away, but he held her tightly.

"Please, Amanda, act happy. This is it!" He nodded, and the tent was whisked upward with the assistance of a block and tackle strategically placed in the tree above. There stood the bus completely redecorated and festooned with banners and streamers, tin cans and old boots.

Amanda was speechless.

Enrique was at the wheel of the ancient vehicle. He started the deep-throated engine, which caught with a grinding roar. The side door swung open, and a bombardment of birdseed shot out over Amanda and Brad.

"We didn't have any rice," Brad shouted. "Come on, let's go." He pulled her toward the now completely revealed vehicle.

Amanda started to laugh. The crowd was shouting for a wedding kiss.

With a small hint of apology and obviously with relief that she was going to be a good sport, Brad looked at her wickedly. He bent toward her cool lips and kissed her primly to the glee of the group.

"They'll never believe that," Amanda said. "If we're going to pretend, let's really put ourselves into it." She threw her arms around him in a very good simulation of passion and returned the kiss soundly. He deepened it. She matched him, tightening her grip. When they came up for air, Amanda stared at him, woozy, her knees weak, reflecting the question in his eyes. Was this the kiss they had wanted last night?

The crowd roared their approval and brought the stunned pair back to their senses.

Amanda and Brad waved *adiós*, turned and climbed into the back of the bus. Each astride a cylinder, side by side, they waved at the crowd. Brad slipped his arm around Amanda's waist like a true bridegroom.

Enrique stepped smartly on the accelerator. The old Ford responded with a mighty roar and lurched forward slowly, out of the courtyard and onto a long lane that led to a deserted country road.

Under cover of the rumbling of the bus and the muted clapping of the cylinders, Amanda said, "That was some idea, Bradford." She wriggled to get comfortable. Though the cargo had been repacked and lashed down, the cylinders were in constant motion.

"Yeah." Brad realized the moment was awkward and removed his hand from her waist. "Thanks for playing along." His cylinder jostled him about, but he rode it easily, as if in a saddle.

"Did I have a choice?"

Brad gave her a crooked grin. "I didn't know how much of a sense of humor you had." A devilish glint filled his deep blue eyes. "Actually, it was Enrique's idea. It clinched the deal." He gestured toward Enrique, who was hunched over the wheel, barely able to see over it.

"Oh, yes, the deal. What did I pay for this wedding bus?"

"It's free and clear."

"What does that mean?" Amanda closed her eyes, instantly suspicious.

"Uh, nothing. I bought it for you."

Her eyes snapped wide. "You bought it for me? You own it? How did you do that?"

"I traded the Jaguar for it."

"That's ridiculous." She crossed her arms defiantly, but instantly had to make a stabilizing grab at Brad.

"Yeah, it is. I must be nuts."

"You must be. How are you and Enrique going to get back to the city?" She recovered her balance and pulled her hands back quickly to the safety of her lap.

"We're going with you to make sure you get there."

"Oh, no, you're not! I took on this mission. I can handle it without you. And I'll pay back whatever I owe you."

"I'm afraid you haven't thought this through. Your company driver's in Mazatlán, remember? You would be a woman alone on a very dangerous road. What if you broke down?"

She took a long look at the rugged terrain and the corrugated road. "I know that. I'll call for another driver."

"That would waste time—and probably endanger him, too. We're all set. Food and water, blankets, a kerosene lantern, the works. We'll make it back in time for your wedding if we keep going. You do want to be back in time for your wedding, don't you?"

"Yes, of course I do. But I was told that your presence would endanger the mission."

"It has already been compromised, or we wouldn't have been hit at your apartment last night. I can't leave now. I know you're capable and afraid of nothing—"

Amanda's eyes turned smoky. "Don't patronize me! Of course I'm frightened. I didn't ask for the job. It was dumped on me."

"Oh, don't I know." He held up a hand in defense. "I did warn you, but I guess I still owe you. I'm trying to make up for what they did to you. Sort of amortizing the payback, as your Harvey might say."

"Leave Harvey out of this. It's your friend Ms. Cullen that did it," corrected Amanda petulantly.

Brad looked at her a long moment.

"Well, it's true." Amanda squirmed under his thoughtful eyes. "Why don't you admit it?"

"I admit it," he said easily. "But why do you sound like a jealous woman?"

"I'm certainly not jealous. I'm—peeved. Now, I want Enrique to stop this bus. I want both of you out."

Brad's features clouded. "Wait a minute, lady. You can't order me off so imperiously. I own this bus. I hired Enrique to drive with us to Tampico."

Amanda gave him a scathing look. "Of all the dumb things to do. Does Enrique have a driver's license?"

"Well, surely."

"You checked that out, right? You can't drag him into this. He's a child."

Brad cocked his head. "Now he's a child. This morning he was a young man with connections."

"What about his job at the hotel? You'll get him fired."

"I'll get him fired! Who phoned him in the first place?"

"I only needed him for a couple of hours."

"Relax," Brad said easily, producing a road map and flashlight from the gear at their feet. "He won't be fired. He called his cousin. It's handled."

"I don't understand. How?"

"His cousin is the bell captain. Enrique got him the job. You don't have to worry; he'll cover for Enrique."

Amanda nodded, frustrated but not convinced yet. "No, now, listen to me. If you wish to endanger your life, that's fine. But you can't risk his."

"You're right. We'll leave him at Tizayuca down the road about thirty kilometers from here."

Though she couldn't see him in the dark, Amanda could sense smugness in his voice. Apparently Brad was taking the situation lightly. He switched on the flashlight again and started to plot a course.

"Fine!" Though Amanda agreed, she had to wonder if she'd won or lost a victory. What if she simply abandoned Brad and his bus when they arrived at Tizayuca. That would put the responsibility right where it should be, with the embassy. But she couldn't abandon the mission.

"May I see the map?" she asked.

"Certainly. I've marked our course. We'll take highway 85 north to Ciudad de Valles, then 110 to Tampico. Easy. We'll be there sometime tomorrow afternoon with any luck."

That sounded good to Amanda. She checked the route and was about to agree to it when she realized bright headlights were approaching rapidly from the rear. Her stomach churned. Even with Brad and Enrique beside her, she was frightened. What would she have felt like if she had been alone? She couldn't bear to think about that. Soon they would reach the side road that would take them into Tizayuca; then it would be on to Tampico. She glanced back at the glaring lights again. She couldn't tell what kind of car they belonged to.

The lights remained about two hundred yards behind their slow progress.

Amanda glanced up as the bus lurched, then began to slow down even more.

Brad muttered an expletive and moved forward to part the curtain to the cab. "What's up, Enrique?"

"Looks like a train stopped on the crossing ahead." Enrique sounded cheerful. He brought the bus to a smooth halt.

Brad was wary. "Better turn off the lights and the engine. We may be here all night." He climbed forward into the cab. "You want a break at the wheel?"

"Sure." Enrique slipped over to the far side of the bench.

Amanda stared back at the dark form of the car behind as it pulled over and stopped a couple of hundred yards back. The lights went off. The silence was eerie.

In the car to the rear, Guando leaned forward to the two men in the front seat. *"Perfecto,"* he said. "I couldn't have asked for a better way to stop them."

"Beats wrecking the car," said Rolando, the driver.

Guando snorted, remembering the wrecked Porsche. "Your luck is holding, Rolando," he growled. "But remember, my friend, she nearly hit you this afternoon."

*"¡Hijo!* I remember," Rolando agreed. "That turn around she made was a disaster. I could barely get away from her. Women are all bad drivers."

"Shall we go take their cargo?" asked Paco, about to light a cigar.

"You light that and I'll slit your throat," Guando said. "How do you know they even have the cylinders. Perhaps this is another ruse. El Tigre won't stand for any more mistakes."

"Go ask them," Paco suggested.

"They know my face, you fool. They might start shooting. You go. Take your cigar with you and ask for a light. See if the cylinders are there. If they are, we'll move in."

"What if they shoot at me?"

"That's an order! Just do it."

Paco moved instantly.

Amanda glanced back. She thought she had heard a door slam but couldn't be sure. Nerves, she decided as she readjusted herself on the cylinders. They had to rearrange the load at the first opportunity so that there would be a place to rest. She shivered and decided she'd be better off up front. "Hey, any room left up there?" she inquired in a falsely cheerful voice.

"Lots of room if you don't mind sitting on my lap," Brad joked.

Amanda eased into the space between the two men and closed the curtain behind her. The seat was cozily crowded. "Well, here we are," she observed with little enthusiasm. "What's the record for a train crossing?"

"Sometimes a week," Enrique teased. "But usually twenty minutes."

"I'll take the latter, thank you." She felt tired, not the least bit adventuresome. "Let's think positive." She turned to Brad and sucked in her breath to stifle a scream.

Outside the window a swarthy face lurked. Black eyes like marbles hypnotized her into paralysis. She had not bargained for this.

Brad swung around to follow her fearful gaze. His reaction was a cross between a gasp and a growl. He took the offensive and rasped with cold politeness, *"Buenas tardes, señor."*

Unperturbed, Paco transferred his beady stare to Brad.

*"¿En que puedo servirle?"* Brad's sharp tone cancelled his formal offer of help.

Attempting an ingratiating grin, Paco furtively tried to penetrate the curtain at the back of the cab. He waved his cigar. *"¿Tiene usted fósforos?"* He wanted a match.

*"¡No! No tengo nada."*

"I have some matches," Amanda responded, cursing the weak quaver in her voice.

Brad took the matches from her, struck one and held it out to light the cigar. The dim glow it shed gave

Amanda the chance she wanted to see the man's face more clearly. She would remember that face.

*"Muchas gracias, señorita,"* he said politely enough.

Brad began to roll up the window, but Paco said hastily, *"Perdón."* He switched languages. "Uh, what you carry, eh, *señor*?"

"Antique bottles." Brad made no pretense at politeness.

"Ah," Paco grunted knowingly. He spat on the ground. "Let me see. Maybe have customer for you." He winked and nodded toward the dark car behind.

"No. Not for sale."

"Better let me take a look." The voice had more than a touch of threat in it. "Pay plenty!" He pulled on the door handle, but Brad had wisely locked it.

Enrique covertly reached across Amanda's lap and tapped Brad's hand with a heavy tire tool. With his fingers securely curled around the cool metal, Brad shrugged and turned his back to the window as if to tell Amanda he was going to open the back of the bus. "I hate to do this," he hissed between clenched teeth, "but I'm going to have to hit him." He turned back. "Buzz off, buddy, or you're dead meat!" The tire tool was poised.

Amanda leaned toward Enrique to give Brad some room. She had never dreamed he could sound so deadly.

Paco brought up a heavy fist. A burst of bright headlights from behind the dark car stopped him momentarily from making a move.

He squinted at the light. Why do anything with an audience? He could wait. "We will see, *señor*." He retreated to the car.

Amanda listened to his footsteps grow fainter. As he opened the car door, the rearview mirror clearly defined his reflection in the bright lights from behind.

Amanda caught her breath and swallowed hard. He had entered a brown four-door Mercedes. She recalled the near miss of that afternoon. "Damn!"

"Better say that again," prompted Enrique, his voice quaking. "We got trouble. Wish that train would go."

The approaching headlights materialized into the shape of an eighteen-wheeler filled to overflowing with produce headed north. The driver pulled up beside the Mercedes and hopped out to stretch his legs and pass the time chatting. Who knew how long the train would be there?

The three men in the Mercedes seemed to have had a conference. The doors to the car opened suddenly, and all three loped out, ignoring the truck driver.

"Hang on," Brad yelled. He dropped the tire tool in Amanda's lap and started the bus. The engine gave a full-throated roar as he shoved the gearshift into reverse, popped the clutch and backed up a few feet.

"Hurry," Amanda urged, gripping the tire tool.

"Go, dammit! Go!" Brad wrenched the gearshift in low, then ground forward with the steering wheel turned as far as it would go. The old bus groaned and shook, the transmission protested, the tires howled, but it progressed, forging a circle on the road. The three thugs were almost upon them when the bus charged back toward them.

Enrique ducked to get out of the way of Amanda, who was brandishing the tire tool with both hands, ready to smash it into any face that appeared at the window. The bus slowly gained momentum and lumbered forward.

The three men leaped aside into a ditch under the astonished eyes of the truck driver, who stood transfixed at the sight.

Brad slammed the accelerator to the floor and prayed. Already the men were hobbling back to the Mercedes, prepared now to run down their foe and give no quarter.

"What do we do now, lady?" Brad yelled over the din. The cylinders in back swayed and clanked like the bells of hell. "I vote for throwing out a cylinder for them to fight over. Maybe it'll explode and blow them to smithereens."

Brad's idea was good, but it might not work. The catalyst wouldn't explode as long as it was under pressure and the cylinder remained intact. "No!" Amanda gasped. Her eyes burned, her pulse rioted, confusion clouded her thoughts. "Not the cylinders. Just stop talking and drive faster. I'm trying to think."

"You'd better think fast. They'll get us in about five miles."

Amanda's hands shook badly. She dropped the tire tool on the floor under Enrique's feet and picked up the flashlight and the map. Between the bumpy ride and her trembling hands, studying the map was nearly impossible. She hated this! Maybe they should all jump out now and just run for it. They couldn't escape!

## Chapter Nine

What would Nathan Perry do now? Amanda raced over their options. He'd probably turn and fight. No! The odds of success were too slim. Pick a better place to fight and then fight to win. She scanned the map again and again. Nothing! She just couldn't think. This road was taking them back to Mexico City, and the hunters were gaining on them. The Mercedes's lights periodically slashed the night behind them as it rounded a curve or crested a hill.

Brad kept the accelerator on the floor. The old engine worked at grinding up the road; all aboard were jostled about. The cylinders shifted and clanked. To Amanda this wild chase seemed all unreal.

But it was real. She watched the twin beams of their headlights cut a jagged, erratic path down the narrow black road. She glanced at Brad, stone faced as he wrestled the wheel around a bend that curved out of sight. She and Enrique searched the darkness ahead.

"Hope we don't hit any cattle," he mumbled just as Amanda glimpsed a country lane, little more than a cow path, before them to the left.

"Turn left!" she shouted abruptly at the top of her lungs.

"Where?"

"There," said Enrique, his hand intercepting Brad's view.

"Now!" she shouted. "Now."

Brad turned the lumbering vehicle sharply, almost missing the mark. Amanda slammed against Enrique, and the two of them held on to the inadequate handrail while the bus skidded and swayed. It rounded a hillock, and Brad doused the lights. They were safely out of sight only moments before the Mercedes, still gathering speed, roared past and continued on the main road back toward Mexico City.

The bus smashed heavily into a boulder just as Brad switched on the lights. Amanda apologized to Enrique for flattening him on the turn. "No problem, Señorita Perry," he joked. "We got away, didn't we? Besides, I'll get you on the next one."

Only Brad didn't find anything humorous in their situation. As he grappled with the wheel, the bus bounced forward on a dusty, potholed, nightmare path that stretched into darkness. They were all being thrown forward and back again in the seat.

"Where does this go?" he demanded.

"Be careful," Amanda screamed, her voice edged with hysteria, suddenly fearfully aware of their volatile cargo being violently shaken up. "If one of those cylinders loses pressure, it could blow up the whole load."

"I'm trying, dammit! Now, where does this road go?" Brad applied the brakes, but the clanking and rattling of the cylinders only increased.

"It probably follows the riverbed," Enrique suggested. To the left he noticed a deep gorge paralleling the narrow path. *"Muy peligroso,"* he shouted. "Very dangerous."

Without taking his eyes off the path, Brad said, "Yeah! It's dangerous as hell." The bus eased to a crawl, and the noise diminished. He wrenched one hand off the wheel and mopped the film of perspiration from his worried brow. "Amanda, did you get a good look at any of those apes in the Mercedes?"

"The only one I recognized was the man you fought in my apartment. He said his name was Detective Guando." The tension in the bus wound tighter at the mention of his name.

"I thought I caught sight of him." Brad shifted into a more powerful gear. "I'm sorry, Amanda. Sorry you were ever dragged into this."

Certain strangers could walk into your life and turn it upside down, Amanda mused. Her hand, less shaky now, lightly touched his arm. "It wasn't your fault. You tried to keep me out of it." Her hand returned to her lap. "And I don't want to blow you up. I'm afraid we've got to stop and repack the load for the sake of safety, before we kill ourselves."

"Yeah." He checked the rearview mirror. "But not now. We may have lost those guys for good, or they may realize their mistake and backtrack. We've got to get to a main artery somewhere. Do you see anything on the map?"

Perhaps he was right. He was an agent, after all, and he had gotten them this far. She checked the map with Enrique. "We're headed generally toward Pachuca. We should cross a road somewhere along here."

Brad made a sudden decision. "As soon as we get to Pachuca, I'm sending you and Enrique back to Mexico City. I'll take the cargo to Tampico alone."

Enrique protested. "I'm the only one who can keep this old bus running. I have to go along."

"I'll keep it running," Brad assured him with unjustified confidence. "There's no use risking three lives."

Amanda couldn't have agreed more. It was logical to send Enrique back; it was logical for her to go back; it was logical for Brad, the trained operative, to continue. She had seen the competence with which he faced that thug. But it was obvious that one person could not make this trip alone. And as much as she wanted out, she couldn't renege on her deal with Ms. Cullen; she couldn't abandon the job to Brad.

Enrique crooked his head. They were both waiting for Amanda to speak up.

She took a deep breath and admitted reluctantly, "It isn't that easy. No one wants to be rid of this horrible cargo more than I, but one person alone wouldn't succeed. I can't let you go alone. I agree Enrique should go back, but I'll see my job through."

"Suit yourself," Brad said. He seemed relieved. "You're an adult. If you miss your big wedding, it'll be your own fault, lady."

"My wedding doesn't concern you, Bradford."

"What's this belittling 'Bradford' you're always laying on me? Brad is my name. I'll decide what we do—"

Something was wrong with the accelerator. It no longer propelled the bus. He pressed it down, and nothing happened. His mouth went dry. He worked the pedal.

The 1937 engine backfired with a thunderous report; all three jumped. Then the engine coughed, sputtered and died completely. No one said a word as the bus slowed to a halt. Brad shut off the lights and cursed softly. A cool wind whispered up from the gorge and rattled the nearby bushes. Pale moonlight cast wan shadows on the surrounding blackness.

"Apparently the bus will decide what we do next." Amanda's stomach ached with anxiety.

"Wonderful. Make a joke out of it. We may be carrying those cylinders on our backs," Brad warned.

"I'm sorry. What happened?"

"How do I know; I'm no mechanic."

"But I am, remember," Enrique interposed. "Probably some no good gas."

"Enrique," Amanda asked hopefully, "can you fix it?"

Before Enrique could open his mouth, Brad leaped from the cab, slammed the door and jerked the hood open. "Bring the flashlight," he ordered angrily.

For the next twenty minutes Amanda held the light and controlled her fear, and her irritation with Brad, because more than anything she wanted that noisy engine running again. Anxiously, she searched the darkness behind them, expecting any moment to see distant headlights slice toward them.

Brad straightened from his cramped position under the hood and brushed some strands of hair back from his face, unaware that he had left a streak of black across his forehead. "Okay, Enrique. Hit the starter again." He rubbed his aching back, transferring another smudge to his shirt. He stretched as the starter ground fruitlessly for a few seconds, then stopped.

"How about a short break?" Amanda heard herself suggest. "There's that food Enrique's relatives sent along. It's sure to be delicious. Then we can try the engine again in a few minutes. Okay?"

Stumped, Brad took a weary breath and eyed her. "Okay." She followed him back to the cab. Enrique looked at them expectantly. From under the seat he pulled a rag for Brad's dirty hands, which Brad took with a nod of thanks. "This is complicated," he told them as he wiped his hands. "To tell the truth, I don't know what's wrong yet."

"Can you fix it?"

"With time—and a little luck." Dejected, he pitched the rag onto the floor and walked to the back of the bus.

Amanda joined him there and said softly, "I know you're trying your best."

He turned to her and in the rising moonlight studied the planes of her face. To avoid his scrutiny, she glanced up. the sky was alive with billions of stars, and—sudden romance.

"Amanda, you have grease on your face."

Her hand instantly went to her cheek. "So do you."

He smiled and said nothing more. He seemed to be memorizing the length of her body. In the pale moonlight, his eyes burned like coals. Amanda inhaled the freshness of the land. Everything around her seemed newly alive. She stood waiting.

Their eyes held for a long moment.

Brad shook his head trying to fight the deep emotion that had laid hold of him. He stepped closer. "I shouldn't do this," he murmured. "It's the wrong time." His eyes swept the sky for headlights nervously, but his strong arms reached around her waist and slowly drew her near.

Amanda felt light, weightless. His very nearness was unbearably powerful. It pulled her body closer.

His arms tightened around her; she molded herself to him. For a moment she persuaded herself that she wanted his reassurance. She was lying to herself. She wanted him.

She lifted her chin, vividly aware of his lips, of the last kiss they had shared. Her swelling emotions eclipsed even her consciousness of their pursuer. She was enveloped by the magic night, the physical attraction of this exciting, unknown man; his will was hers.

She felt the sweet warmth of his soft lips as they touched hers, but before the kiss deepened, he lifted his head and whispered, "I wish we could all three walk away from this."

Amanda stayed poised for his kiss a moment longer, and then with a sigh drew her body away from Brad's.

"We can't do that. We'd better get something to eat and try to solve our problems." As though in answer, the starter turned over. As the engine faltered and coughed, then sprang to life, they jumped apart.

"Well, I'll be damned," Brad muttered. "That Enrique's a genius."

"Thank goodness!" Amanda murmured, peering into the distance. "Look!" Far away, a pair of powerful headlights angled to the sky, then dipped down and up quickly as if a car had come upon a very bad road.

"I'm afraid they've picked up our trail." Brad's deep voice hardened with anxiety. "Let's go!"

They both ran for the cab.

"Hit it," Brad instructed Enrique as he slammed the door behind him.

"You bet!" Enrique ground the gears into low and floored the accelerator obediently. It was the wrong thing to do. The engine backfired, then stalled.

A cold silence paralyzed the cab.

"Damn!" Brad muttered, checking the distance between them and the approaching headlights.

Amanda felt faint. It was over. They had failed.

"Ayeee!" Enrique moaned, his hands clenching the wheel. "I swear I fixed it. I fixed the fuel filter." He hit the starter again. "Start! Start!" he pleaded. The engine coughed to life. The bus jerked, then slowly rolled forward, gathering speed, though faced with a steep ascent. All three of them urged it on. Laboriously, it crested the rise and then, its engine running smoother, flew down the other side.

"We're gonna make it," Enrique chortled. "I told you I had to stay."

Amanda was fed up with problems. "If we're lucky enough to reach Pachuca, I'm buying a truck."

Enrique looked hurt and let up on the accelerator. "Why? I'll get us there."

The engine backfired from lack of fuel. Amanda's heart sank. The bus was coming to a halt.

"She's only kidding," Brad yelled over the din. He patted Enrique's shoulder, urging him to step on the gas again. The engine smoothed out. "We're a team; we can do it!" he assured him.

"Right!" Amanda hastened to add. "I didn't mean it," she amended, checking behind them. "Just keep going; don't stop, whatever you do."

"Yes, *señorita*." Enrique grinned, enthusiastic again.

He seemed to have no thought for the danger they were in. He was consumed by the driving. But he had no need; she was worried enough for all of them.

They bumped along over countless miles, Enrique at the wheel, Brad as vigilant as an Indian guide, Amanda squeezed in the middle, grateful for their body warmth, for it was colder now. She held her breath every time the engine faltered. Her tired mind was constantly aware of the slowly shrinking distance between the bus and the tracking headlights.

Here she was, trying to keep her word because she was a fool—no, because she always kept her word—to deliver these cylinders. They were explosive politically as well as chemically, and she might be dead at any minute.

What if they ran out of gas? What would it feel like to have a bullet strike you? She shivered. She would be fortunate if they only killed her. They might torture her. If only she had a weapon! Her mind immediately flinched away from the thought. She must never let herself be reduced to the level of wanting to kill.

*Think positive,* she lectured herself. After all, they were still alive. Her spirits took a small spurt upward, then tumbled. Alive, yes, but for how long? Certain death was closing in. She realized the bus was slowing.

"What's the matter? Don't stop!" she cried, her voice tight and cracking.

"We have to," Enrique apologized. "I don't know if we can get across."

Brad gave a low whistle. "Look at that."

Directly in their path ahead lay water, angry, swift-moving water. This was the end, the end of the journey.

"It's more than a creek. Looks like a raging river," Brad decided. "I'll check it out. I don't know if we can get across. It might be too deep." He jumped out and ran to the edge.

"Put the bright lights on," Amanda said. Enrique complied, and she could see the river wasn't very wide. Perhaps there was a bridge somewhere up or downstream, but which way to go?

Brad ran back. "It's pretty rocky at the edge. I can't tell how deep it is, but we don't have many options. We can go either left or right, and we may find a better place to cross. But that water looks mean to me." He paused. "We could abandon the bus and run like hell. What do you say?"

Seconds fled by while Amanda agonized, then made a firm decision. "Get in, Brad. We're going across. Right here."

Enrique shook his head. "We'll never make it."

"I agree. We're wasting time. Turn right," Brad ordered. "At least we can keep going for a while."

"No!" Amanda snapped. "We'll try for it right here. It's the only choice." She looked them in the face one after the other and said, "If you can't handle it, I will."

Enrique ground the gears. "I can do it. Sure, Señorita Perry." Brad just shook his head in despair.

"Slowly, now! But don't stop moving, no matter what happens. We'll make it," she said, forcing confidence into her voice. "Angle downstream a little and keep going as if our lives depended on it. Go!"

"I don't think you're—" Brad began.

Amanda glared at him. "Do it!" The tension in her voice crackled. Her eyes locked in conflict with his. The seconds ticked away. Enrique let out the clutch, and the bus picked up speed. Brad's face was still a grim mask of doubt, but he didn't countermand her order again.

The bus plowed into the water, moving steadily at a slant. It bounced when it hit an underwater depression. Water spewed, and steam hissed upward. Amanda's breathing was rough. "We've got to make it," she muttered. The tires caught and spun, then suddenly the cab tilted dangerously to the left, throwing Amanda and Brad toward Enrique, but the bus kept moving forward. With gurgles and thumps, the vehicle righted itself and plunged onward.

Now they were at the center of the flow, barely moving. Water was sloshing noisily just above the bottom of the door, but they weren't across yet. The riverbed was solid, thank goodness. If only their luck held for a few more minutes, they'd be over.

The hood of the bus lurched downward as the tires hit a depression near the far bank. Water gushed into the cab up to their ankles. If the engine was flooded, it would stall at any moment.

Enrique fought for control of the faltering vehicle. "Please, let us make it. Don't let the luck leave us now," Amanda murmured. She grabbed the wheel and helped him as the bus miraculously climbed up onto dry land.

"We made it!" Enrique yelled. "I knew we could."

"Don't let up on the gas," Brad cautioned. "Just keep moving."

Amanda let out a sigh of relief. Brad was watching her. "That was a gutsy call," he said quietly. "We could have lost it all right there."

"No, I don't think so. I just didn't have time to debate. I'm sorry if I sounded irritable."

"No problem. I expected it." He glanced back. There were no headlights in sight. "It's academic now," he admitted. "The bus engine didn't get flooded because it's so high off the ground. But that Mercedes will never make it across. You can relax."

His words both disturbed and elated her. "Really?"

"No doubt about it. They'd need a stunt driver to get across."

"What do you mean?"

"If he had the guts and the skill, he could back off, angle upstream where the bank slants the right way, then drive like hell and try to jump the river." He laughed at the absurd thought, his mood improving.

"Do you think they can do that?"

He shook his head. "No way! Even with a stunt-man, they'd have to be extremely lucky to make it."

His certainty should have calmed all Amanda's fears, but it didn't. She had seen how the Mercedes was driven that very afternoon. Whoever was at the wheel was exceptionally good.

Brad made her exchange places with him so that she could get a little rest, but it was he who leaned back and closed his eyes; though his head bounced on the back of the seat, he seemed serenely relaxed. Amanda spent the next hour fearfully watching the rearview mirror until her eyes burned.

She began to feel sorry for Enrique. "Do you want Brad or me to drive?" she asked, not really feeling up to it.

"No," he answered quickly, "I like this. It's like I'm in a tank going for the blood."

Amanda was horrified. What had she done to turn this child to thoughts of destruction? "You don't really mean that, do you?" she queried.

"Aw, no, Señorita Perry," he said with a laugh, "I just use my imagination to keep from being bored, or sleepy. Don't worry. I'm no killer."

"You just get some rest," he advised, wise beyond his years. "Then in the morning you can drive, but night is my time of day."

Amanda nodded. Enrique was creating a private fantasy, even though the pursuing danger was real enough. But he was right. She had to relax a little; she was doing no one a favor by exhausting herself looking for a Mercedes behind them. She would sleep. She glanced in the rearview mirror one more time just to make sure no headlights were approaching from the rear. Nothing. Brad was correct. The car must be stalled at the stream. She turned her eyes to the front again and froze where she sat.

The bus's headlights illuminated blazing demon eyes backed by shadowy figures.

"¡Diablo! God in Heaven!" Enrique mumbled. He slammed on the brakes and twisted the wheel, throwing his passengers sharply against the dashboard. The cylinders crashed forward with a unified rumbling thump. The bus halted abruptly. A swirling cloud of black dust filled the cab.

Brad, not properly awake, thrust Amanda roughly out of the way and tumbled, choking and coughing, from the cab. "Where are they?" he shouted.

The sound of hoofbeats filtered through the dust.

"It's okay! It's okay. I missed them," Enrique yelled.

"Thank God," Amanda murmured, collecting herself from the floor. "Cows, Brad. We narrowly missed some cows. Thank goodness for small favors."

The noise abated. The calming, distinctively earthy odor of cattle filled the cold night air. They could even smell the greenery the wild cattle had been feeding on. Above, stars were shining.

Amanda laughed nervously, thankful for Enrique's fast reflexes. "Get in; we're still safe and sound."

Brad rose from his crouch, dusted himself off and glanced around.

"The hell we are. Get going, fast!" He jumped into the cab, pushing Amanda roughly into the middle of the seat.

"Hey, just relax, will you," she complained. "It's nearly morning, and we'll be there soon."

"Yeah, fine, look in back of us. Drive, Enrique, go!" The bus moved forward, gathering speed on the now-empty path through a gorge.

Amanda checked the mirror. Far behind, lights arched up briefly toward the sky, then disappeared from sight.

# Chapter Ten

Guando rubbed the lump on his head. When the Mercedes had leaped the river and landed crosswise on the far bank, he had been flung across the car. Only Rolando's quick reflexes had saved them from rolling over. The gods were still with them. "You nearly killed us with your reckless driving, Rolando," Guando growled. "I thought you said it was an easy jump. We barely made it."

"Forgive me, Guando," Rolando whined. "The river was wider than I thought. The ground was uneven. I miscalculated."

Guando drew a hand across his nose and brought it away covered with blood. "We're fortunate to be alive. Now step on it. Catch that miserable bus or I'll break your head open like you broke mine."

Obediently, Rolando pressed harder on the accelerator, nosing the car down into a ravine, then climbing up on the other side. The terrain was killing, even for a Mercedes.

Guando knew he would soon have his quarry. The taste of blood focused his senses. "Faster, Rolando! Faster," he hissed. He would make them pay, the woman especially. She would suffer for this.

Paco sensed Guando's blood lust. His breathing quickened as he anticipated the moment of the kill. "Eh, Guando," he said in Spanish. "When we catch them, how about I get the woman first."

"You'll get nothing. I'm going to put her out of her misery quickly."

"That's a waste. What will El Tigre say? El Tigre might have plans for her. You know what I mean? Better not kill her; just make her suffer a little."

"Shut up and keep watch," Guando ordered. "Thanks to you, we don't even know if they have the catalyst or if we're on another wild-goose chase. El Tigre won't tolerate that. Have your pistol ready when we see them. They won't escape this time."

Far ahead, Amanda's skin crawled as though someone had walked over her grave. With morbid fascination, she watched the distant headlights. "I thought you said they couldn't make it?" she mumbled.

Brad said sarcastically, "Well I'm sorry they're smarter than I thought. Just let me out and I'll wait here and throw rocks at the bastards."

Enrique laughed, and even Amanda smiled in spite of her fear.

"I'm sorry," she said. "Don't get out. I didn't mean it was your fault. I'm just scared."

Brad relented, feeling foolish. "I'm sorry, too. Don't worry. I wasn't really going to get out."

"You weren't?"

"Are you kidding? What chance would I have against them? Truthfully, I'm as scared as you are."

For a while Amanda stayed frightened and sank so deep into despair she was sure they would never live to see the dawn. But on reaching this point her mood began to change, and all at once she felt too calm, too alive and well and healthy to be in any real danger.

"Brad," she said, "it's really strange to suddenly feel good when things are so bad. I mean, I know I'm frightened and running from certain death, but suddenly I'm not scared."

"It's a false feeling," Brad explained. "Caused by the altitude. Not enough oxygen to the brain. Like divers' euphoria."

"No, there must be a better reason," she objected, depressed again.

As the night wore on, they talked little and smiled less, though once Amanda actually laughed when Brad suggested pouring their wedding wine into the fuel tank if they ran out of gas. She hadn't realized he was serious. Then she plummeted into depression again at the irony of carrying a cargo of catalyst to save the world with cheap gas in a bus that was running out of gasoline. Brad thought this very humorous. Everything was out of kilter. Moments of near hysteria were followed by sudden flushes of unwarranted euphoria. It was the uncertainty that was telling on her.

Enrique pulled the bus to a stop. Amanda jerked upright, instantly alert. "What's wrong? Where are they?"

"It's okay. We have to cut a fence," the exhausted Enrique mumbled. "Then we're home free. That's the highway to Pachuca on the other side."

Brad opened his door and jumped down to contemplate the six-strand barbed-wire fence that stood forbiddingly before them. To the east the sky was brightening quickly.

"They can't be more than a half mile behind us." Brad seemed irrationally calm.

"Enrique, drive through the fence," Amanda ordered. "We don't have time to cut it."

Brad stared at her darkly; then his face crinkled with admiration. "She's right!" He jumped aboard. "But line up with one of the posts down the middle so that we don't risk barbed wire tangling with the drive shaft."

"Gotcha." Immediately, Enrique eased up on the clutch, and the bus lunged forward, easily pushing over an iron post. Beneath the cab, the noises coming from the tortured fence made Amanda pray that the tires wouldn't be ruined. When the bus had crunched over the last strand of the wire, Enrique gunned the engine, and the tires clawed their way onto the shoulder of the highway.

"Just a moment," Brad yelled. He threw open the door, jumped down and rushed back to the fence. What on earth did he have in mind? With a mighty effort, he hefted the post into an upright position. He looked up and blanched. Not three hundred yards away, the battered, dirty Mercedes bore down on him. He ran for the cab. "Go, Enrique," he shouted.

The bus responded, jerked and bumped, and slowly began to gain speed, its engine straining. It had not traveled fifty yards when the hurtling Mercedes hit the fence head-on. The barbed wire snapped with explosive reports.

Peculiarly detached from the scene before her, Amanda observed it with only minor interest in the inevitable outcome. In seconds the car would be upon them. Although they would be at the mercy of killers, she had no fear.

Amanda suddenly felt she had the answer to all the questions that had ever plagued her for explanation. She knew how Nathan Perry had survived and why, in his last act of courage, he had failed. The answer was luck.

The relentless Mercedes, with men hanging out the windows, guns in hand, sprang forward and then, astonishingly, stopped as though it had hit an iron wall. It sloughed around in a cascade of churning dust, then halted, its battered rear end ignominiously facing the road.

The aged bus limped away with agonizing serenity.

"We did it," Brad shouted. "We did it!"

Amanda snapped out of her dazed reverie. "What's happened? How did we do it?"

"Oh, Lord, Amanda, it was absolutely the most beautiful thing I ever saw." In his exuberance, Brad beat a drum roll on the dashboard. "A few more miles and we can disappear into Pachuca. Those guys have had it."

"What stopped them?" asked Enrique, his bloodshot eyes glued to the much smoother mountain road ahead.

"Beats me." Brad shrugged. "But I think they got barbed wire wrapped around their drive shaft. They came to a mighty swift stop. I think—this time—they're out of the running."

An enigmatic smile formed on Amanda's lips. She was sure that Nathan Perry had saved them by performing a miracle when her mind had fastened on him so powerfully. Not only had the enemy been destroyed before her tired eyes, but also in that moment of truth she'd learned the secret of life.

"Are you okay?" Brad asked, staring at her.

"Yes, I'm fine. Exhausted but fine. Do you want me to drive for a while, Enrique? You must be completely worn out."

Enrique grinned, game to the end. "No, I'm just getting my second wind." He glanced at her through red-veined eyes as the bus weaved all over the empty road.

"I'll drive for a while," Brad volunteered.

"No way," Amanda protested. "I will. Pull over."

"*¡Sí, Señorita Perry!*" Enrique stopped abruptly, killed the engine and leadenly abandoned the driver's seat. He rolled into the back behind the curtain, and Amanda swore he was asleep seconds after he lay between the cylinders.

As she slid into the battered and peeling leather seat, she had her first misgivings.

"Six on the floor." Brad yawned, intending to help her master the gears quickly.

She looked down at the dusty pockmarked floor and the gearshift. "Six on the floor," she repeated. And she had threatened to drive this across the river?

She reminded herself that they had just been delivered from what looked like a certain fate. Could anything ever stop her again? Never!

Brad gave her a brief introduction to clutching in order to pull heavy loads and gain momentum, in the process discovering that years of lazy drivers had cut down the six to a mere four on the floor—reverse, first, second and fifth.

Amanda started the engine on command; her left foot strained to hold the clutch to the floor as her right revved the old engine. Brad's hand on hers pushed for first. The ancient metal gears ground against metal.

Amanda shook her head. "It's a wonder this bus runs."

"Ease up slowly on the clutch," Brad shouted, then removed his hand from hers. The ancient vehicle jumped forward.

Amanda worked the big grimy wheel back and and forth; it was nearly impossible to steer. The bus responded sluggishly, like a tank. However, in a mile or so, she became accustomed to the play of the wheel and steered more evenly, albeit cautiously, especially on the curves.

Fear was forgotten as they rode along peacefully. After the emotional ups and downs and adrenaline-charged bursts of activity of the previous two days, peace was a letdown.

"I wish we could stop somewhere and sleep," she said wistfully to no one. Enrique now slept like the dead on his nest of cylinders, and Brad, his head on the seat, eyes closed, was at peace with the world.

On the one hand, it was nice that Brad trusted her driving and their safety enough to fall asleep. On the other hand, Amanda was lonely. She wanted to talk to someone to stay awake. She began to feel like a martyr at the wheel. Why should she have to drive after her harrowing experiences in the night?

But she was driving because she insisted, her inner voice reminded her. Brad and Enrique had accepted her and now she was one of the boys.

Perhaps being pampered by Harvey wasn't all that bad. Brad tended not to pamper. Of course, she had made him treat her like an equal, and he had obeyed her for the most part.

Her jaw snapped in a sudden yawn. She'd caught herself nodding. Her head jerked forward, then back as she took a deep breath.

"Brad!" she said sharply.

"What!" He sat bolt upright, instantly alert. "What happened? Where are they?"

"Nothing happened, and no one is following. I'm sleepy."

"Oh, okay. I'll drive," he said, relaxing. "We need to get some strong coffee. Where are we?"

"We must be coming into Pachuca. Look ahead. I can drive fine. Just talk to me." She yawned again.

Pachuca, situated in the hills ninety miles from Mexico City and not very far off the route to Tampico, was still sound asleep when the bus rumbled through the deserted streets.

"Sure." Brad squinted, glanced around and yawned. "What do you want to talk about?"

"The universal truth."

"Okay," he began in a sleep monotone. "Universe. The big bang. Happened somewhere about twenty billion or so—"

"No big bang."

"Fine. What?"

"The meaning of it all. Haven't you ever wondered why it all happened? I mean where are we going? Why we're even alive? Who are we?"

Brad leaned back. "Yeah, all the time."

"It all came clear to me back there at the wire. I know who I am, and I know why some people are heroes."

"Well, don't ask me. I couldn't give you the answer."

"You don't have to. I can tell you."

"Good." They were approaching a service station; a welcome yellow light glowed in the window. "How's our gas supply?"

"Riding on the red just above empty. Do you want to hear my new theory? I'll pull in at that station and fill up."

"Certainly. Sounds good to me."

Amanda wheeled the bus into the dusty driveway, downshifting as Brad instructed. A sluggish attendant ambled out to greet his first customer of the day.

"They must open at six."

"It's luck!" The bus bumped onto the hard dirt in front of a pump. Amanda slammed on the brakes, and the engine died with a wheeze. They had stopped.

"You can say that again. This is probably the only station in the whole state that's open this early."

"No, silly!" Amanda laughed. "That's the secret. That's how heroes are made. Luck! Luck is the secret. It makes some people different from the rest of us. I realized this back there when I was so tired. Look at Zena Ballanger. She has luck. My father had luck almost all of his life. Success or failure is not only a matter of work and skill; it's a matter of luck. The greatest word in the entire universe. If you have more of it than the person you face, you win. If you have less, you lose. Luck makes the world go round."

Brad leaned over close and kissed her lightly on the cheek. "I couldn't agree with you more."

"Don't patronize me. I'm not oxygen starved right now."

"I know. I kissed you. I feel lucky. I didn't get slugged, did I?"

"Well, don't feel too lucky. It's daylight now. And I see things more clearly."

"I doubt that," Brad said.

The attendant approached the cab window with a big grin on his face for Amanda.

"Now I will show you real luck," Brad said. He leaned out to the attendant. *"¿Café, señor?"*

With an even broader smile he pointed to a coffee pot brewing inside the station door.

"Excellent," Brad enthused.

Amanda rubbed her tired eyes and ordered the attendant to fill the tank with regular gas.

*"Sí, señorita."* The attendant went to the gas pump.

"Finding coffee at this moment, Amanda, now that's luck."

"Exactly! I'm serious, Brad." She stretched her arms over the wheel and lifted her stiff shoulders to her ears.

He nodded. "I know it. And I'm not so sure that you're not right. I had an eerie feeling out there when everything seemed hopeless and then that Mercedes just stopped dead. I don't think I can figure it out right at this moment."

This was the first really meaningful conversation they had had so far. It wasn't much, but it was a beginning.

# Chapter Eleven

The gas station was a real oasis. While the attendant fueled the bus, they had each taken a turn in the bathroom. Amanda always traveled with a bar of soap, a towel and tissue, for toiletries were rare in Mexico's public facilities. The station attendant shared his *café con leche* and Enrique hurriedly unpacked his relatives' basket of food. They had a quick picnic with the generous attendant, standing around a grimy table that served as his desk. Although Brad would have preferred some ham and eggs, they enjoyed the impromptu breakfast of bananas, mangoes, oranges, almonds, pecans and home-baked breads heartily spiced with cinnamon and cloves. They repacked the wine and spicy sausages for later.

Amanda paid the attendant and slid into the worn seat behind the wheel. "Any sight of a brown Mercedes?"

"All clear," Brad assured her. The engine coughed to life.

"This town has a great marketplace," Enrique hinted. "We might get something else for a little later. They have great chocolate and fruit pastes and caramels."

"I'd settle for a motel and a bottle of scotch," Brad said.

Amanda yawned and steered carefully onto the road. "I'd like a hot shower and eight hours' sleep."

"You deserve a rest," Brad said. "Why not stop? I'm sure we can find a place with two rooms somewhere in this town."

Amanda's brow quirked. "Three rooms!"

"I meant, Enrique and I will share a room." Brad smirked.

"I know what you meant." What was wrong with her? Words were coming out of her mouth much too sharply. She should be in control. Emotions she was too exhausted to analyze were taking over. So why not find a motel? She was in charge; she was at the wheel. No, it would be too risky to stop to rest. The men in the Mercedes might not be the only people on the trail of the catalyst. "We'll keep going for now. You'll have to make do with that magnificent basket of goodies your relatives gave us—I must thank them properly when we get back. But, we will stop for some chocolate later," she promised.

"Okay," Enrique agreed easily. "I've got relatives in Molango. It's about a hundred kilometers up the road."

"Fine. We'll stop there."

Enrique was always good-humored. What a treasure he had turned out to be. His choice of the old bus seemed perfect now, Amanda admitted to herself as she guided it smoothly through the slowly awakening town. No one gave the dusty, battered old vehicle a second look.

The bus was nearing a large open-air market. Enrique was correct. It was a wonderful, exciting-looking place, spilling over with produce stands and open-air shops. Even though there were few early-morning customers, the market was already coming alive. Merchants were displaying their wares, farmers setting up stands heaped with colorful fresh fruit and vegetables that glistened in the morning light.

A veil of mist, not yet burned away by the sunshine, still hung stubbornly in the crisp, clean mountain air. The town, unpolluted and vastly different from the big city, held tantalizing aromas of exotic cooking that drifted into the bus and teased Amanda's senses.

The scent of new-mown hay being unloaded from a truck at the far edge of the marketplace carried with it a rush of wistful memories from her past. "Doesn't that smell good?"

"Yeah," Brad answered laconically. "Actually, that hay would make a good cushion for the cylinders."

Amanda wheeled the bus around a corner onto a secluded side street and parked under the shade of some trees. Brad glanced at her, a question mark in his eyes.

"You're right," she said. "We'll get the hay. We really need to repack the cylinders more carefully." She winked at Enrique. "And while we're at it, we'll buy some of that chocolate, and whatever else you mentioned."

Enrique was delighted. Amanda and Brad conferred. She rummaged through her purse for pesos and handed them to Enrique with instructions to bargain shrewdly. He leaped from the bus, straightened his shoulders and strolled away with a cavalier swagger.

Brad and Amanda watched him for a moment in mutual silence. Amanda took a deep breath and slumped down in the seat. Her eyes closed. An insect buzzed through the cab. A cicada gave its distinctive mating call somewhere in the distance, and the sound drifted through the silent bus on a cool breeze. The soft rustle of leaves filled the air and filtered a distant rumble of voices. Amanda drifted on that delicate border between being awake and asleep.

Brad was also relaxed. He used the rare moment to enjoy looking at her in repose. He smiled at the small dark head, capped by short ringlets. The haphazard curls ventured onto her high forehead and teased at her temples. She wore the small gold hoop earrings she'd had on when they first met. He drew closer. She had almost no earlobes. He liked that and her pale freckles, so healthy-looking across that button nose. Lips like a valentine, he mused, sorely tempted to lean over and try them. He recalled the kiss they had barely begun—was that just last night? God, what a wild time. How lucky they were to be alive. What lay ahead? How soon would they reach Tampico?

Amanda stirred and brushed at an insect tickling her ear. Since she was already disturbed, Brad stole the opportunity to say quietly, "I don't want to be at odds with you, Amanda. I'd really like us to talk, you know, seriously, about some things."

Amanda glanced up and nearly drowned in Brad's inviting blue eyes.

"I want us both to be honest with each other." Brad moved closer. She could feel his warm breath fan against her cheek.

"Brad," she murmured, "I—"

"Señorita Perry." Enrique, wreathed in smiles, his mouth rimmed with chocolate, pulled open the door of the cab. Brad and Amanda separated from each other with a guilty jerk. If Enrique noticed, he was too excited by his adventure to wink. "Look at all the bargains I got. And you still have lots of money left."

He handed them a bag of fragrant hot tamales and opened a large white sack to reveal squares of dark chocolate thick with almonds. "The best, I guarantee. And in this sack, strawberry paste and caramel and..." He pulled from under his arm something red and black, trimmed with gold threads. "I figured I needed a disguise," he explained. "No one will know me as El Diablo!"

Not far behind Enrique came two men, each carrying a bale of green hay.

Obviously, any serious conversation with Brad would have to wait, but so far Amanda liked what he was saying.

Thirty minutes later they had padded the cylinders with hay, eaten the tamales and sampled Enrique's sweets. Thoroughly prepared, they were on their way again. Brad had taken the wheel, and Amanda studied the map. The pungent aroma of the rich Mexican earth and its crops permeated the bus. With the hay covering their cargo, everything seemed less sinister.

Neither Amanda nor Brad brought up the subject of buying a truck and abandoning the bus. Neither had they reverted to the idea of Enrique's being sent back to Mexico City. The status quo was better left undisturbed, Amanda decided. After all, they could reach Tampico, even if they stuck to side roads, by nightfall, or morning at the worst. Then they would make contact with the fishing boat and off-load the cylinders and end their odyssey.

Brad maneuvered the bus skillfully in accordance with Amanda's map reading, aided and abetted by

Enrique. By noon they had traveled past Atotonilco and were on a mountainous, little-used back road, winding slowly higher to an altitude of nearly eight thousand feet. Beyond this point, the road descended slightly, running through the sleepy little towns of Metzquititlán, and Zacualtipan.

Enrique had curled up at midday and slept contentedly on his hay bed among the cylinders, quite a comical sight in his red-and-gold devil's costume.

"Enrique's still sleeping," Amanda observed as she refilled Brad's cup with bottled water. They were both rather thirsty from the tamales and the sharp mountain air blowing into the cab. "He's got the right idea."

"How about your doing the same? I can let my navigator get some much-needed rest," Brad said.

For once Amanda didn't argue.

"Put your head right here," he insisted. She snuggled down, her head resting lightly on his hard thigh, her knees bent to her chest. She relaxed, cramped as she was, but knew she wouldn't be able to sleep.

The next thing she knew, she was being awakened by Brad's leg moving under her head. "Sorry. Got to shift. Road's steeper now. Save these old brakes."

She sat up and waited for the cobwebs in her head to dissipate. The weather was much warmer now than before she fell asleep, so she struggled out of her blazer. She studied the sloping terrain, stark and beautiful and patched with wildflowers.

Earlier in the afternoon, Brad, too, had removed his jacket and tossed it in the back. His bare tanned arm was propped confidently on the open window. He was beginning to need a shave. Abruptly, he downshifted as the road inclined, and they continued their descent from the rugged high country. He clenched his jaws, too intent on the road to appreciate the stark beauty about them until Amanda called it to his attention. He gave it a cursory glance, and his face relaxed.

"Someday," he said, his voice scratchy and tired, "I'd like to take the time to hike through this country." He yawned and stretched.

"You like to hike?" Amanda asked, noticing that the road was leveling off into a valley. Though she didn't feel like driving again, she thought she had better get him away from the wheel before he fell asleep.

"Sure do. Hike, jog and swim." He leaned forward, resting his forearms on the steering wheel.

She waited, but he volunteered no more.

"I'll take over," she said, adding quickly, "if you'd like."

"Sure you're up to it?"

"In the pink," she lied.

He made no objection and pulled the bus over to the side of the narrow dirt road. As they passed each other at the front of the bus, changing places, Amanda stretched a moment, and all her skin twitched in the dry, still air. The afternoon was uncomfortably warm and dusty. Her lips were chapped by the wind, as were her cheeks, and her lungs felt parched. The cloudless blue sky seemed to go on forever.

Rounding the bus, she was attacked by a cloud of nasty little black mosquitoes with a ferociousness that made her jump behind the wheel and quickly slip the bus into gear.

Brad had walked stiffly around to the other side of the bus, immune to the insects, and was still stretching and yawning. "I could use a little sleep," he admitted. He eased onto the seat and closed his eyes.

Amanda ground the gears in her rush to be moving again. The mosquitoes soon disappeared on the wind that rushed through the cab.

Half an hour later, arms itching and aching, eyes leaden, she was exhausted but determined to stay at the wheel a while longer. Suddenly, she began to experience a light-headedness very similar to that of the previous night. The sensation increased moment by moment, only this time she didn't feel she was about to uncover a great truth. Uneasiness gripped her.

She noticed a highway sign farther along the road. It indicated there was a steep grade ahead, but to Amanda, it carried a hidden warning.

She glanced at Brad. He looked so peaceful that he might as well be dead.

That was it! The warning. He was dead. "Brad!" she cried, her voice strangled. "Look! Oh, no!"

He jerked up. "Amanda, you okay?"

He eyed her cautiously. She was breathing erratically. Was she cracking under the strain or just extremely tired. He moved closer to comfort her. She pulled away.

"That sign," she gasped, raising her foot from the pedal to slow the bus. "It says, 'Death ahead.'"

His skin prickled, but as he glanced at the sign, which they were now passing, he smiled. "It's okay. It's only a steep grade. We're in good shape."

"But I saw it!" Amanda persisted. "It was as clear as day. A skull—a premonition of death."

The grade ahead didn't look dangerous. No one was following. The bus was running smoothly. Brad approached the subject gently. "Just calm down," he said in a soothing voice. "You're tired. You're talking strangely. Everything is fine."

"No! Something's wrong; I can sense it."

He glanced around, assessing the depth of her distress. "Well, whatever it is, I don't see it yet."

She averted her eyes from the road for a brief, solemn glance at him. "I don't, either, but I feel it inside." She calmed a little. "I'll try to explain if you like, or would you prefer me to say nothing? I've never experienced feelings like this. My energy may be depleted, but I can think. I've been getting waves of strange feelings. Of course I'm worried. If you aren't, just go to sleep like Enrique. He's the smart one."

"I was asleep," he reminded gently. "But I'm not taking your premonition lightly. I don't want you to drive us over a cliff. I'm a little nervous when you talk like that."

"All right. Then you'll listen?"

Scanning the road ahead, Brad could see nothing but the ruins of a large old mining operation off to the right near the bottom of the hill. Several weathered structures, deserted and dead, paralleled the road.

"I promise to listen carefully."

The bus started down the grade, gathering speed. Amanda gripped the wheel tightly.

"More and more during this trip I've been getting strange feelings. When the Mercedes was stopped, I knew what stopped it. Then, just a minute ago, I felt as though a cold hand had reached out and touched me, warned me that danger was—"

A mournful wail cut Amanda off. A single loud bang followed, then a chorus of clangs and bangs. Amanda fought the wheel as the old bus swerved and headed, uncontrollably, off the road, through a patch of soft gravel and made directly for the side of a long, delapidated wooden building that appeared to be on the verge of collapse.

Brad made a grab for the wheel, but he was thrown into Amanda's arms, and the two struggled in an unwelcome embrace. Enrique, jostled awake, tried to come forward but was deposited in a heap of hay in a corner.

"Hang on!" Brad shouted hoarsely as he tried to shield Amanda from the imminent collision. "We're going to hit the—" His words were devoured by splintering wood, a cacophony of smashing sounds and then suddenly complete silence.

Amanda's ears rang. "Brad!" she moaned.

He held her tightly. "You—all—right?" His voice was a raspy whisper.

"No, you're crushing me." She moved her legs awkwardly.

"I—can't move," he said weakly. "Breath—knocked—out of me."

Amanda tried to untangle herself. "Enrique!" she called.

"*Sí, señorita.* I'm fine," came his disembodied voice. "You guys make it?"

"Yeah!" Brad mumbled. He sounded terrible. "I—think I totaled Amanda." He groaned and eased away from her.

"I'm not hurt," she assured him. "A little shook up, but I don't think anything's broken. How about you?"

"Bruised," Brad said. "At least we're alive. What the hell happened?"

Amanda felt too relieved to be alive to worry about what had happened. "I don't know. Something grabbed the steering wheel and shoved us into this shack, or whatever it is. I swear I thought we were dead.''

Filled with trepidation, the three of them cautiously picked their way free of the wreck. Once on solid ground, they found the bus had come to rest in the middle of the crumbling old building. Dust and debris danced in the shafts of brilliant gold sunlight that slashed at odd angles through holes in the roof.

They carefully inventoried the damage to the bus. The front right wheel sat hunched over at an impossible angle. The vehicle seemed crippled, in ruins.

Brad, bruised and dirty but feeling better, slid underneath the bus and checked it out. ''We're missing a spindle hub nut and a locking washer. Without those, the wheel came off.'' He grimaced as he came out from under the bus. ''I wonder when we lost that cotter key? Could have been that cross-country jaunt we took last night. Bad luck.''

''Not bad—disastrous,'' Amanda said, beginning to think again. ''But at least we're not dead.''

''True, but we're stalled out here in the middle of nowhere. That was my worst fear.''

''My worst fear was being caught by that bunch of goons,'' Amanda had to admit. ''When they were stopped, I felt it was by some...power. This is so strange, Brad. I knew something was going to happen when I saw that sign.''

''Don't get superstitious. Remember, we're stuck.''

''No, there has to be a reason for all this. Something has taken us this far safely. It's as though we're being watched over.''

''Amanda, you're just overtired and hallucinating.'' He touched her head. ''I think you have a fever.

The next thing you'll be telling me is that the dust motes are square and they're little universes in the air," he said wryly.

His words bore consideration. She gazed up at the majestic spectacle of the dust filtering down and touched her brow. "You may be right. You may not believe me, but I saw the death's-head, I swear. I'll have to think about the dust." Her forehead was slightly warm and gritty with dirt, but she didn't feel ill.

Brad's features hardened. "Squares, death's-head warnings. Ridiculous. Wake up, Amanda."

Enrique stood next to them, shaking his head, first in agreement with Brad, then in agreement with Amanda. "You know," he said, "that dust does look square. Maybe we're all *un poco loco*."

Brad smiled sardonically. "Enrique, there is nothing magical about being stranded in—" His eyes were drawn toward the hole in the building through which the bus had crashed.

From the road fifty yards away came the sound of a car approaching—a damaged car, for it was laboring along, making a fearsome noise. As it grew louder, he saw Amanda's eyes widen, terrified. She shrank back instinctively. Enrique ducked under the bus. Then Brad caught sight of the dark brown Mercedes, bruised, battered, windows broken and dents everywhere, still trailing wires. Three stark figures inside could be seen with heads turning, searching. Brad held his breath. He was helpless to stop them. Though moving slowly, the vehicle of death was free enough to continue its relentless pursuit.

Time slowed to match the Mercedes's pace.

# Chapter Twelve

No one breathed. Mercifully, the Mercedes kept moving forward. For long minutes after it was out of sight and the noise of it diminished to nothing, the trio stood frozen in silence. Finally, Brad spoke.

"Damn!" he exclaimed, shaking his head. "If we were still on the road, they'd have had us for sure." He looked up and with a nervous grin half apologized. "Just keep hallucinating, lady."

Amanda crammed her hands stubbornly into her back pockets. "I wasn't hallucinating. There's an explanation."

Brad turned to the bus and took charge. "Okay, it broke down at the precise moment it should have—magic. The African Queen, Detroit style. Now, how far are we from civilization?"

Enrique beamed. "We're in the old Chauta mine shed less than a mile from Molango."

"Okay," Brad announced, knocking dust off his chinos. "I'll hike into town and with any luck get a spindle hub nut, locking washer and cotter key. That's no problem. The spindle hub's a big, long bolt that holds the wheel on. One end is machined into threads like the end of a garden hose. A washer that looks like a little steel doughnut fits under the nut. Then the cotter pin fits through the nut and locks it in. It looks like a nail. Hey, a nail would do it."

Amanda's mind was moving ahead, recalculating the journey. "I understand. Now, how long before we can be rolling again?"

He thought a moment. "We'll jack her up, put the wheel back on and maybe be on our way in a couple of hours."

"Sounds too easy." She dropped her head forward and massaged the back of her aching neck.

"There might be something else wrong, too," Enrique warned. "How about I go get my uncle Pablo? He runs a junkyard on the other side of the town."

"I might have known you'd have an uncle here." Brad scratched his head thoughtfully.

"Thank goodness for that." Amanda sighed. "We certainly aren't getting any help from our uncle."

Brad glanced at her sharply as though she had let some great secret fall into Enrique's young ears. "You knew we wouldn't get any help from our uncle," he said guardedly.

Enrique intervened. "Hey, look, if you two mean Uncle Sam, you can stop talking in code. Okay? I know we're on some kind of secret mission. I mean, it can't be Tri-Cola syrup in those cylinders. You'd have dumped it by now. You wouldn't have said they might blow up back there when those hoods were chasing us. I may only be fifteen, but I wasn't born yesterday, as they say. You know, I've crossed the border a few times myself."

Both Brad and Amanda laughed at once, shamefaced, and Amanda acknowledged, "Okay, partner, we're in this together."

"Right," Enrique continued. "You guys stay to guard the bus and the cylinders."

"One of us should go with you, Enrique," Amanda volunteered.

Enrique pointed out, "I could go much faster alone."

That made sense. She acquiesced and watched him jog away over the hill that stood between the mine and the town below.

She and Brad sat back in the bus in silence. Amanda was tempted to walk back up the hill and check the danger sign but didn't dare go alone; she didn't want to leave the bus. Besides, her ankle could still do with the rest.

Deep in his own thoughts, Brad retrieved another bottle of water from the back, found their plastic cups, which had bounced out of sight, and filled a cup for them both.

As she gratefully accepted hers, nodding her thanks, Amanda asked, "Would you care to continue our talk—or explore our options?" Too late, she realized the implication of her question. "I mean the countryside," she added lamely.

"I don't know about you—" Brad sighed, completely missing any second meaning "—but I'm bushed. I think I'll get some sleep."

"Sleep? How can you sleep with that car prowling the countryside looking for us?"

"I don't know. Maybe I can't. Do you want to try? I'll stand guard."

"No." She sipped her water. "I couldn't. I'm too tired, too keyed up."

"Well, give it a try. Lie down on the seat. At least it's padded." He got out and sat on the ground beside the open door. There, slumped against the side of the bus, he drank the rest of his water and continued with his thoughts.

Amanda shrugged and stretched out on the seat. She tried to relax. The bench seat wasn't too bad, but after ten minutes questions began swirling around in her head, unanswered questions that demanded answers.

"Brad?"

"Yes?"

"Who are you?"

He paused. "A little late to ask that, isn't it?"

She squirmed to get more comfortable. "I suppose so, but I just want to know. How did you get into this business?"

"What business?"

"The spy business."

"Amanda, I'm not a spy." He paused again, took a breath and decided to tell her what she wanted to know. "I'm a businessman visiting Mexico City on a holiday, with a few business meetings thrown in for good measure." Some business meetings, sitting beside a stranded bus.

She thought about that a moment. "Okay, I accept that. I'm a businesswoman. But you people did approach me, did ask me to do this trip with the catalyst. Is that what Ms. Cullen did to you? Or are you involved in other ways? I suppose you don't have to tell me if you don't want to."

"No, I'll tell you everything you want to know, but I'd like to know a few things about you, too. Flat truth."

"Fair enough. Question for question?"

"Agreed, but you may not like what you find out."
Brad didn't feel sleepy anymore. He rose and stood
facing Amanda, who raised herself up on her elbows.

"You may not like what I say, either," she warned.
"First, is your name really Bradford? Or is that a
cover name?"

"That's my honest-to-God real name."

"Good. Next—"

"No, it's my turn, right?"

She shrugged. "I think you know everything about
me."

"No, I don't," he shot back quickly. "Do you
honestly love Harvey? Truth!"

His question shocked her. "I—uhm—yes." She
studied his face for clues to why he had asked the
question. His face was honest and open. She couldn't
lie. "Yes, I love Harvey's stability, but I don't seem to
be able to—" She paused. Truth! "I'm bored with
Harvey. All we ever talk about is banking and business, and I can't stand it at times."

"Why?"

"Frankly, I sometimes think he's more excited
about how much money I owe the bank and how I
work out plans to repay and build more and borrow
more than he is by me."

"You're not serious, I hope."

"I'm serious. You just don't know. I didn't really
realize it before, but I'm serious. Bankers are bores,"
she added vehemently. "My turn."

He nodded.

"Do you love Ms. Cullen?"

He frowned. "What the hell kind of question is
that?"

"The kind that gets answered by the truth."

He nodded. "Suit yourself. Of course I do. But wait a minute; I want to talk about your banker. Don't you trust him?"

Amanda bristled slightly. He was avoiding the issue. "That is not the current question. We're talking about Ms. Cullen. And how you don't trust her," Amanda supplied, a bitter feeling goading her to force the issue. "You said as much. You advised me not to get mixed up with her."

"That's true. She's a zealot, a superpatriot, but that's no reason for me not to love her."

Amanda felt her breath quickening. She sat up. "Then how can you come on to me when you're in love with another woman?"

"Oh, Amanda. You're talking apples and oranges."

"A double standard. Typical in this country. I'm good enough for a roll in the hay, but—"

"Whoa! Wait a minute. What is this? I haven't tried to roll you anywhere." Suddenly, Brad laughed. "You're jealous of Margaret Cullen? I can't believe this." He slapped his thigh, threw back his head and had a great uproarious laugh.

Amanda burned. "Not jealous, simply pointing out a fact. You live with her."

"I've been staying in her very comfortable fourteen-room hacienda while I'm here for pleasure and business."

"I suppose you're not going to admit that she's your mistress. I heard that over-concerned tone in her voice when she talked to me at the airport."

"Ah, Amanda! Amanda!" He was shaking his head, grinning and neatly infuriating her.

"Don't Amanda me, Brad."

He tried to sober his face, but his eyes still twinkled. "I'm sorry. It's just—you're so fired up. I mean, you're engaged to a banker, and you're bored, yet you're badgering me about—" He stood on the step and tried to take her in his arms, but she avoided his embrace.

"No!" she snapped, hurt and humiliated. "And leave Harvey out of this." Her hand snaked out to slap his smiling face. It connected with his cheek before she could stop it, and instantly sorry, she snatched it back to press it against her lips.

He recoiled. "Is that what your wonderful father taught you?" he growled, a red patch rising on his cheek. His eyes narrowed dangerously. "Strike out with all your pent-up frustration? Give the enemy no quarter?"

"Leave my father out of this."

"Why should I? You can bring up anything you want, make any outlandish charge. Aren't I allowed to say anything?"

"Yes, but you've compared me with my father before. I just have a job to do."

"And you'll do it. Of that I have no doubt." Their eyes locked in painful confrontation.

She lowered her gaze and murmured, "I'm sorry I slapped you. I—" She looked out the window. "I'm not at my best."

"Neither am I," he retorted bitterly. "Now, I was about to say—"

The growl of a heavy truck downshifting and climbing the hill that led from the town to the mine stopped him. He turned toward the sound, then glanced back at her. "I was about to say, I'm sorry, too. We'll talk later."

Amanda tried to smile but couldn't. She jumped down and rushed to the new entrance their bus had made.

Outside, two trucks loaded with people, Enrique sitting on the hood of the first, were pulling into the gravel drive.

Enrique waved his hands in the air. "Hey, I got the nut."

"Looks like more than that," Amanda murmured in a daze as she watched people gaily spill from the vehicles and approach the building, chattering happily.

In quick order Enrique explained the obvious. He had brought not only his uncle who owned the junkyard but his aunt and several cousins, with gurgling babies, as well. Tools were being laid out and lunch baskets opened, children were raising a volley ball net, and a couple of teenagers were making sweet music with a flute and a guitar.

Enrique had explained his situation to his relatives. Amanda and Brad were eloping to escape the wrath of the gringa's sadistic brothers, who had vowed to stop the wedding at all costs.

It would be too bad for Guando and his men if they showed up now.

There was a slight thaw in the frosty atmosphere between the prospective bride and groom.

Work was not the first order of business. Food was. Then came a much-needed siesta for everyone. Then several of the women discovered that water was still flowing from the water tower behind the building, and they had uncle Pablo rig a private shower. Amanda decided she would take a shower later.

Finally, the job of repairing the bus began. The work progressed fitfully. The spindle hub nut was the wrong size, the outside bearing was bad, and there were threads that had to be redone.

Enrique's uncle lifted his stooped shoulders with stoic Latin dignity and went out to find other parts.

Three times he returned to his junkyard to find parts for the growing number of problems he uncovered beneath the bus's gaily decorated exterior. Each time he returned, he brought a few more friends and relatives, food and drink. Each person was introduced to the bride and groom, who managed to perform to a willing and enthralled audience, becoming more and more adept at their roles as the day sped onward.

Amanda was nonetheless more worried than ever. She now added Brad to her list of problems. Despite their terrible disagreements, she wanted to know him better, wanted to be near him. He charmed the crowd of well-wishers and to Amanda was gallant, respectful and kind. They dined side by side. He was still shrouded in mystery, but in response to eager questions he revealed goals for home, family, and future that matched hers. Was he only acting, telling Enrique's relatives what they wanted to hear? Or was he talking to her through them?

He seemed to care for her. She liked the way she responded to him. The chemistry between them was stronger than ever, yet in spite of the abnormal experiences they'd shared so far, their response to each other was much more than only physical attraction. She could no longer deny her feelings. She had been falling in love with him ever since they met.

If he were to make an advance, should she hold him off? But there was no need to make a decision. He wouldn't.

What about his relationship with Ms. Cullen? He'd laughed off her accusation earlier. A typical evasion. She had better steer clear of that subject from now on. Brad would only disappear after this journey, anyway.

Should she break her engagement to Harvey or take her medicine and go through with the wedding? No, she couldn't go through with it. She'd faced that when she and Brad had talked earlier. The wedding was off, permanently.

On top of all her other problems, late in the day she heard the telltale sound of the Mercedes coming back along the old highway. Although the bus was safely hidden in the building and the party outside drew no interest from the men in the car, Amanda still worried. Safely concealed, she watched the vehicle pass by. It was terrifying, like a bloodhound trying to find a trail.

The car kept going. Luck was still with them even though darkness had approached and the work was not finished.

Finally, one by one, the relatives began to leave. And then Enrique's uncle pronounced the job completed. He left happily with a large wad of money Amanda forced him to take.

Exhausted again, Enrique curled up to sleep among the cylinders and hay. Outside, alone for the first time since the work began, Brad and Amanda faced each other once more. Beyond mere exhaustion, they eyed each other awkwardly.

"About this afternoon—" Brad said. "I've been thinking."

"So have I. Let's just start fresh. Tomorrow, when we reach Tampico, we'll look back at all this and laugh."

"I hope so," he agreed. "It's going to be morning before we can hit the road. Why don't you get some sleep. I'll stand watch."

"I feel too grimy. I'm going to try that shower first," she confided.

He nodded and murmured, "Sounds good. I think I'll take one after you finish." He turned away to busy himself with the map.

Amanda climbed down from the cab with her luggage, and by the light of a crescent moon and a billion stars, made her way to the water tower. She set her suitcase in a relatively private spot, undressed and packed her dirty clothes, then with soap and towel in hand, found her way into the shower setup. Once she had figured out how to make the pulley system work, she luxuriated in the water, which, heated and purified by the sun, was like healing balm to her parched skin.

Unconsciously humming refrains the guitar and flute had played, her hips moving in rhythm, she soaped her body and massaged in the lather from her scalp to her toes. It didn't take long before she realized her breasts had firmed and budded. A part of her wantonly wished she wasn't completely hidden from Brad's eyes. She could see him outlined against the front of the building, back lighted by the flashlight by which he studied the map.

She watched Brad stand up and stretch, then arch eloquently. Instinctively, she arched with him, though he was more than thirty yards away. She wanted him to come to her so that she could lose herself in his arms in an endless embrace.

Magic was needed. Silently, she willed, "Come to me!"

He didn't even look in her direction.

She closed her eyes and let the water cover her face and course smoothly downward, stroking her breasts, waist, thighs. His hands would slide over her with that warm, sinuous touch. If only—

"Amanda." Brad's deep voice was close beside her.

Her eyes snapped open and blinked to clear the water. Her heart skipped a beat.

"Yes," she said softly, her voice steadier than it had a right to be. She could see him now. He had crossed the gap and come to her.

His face betrayed his anguish, his love and desire. "I'm sorry. I know you're an engaged woman—"

"No, not anymore. And don't be sorry," she murmured quickly, without guile. "I willed this to happen. I—I want—us—to happen."

He was a dream standing at her fingertips—shirtless, his gray chinos tightly molded around the outline of his obvious need, breathing fast, defenses abandoned.

"No one like you has ever happened to me before. I don't know exactly how to take you, but—I want you in the most natural way—I shouldn't, but—"

"You don't have to explain." She held out her hand to him.

He walked blindly forward into the heavy spray of the shower, his hands caressing her body, and slowly tightened his arms around her naked hips until he was hard against her.

The right man, the right time in her life, maybe even the right place. Amanda rubbed her cheek against Brad's chest and impulsively kissed the warm flesh, while she unsnapped the waistband of his pants and slowly lowered the zipper. In an instant, he had peeled them off and was tenderly embracing her again. His hardness throbbed against her.

"Wash me and help me cool down," Brad muttered, freeing her.

Amanda lathered her hands and complied, bringing groans of pleasure from him.

"Take it easy," he cautioned. "I'm a volcano again."

Her slippery palms stopped. "Remarkable things, volcanoes," she whispered, her eyes locked to his.

Gone were the fears and the stark world outside their small, private waterfall. Brad's lips found hers, and he carried her out of the shower to where he'd thrown down his shirt on the grass. She clung to his kiss as he sank down with her. Their lips parted only to say each other's name again and again.

Brad plucked a long stem from the tall grass that hid them from the bus and drew an erotic trail across her taut stomach, teasing, tantalizing.

"Oh, lady, if I could only have found you years ago."

Amanda gasped at the feather touch of the grass on her thighs and circling her swelling breasts.

In perfect harmony with the universe, a blaze of stars above, the rich earth below, Brad and Amanda lay together. Lips burning, tongues darting in ecstasy, they drank hungrily from their kiss, moving swiftly to the edge of the precipice. Brad's strong, smooth hands slowly parted her thighs. When their lips met again, they were all that existed. None had been before; none would come after. There was only now. They clung together in long, slow thrusts that built to a faster rhythm.

Her arms tightened around him. "Oh, Brad, love me! Love me!"

"I love you, Amanda. I've loved you since the moment I first saw you."

Together they crested, clinging like two made one in a molten world of shared love.

## Chapter Thirteen

To Amanda, life had never been more magnificent or more complicated. Everything was different now. She nestled close beside Brad while he drove. They often shared an affectionate glance and a sweet touch, but most of the time her mind replayed events and tried to reason through all that had happened.

In the back, ignoring the romance in the front seat, Enrique pored over the map, searching for a suitable back road to Tampico.

There had been no sign of the Mercedes all morning. Before today's trek began, the trio had taken time to check the cylinders and to breakfast from the restocked picnic hamper. A little after ten, Brad had backed the bus out of the mine building and retraced their path up the grade at Amanda's insistence. Warily, she climbed down from the bus and studied the sign that had saved their lives. She could have sworn it had given her a hidden message. But it was only a battered old roadway sign.

Brad and Enrique came up behind her. "I was so sure I was seeing a death's-head," she said, her voice listless. "I don't understand."

"I don't, either." Brad patted her arm. "Better be on our way."

She shrugged and fell into step with him. Enrique backed rapidly away from the sign, then jumped up into the driver's seat. "Hey, look at it from this angle," he called.

They jogged back to the bus and got in. At first, Amanda couldn't understand Enrique's excitement, but then she caught sight of the sign from the angle at which it resembled a skull and crossbones. "That's it!" She sighed with acute relief. A small mystery solved. "I wasn't crazy."

"I never thought you were." Brad touched her hand, and a rush of warmth poured over her. "It was an optical illusion. But I'm grateful you saw it. It made us alert enough to save ourselves. No magic involved."

"I don't know about that," Enrique said soberly as he climbed to his nest in the back of the bus. "How did that thing get dented that way? Very strange, even miraculous."

"I have no idea." Brad settled behind the wheel. "We'd better get moving now and worry about miracles some other time."

Now, three hours later, the bus was proceeding along a route of dirt roads. As the rugged miles passed, Amanda recreated the night and her dream-like discovery of Brad. With each remembered moment, her head quickened. She felt again their naked bodies in the shower, his flesh on hers as they lay in the tall grass, his powerful kiss, their ultimate soaring through the stars.

Harsh sunlight penetrating her eyelids had awakened her, shivering, to indistinct bird song and mosquito bites on her arms. A chill wind thrashed the surrounding grass; when she tightened the blanket around her, Brad had stirred. Instantly, she had recalled everything. Wide awake, she turned toward his blond head, feeling a rush of contentment, and snuggled closer to his radiating warmth. He sprawled on his side, facing her, princely in his sleep.

The blanket—removed surreptitiously from the bus last night—was damp with dew. In love and brimming with plans, Amanda had studied this beautiful man beside her and admired the rise and fall of his broad, hairless chest. Except for his darkening beard, his face was smooth; his skin appeared flawless but not leathery. His dark lashes were indecently thick. He was magnificent.

What kind of life had he had? Probably he was a lady killer, with his looks. Then Amanda had spied one tiny mole below Brad's eyebrow. Instead of being a flaw, it simply added to his distinctive appeal, accenting the symmetrical planes of his face.

Even at this early stage, Amanda knew he was her perfect match. After the haunting uncertainty she'd borne with Harvey, the knowledge thrilled her. She loved Brad, and in spite of their clashes that feeling had intensified moment by moment since they'd met.

The breeze toyed with a lock of his hair, which fell across his forehead, tantalizing her. Just as she had reached out to draw her fingertips through it, a noisy squawking rose in the area where the remains of their picnic had been tossed. Amanda sat up. In the distance a dozen buzzards were flapping their immense wings and arguing loudly in competition for their find.

Brad had bolted upright beside her. "What—what? Cylinders!" He realized what was happening and laughed, then pulled Amanda back under the blanket to share a tantalizing kiss. When they had remembered Enrique, they hurriedly dressed behind the water tank. Brad's trousers had dried. As he tucked in his dirty shirt, he said, "I hope we can take time at the next town to buy me a change of clothes. This one-day trip is taking a while."

Tying the drawstring to her gray fleece warm-ups, Amanda had told him, "You look wonderful. You couldn't look more elegant if you wore a tuxedo." The glitter in her eyes had told him more.

"Amanda," Brad said. The wind rushing through the open windows of the bus made his quiet voice hard to hear, but Amanda snapped back from her reflections at once, her eyes riveted to him. He bestowed on her a breathtaking look of love, his lips relaxed, his deep blue eyes vibrant. She slid closer; he squeezed her knee, exciting her immediately.

"I meant what I said last night," he assured her, then cut his eyes back to the road.

She knew exactly what he meant. "And I'm a new person, frightened, excited, bewildered and...awfully happy," she said close to his ear so that he could hear. She was not at all the same steady, reliable Amanda Perry as before.

The kilometers rolled by while Amanda ranged through her feelings for Brad. From the very first time she'd seen him, she'd fought her attraction to him. Remembering all their conflicts, how could they have suddenly come to this great new place, this rare oneness, this wholeness? And remembering what they had shared, how could she even question it?

Lost in her thoughts, she hummed a tune recollected from last night's festive guitars.

Brad listened to her song and reminded himself that when she sings, a woman is happy. He was fairly certain he could take the credit. He just wished they had had that talk. What would she do when she found out everything? How would she take it? No big deal, really, but— Maybe he should have that talk with her—after Tampico.

She stole a glance at him. He was tender, he was stubborn, loved to bait her, he was tough…and he was still a mystery. Indeed, her world had been upside down from the moment they'd met. It was hard to acknowledge that her life now felt truly meaningful because of him.

Her engagement was ended, of course. She was glad she'd decided to break the engagement before last night's tumultuous experience. Even if she lost Brad, she'd never marry Harvey. Other than business, they shared nothing of value. But she couldn't contemplate losing Brad. They were just beginning.

She stretched her legs to the floor, her muscles felt wonderful, her ankle too. She'd love a workout this morning.

Then an insidious thought wormed its way into her sunny moment. Was this euphoria due to the danger they were facing? Was theirs the heightened camaraderie of people under extreme pressure? God, that disturbed her. A long-forgotten pronouncement made by her father swam into her mind. He'd spoken of danger being the greatest stimulant, the ultimate elixir of youth. Could anyone actually be turned on by danger? Without the danger, would Brad be as dull as Harvey? No! She shook her head. She rubbed her moist palms on her fleece pants and vowed their relationship would survive the danger.

Enrique had fallen asleep. They all bumped along in silence. Brad seemed deep in his own thoughts as Amanda brooded. She wondered what he was thinking about and why he didn't talk. Perhaps he didn't want to shout to be heard. Enrique might wake up.

But her mood darkened, and the relentless miles flew by as if hurrying to bring their idyll to a conclusion. Soon the journey would be over. Would they return to Mexico City and resume their lives as before? No commitments had been made, no vows. What exactly did Brad mean by "I mean what I said"? Maybe she had misunderstood him. He and she still lived in different worlds. Soon he would leave hers forever to go back to Washington. What then? Her future prospects loomed drab and depressing.

Even the weather was gloomy and cloudy when Amanda, Brad and Enrique reached the swampy flatlands of Tampico in the middle of the afternoon without incident. They were just tired, dirty and hungry. Amanda was terribly tense. Her bites itched. It had been a long trip.

Amanda knew her way to the bottling plant, but it took the map and Enrique to find side streets removed from the two crowded downtown squares through which Brad could maneuver the bus.

Finally, they arrived at the dock district and stopped two blocks from the area where the pickup was to be made. At the edge of a massive dock complex, Brad parked the bus in a hidden spot among a covey of deserted warehouses. The area was bathed with a humid, salty breeze off the gulf. Rain was not far away.

The place made Amanda feel strangely melancholy. "Home free," she announced unenthusiastically. Enrique and Brad wearily agreed.

In cautious silence they made their way toward the none-too-scenic dock where they found the *Grand Finale* tied up. In the dark shadows of an open concrete warehouse permeated with the vile smell of cowhides, they watched the boat. After a while they edged forward and hid behind stacks of wooden cargo pallets, debating whether to approach. All was not well.

Amanda shrank farther back behind the pallets. She dared to whisper, "I don't like the looks of it. There was supposed to be a red telltale flag flying if everything was go." Brad and Enrique nodded in mute agreement. All three stared at the deserted little fishing vessel only a few yards away. It bobbed lazily on the tide, its moorings lax at the dock.

Brad motioned for them to follow him. Once they were safely on the other side of the warehouse, out of earshot, he pointed out warily, "There's no blue telltale flag flying to warn us off, either."

"You want me to go see if the guy is there?" Enrique volunteered.

"No!" Brad said sharply. "I'll go. He's probably down below, having a beer."

"No, logically I should go. I'm the one he's expecting," Amanda reasoned as she tightened the laces in her jogging shoes, preparing for the job. She considered the matter settled. It felt good to be active again. Her mind cleared of morbid thought, she gave Brad's hand a loving squeeze. He refused to let go.

He was skeptical. "If he's there . . . That boat looks deserted. I'll check it out."

"Maybe it's the wrong boat," Enrique suggested, trying to keep his voice down.

"Well, it says *Grand Finale*, all right," Amanda muttered. "But it surely doesn't look very impressive." She glanced at Brad accusingly. "You'd think the government could get a better boat than that."

He held his palms up defensively. "Don't look at me. It's anonymous looking. I guess that's why it was chosen. I'll check it out."

"Look," Enrique jumped in, "I should go. Who's gonna think a little Mexican kid's a secret agent?"

"Shh!" Amanda said reprovingly. "You're not a secret agent."

"I'm not? What am I?"

"He's got a point, Amanda."

"Yeah," Enrique added. "I'll just go over there and kick a can around. You know, act natural. In this outfit, my own father wouldn't recognize me."

Amanda bit her lip. He looked so small and inoffensive, but that was all to the good. He blended into his surroundings, dressed as he was in the old raggedy clothes, donated by his aunts, that had replaced his garish devil costume. And the boat did seem deserted. The sooner this was over the better. She relented. "Okay, but be extra careful. You've a world of relatives that'll have my head if anything happens to you."

"You noticed," he said, grinning. He rubbed his hands together. "Just watch my smoke!"

Brad and Amanda hid again in the smelly warehouse, sheltered from the brisk breeze, and watched his every move. Once on the dock, Enrique strutted confidently. He sang softly to himself and ambled forward into view, then herded an old beer can aimlessly as he inched closer to the fishing boat.

Amanda and Brad hardly dared to breathe.

Carefree Enrique picked up a stone and spun it at the water and threw another when he got up to the boat. Then he froze as a stream of heavy Spanish expletives hit him. *"Sí, señor,"* he said, and backed away as if frightened. He ran back along the dock, away from the fishing boat.

Amanda's heart was pumping furiously; she feared that someone was going to pursue the boy.

"Come on!" Brad hissed. "We have to get out of here."

"No! Enrique might get lost."

"Don't sweat Enrique. He'll be back at the bus before we are," Brad insisted calmly, half dragging Amanda away from the area.

The instant they opened the bus door, Enrique hissed, "Hit the deck." He was crouched behind the wheel. Brad and Amanda lunged over the seat and into the back with the cylinders.

"What happened?" Brad demanded as Enrique popped the starter. The bus coughed to life and pulled slowly away from the warehouses.

"That guy from the Mercedes, the one with the scar," Enrique said, "he was there, and I caught sight of another one on the deck around back." He laughed nervously. "They waved me away a couple of times before they yelled."

"A trap!" Amanda's blood chilled.

"Sure was." Enrique shook his curly black head. "But I could have mowed them down before they made a move. All I needed was a machine gun."

His words struck Amanda with the hard side of reality. "Don't talk like that, Enrique," she ordered. "You're lucky they didn't chase you."

"Not a chance. I could have outrun them." He was full of overblown confidence.

"What do we do now?" she wondered aloud.

"I don't know," Brad admitted. "I suppose we could toss it back into the embassy's lap." He glanced at Amanda.

"That's not even a possibility." She was equally angry and frightened. "Do you realize someone at the embassy must have tipped off Guando, or he wouldn't have been there? No wonder we haven't seen the Mercedes all day."

"You're right," Brad agreed. "They must have gone directly to the boat, knowing we'd get here sooner or later. Somebody at the embassy must have talked."

"Right!" Amanda's mind was spinning. Ugly suspicions darted through her mind, distracting her from a clear direction. She had only signed on to get the cylinders to Tampico. All day she'd believed she'd be free of responsibility tonight, able to get on with her life. Have a bath, dinner and finally some real conversation with Brad, but now— Carefully, she pulled herself up onto a cylinder. "If the embassy can't even keep a boat secure, they'd never be able to get this stuff back to the States safely." She paused as Enrique took a sharp corner. "But we will!"

"We will what?" Brad repeated as he cautiously sat up on a bundle of hay.

"We'll take the cylinders all the way to Padre Island. That's where they were going, weren't they?"

"Yes, but Amanda—!" He stared at her in disbelief and scratched his three-day-old beard. "That's easier said than done. You know they'll be watching all the border crossings. We'd never get this bus across without being spotted. We don't even know who we can trust or who we're running from."

But the more he talked, the more she believed they could complete the job. "True, but once we're across the border, we'll be home free. It's a milk run to South Padre from Brownsville. We're already headed in the right direction up the coast. All we have to do is sneak across the border. People do it all the time, don't they, Enrique?"

"Sure!" he agreed, driving more slowly so as to follow the debate.

"But we can't risk being caught on the U.S. side, either," Brad argued. "This stuff has to go to the right people, not be impounded by a county sheriff somewhere, or immigration. Too many questions would be raised. That's why our own government was virtually smuggling it into the country. We may be running from the CIA or the KGB or both, for all I know."

Amanda swallowed nervously at the chilling possibility, then chewed her lip. "Well, come up with an idea. You're the trained agent here."

"Oh, no, not that again. Let's just keep this an open forum." He looked worried. "What would your father have done?"

"What was that? What did you say?" She squinted at him, appalled at his having brought her father up again.

"Just a thought. What would your father have done?"

Amanda laughed, a hard raspy sound.

"Sorry! Are you cracking up again?"

"No!" She shook her head. "It's just so weird. When I was young, I admired everything my father did. Then I became disillusioned. But now, suddenly, I feel I'm begging him to take control of my life again. I don't want to feel that way. It's frightening. But I feel lucky that we're alive—I don't know. I—I should be depressed, but I'm not. I was depressed when we arrived, but now I think we can win. With his help, I think we can beat them. Do you understand, Brad?"

"That's what worried me. I think I do. Borderline hysteria, and I've got it, too."

"You?" Amanda said, her headlong explanation arrested. "You in emotional turmoil? But why?"

"Well," Brad replied evasively, "there are a lot of things that have to be solved."

"Besides the embassy information leak, what, for example?"

"Harvey for one."

"Oh, yes, Harvey." She was stopped momentarily, then waved off the thought. "Harvey is solved. I wish I had talked to him before I left, but I'll talk to him later. Right now we have to invade the United States without getting caught by anybody. I'm open to suggestions."

"How about dinner?" Enrique threw in, glancing back over his shoulder at Brad and Amanda. "We're almost at the edge of the city."

Brad looked blank.

Amanda exhaled impatiently and scratched at a welt on her cheek. "I can't think about food in a crisis like this."

"Just a thought." Enrique shrugged, then offered, "Well, if you're going to invade, you need to go in by sea, right?"

"Yes," Brad agreed. "We need another boat. Have you got any relatives with a boat?"

"No, not a real boat," Enrique replied thoughtfully. The threatening weather was closing in. It was getting dark, though it wasn't dusk yet. He switched on the headlights.

Brad interjected morosely, "We better head over to highway 180 and try to sneak across the border at Matamoros. It's dangerous, but we have no choice. No telling if that Mercedes'll show up, either."

"What kind of a boat is it?" Amanda queried, catching Enrique's significant tone.

"Oh, it's nothing. It's just an old landing barge converted to carry tourists out to scuba dive in the Gulf."

"Are you serious?" Brad exclaimed.

"I think he's serious." Amanda clapped her hands. "Enrique, you're worth your weight in gold. Where do we find this relative and his boat?"

"Up the coast about twenty to thirty kilometers. We'll need a good story or *mucho dinero*, a lot of money."

Amanda lifted her chin in thought, a plan forming in her mind. She knew of only one way to get a great deal of money quickly enough to do the job. "Pull over when you see the first public phone," she said. "I'll get the money. But just in case I fail, you two cook up a story."

## Chapter Fourteen

"Well, certainly, I can, Amanda." Harvey leaned on his pristine desk, more than a little irritated. "But give me one good reason why I should."

Standing at the roadside phone, nervously exposed to everyone who drove by, Amanda fell silent. Harvey had balked. He was right. She had absolutely no good reason to give him.

The telephone conversation had gone from bad to worse. She'd caught him working late in his office in Mexico City. He'd accepted the collect call, and now he knew she was on the northern outskirts of Tampico.

At first he'd been calm and cool, but when he'd forced her to admit the wedding would be postponed again, he'd said, "If you postpone it one more time, it's off for good!"

Amanda had stammered, preferring to tell him the truth in person, but finally admitted that the wedding was indeed canceled for good. Harvey had become very calm and said, "I expected as much when I met Tri-Cola's French representative. He was overweight and sixtyish and definitely not that man I saw you with, Amanda."

She had admitted there was another man in the case. That rubbed salt into Harvey's wound. When Amanda finally asked him to send her a large sum of money from her account at his bank, she wondered why he didn't just hang up on her.

Harvey sighed at length. "Amanda you sound as though you've gone crazy. How can you throw me over by phone and then expect me to rush you such a sum when you seem to be entangled in some way with a man who—"

"I'm sorry, Harvey. I know you're right. I wanted to wait. I planned to tell you when I saw you again. But you forced me to tell you now." She felt defeated. She didn't know where to turn.

"But I am a reasonable man." His voice softened. "And it is your money. Though I must emphasize that as your banker, I'm against panicky withdrawals from your account."

"I know. I'm sorry I called. Goodbye, Harvey." She started to hang up the phone.

"Wait a minute, dammit!" Harvey was shaken out of his normally smooth style. "Amanda?"

"Yes, Harvey?"

"You'll get the money. It's the least I can do."

"Oh, Harvey, I love you for this."

"You do. Then I'll go one step further. If I hurry, I can get you a draft on the flight from here to Tampico tonight."

"Well . . . a draft won't do. I need cash."

"Cash!" He was silent for a moment. "Very well. Be at the Tampico airport in two hours. I'll send cash."

"Oh, thank you, Harvey. I won't forget this." Amanda flung the receiver back on the hook and raced back to the alley where the bus was hidden.

"We've got the money," she shouted, hugging Brad and Enrique jubilantly. "It'll be at the airport shortly."

"Well, I'll be damned," Brad exclaimed, awed. "I didn't believe you could do it. Then we won't need the story."

"I hope not, but I haven't got the money yet." She grinned at Enrique. "Don't you people ever get hungry? Let's eat. And Brad, you wanted to buy some clothes."

HARVEY SAT FOR A MOMENT with the telephone receiver still in his hand; then he shrugged and placed it in the cradle. "I knew it! I finally got her to admit it," he mumbled to himself. "So that's it, Ms. Perry."

He glanced up sheepishly, having forgotten the interview that had been in progress. Thank goodness Zena Ballanger had gone into the outer office. He vaguely remembered that she'd discreetly gotten up and left the room when she realized he was having an argument with his fiancée, Amanda Perry.

Harvey went to the door and opened it. "Sorry about that," he said. "Where were we? Oh, yes." He laughed derisively. "We were talking about Amanda."

"Perhaps we should make it another time." Zena flipped her blaze of hair back from her face. "I feel I've chosen the wrong time to talk to you. Not bad news, I hope?" she probed, the journalist in her coming to the fore.

Harvey sighed. Zena was such a lovely person. So concerned, poised and vibrant, so dedicated to her job. In a way she was like Amanda. She had spent endless hours working on the Tri-Cola story, even going so far as to interview Amanda's tiresome assistant, Chris Hubbard. "Oh, no," he said. "That was Amanda. We, ah, have a little problem."

"I'm sorry," Zena said sympathetically. "I'll leave now. We'll talk some other time."

"Yes, that will be best. I'm sorry, but Amanda has—a little financial crisis I have to take care of. I hope you understand."

"Of course I do. Nothing serious, I trust?"

"Oh, no, no, no," he hastened to assure her. "Purely—" his face darkened "—personal. But I must rush."

"Is there anything I can do to help?" Zena offered.

Harvey brightened. "As a matter of fact, there is."

"Name it and I'll do it."

"I'd like to take a rain check on that drink we were going to have."

"I'd be honored to have a drink with the man who rescued me from George Slater." Zena had a subtle way of smiling with her green eyes.

"Oh, yes, him. Incidentally, I saw Slater this morning."

"From a distance, I hope."

"No. He practically ran me down in the hall over at the U.S. embassy, as a matter of fact. I was there to check out a little rumor I'd heard. Slater was with that ambitious little assistant of Amanda's, Chris Hubbard."

Zena's eyes widened at Harvey's slightly tainted description of Hubbard. "Oh, I interviewed Mr. Hubbard this morning."

"I know," Harvey said sourly. "Anyway, the two of them, Slater and Hubbard, were up on the second floor, as thick as thieves, going into the computer section. Hubbard couldn't even meet my eyes when I walked up. Amanda had better watch that one, or he'll skate her job right out from under her."

"That's a shame," Zena said. "Not being able to trust one's own people is terrible." She extended a graceful hand. "You have things to do, and I'm keeping you from them. Thank you." Their hands met, hers radiating warmth. "Harvey, you're a fine man, a loyal friend."

Harvey blinked. The gentle compliment was exactly what he needed. Amanda would soon realize what she had lost. "Thank you, Zena," he said politely. "You're a very understanding person. Now, I must hurry, or I'll miss the Tampico flight."

TRUE TO HIS WORD, Harvey got the money to Amanda on the last flight of the day. He delivered it personally. When he came off the plane, he was greeted by a poorly dressed peasant woman. "Amanda?" he stammered, not believing his eyes. Beside her stood a ragged urchin and a shabbily dressed American who looked like the same man who had driven off with her in that flashy car that dreadful day. So he was the one. Harvey stopped dead, then made a quick recovery and came forward stiffly.

After awkward introductions and the coolest handshake, Harvey handed Amanda a briefcase. His chin high, his back straight, he carefully avoided looking at anything but Amanda. Her eyes seemed like the eyes of a stranger, furtive and sparkling. She was certainly not her usual poised self.

"Thank you, Harvey." She kissed him softly on the cheek. "I do love you for this."

"Ha!" he said with a wave. "You ought to. I went to a lot of trouble to do this for you. And what's more, you're missing out on the best deal of your life. I'm a—a fine man—and a loyal friend—when you get to know me." There was a slight catch in his voice. It was an accurate quote, he thought. Accurate and true.

Brad and Enrique walked away to give Amanda and Harvey a few moments alone.

"I'm sorry, Harvey." Amanda felt awful. Harvey really was a very nice person. "Things changed very quickly. I'm a little off balance yet."

That was an understatement, Harvey noted. He decided not to question her. "You want to know the truth, Amanda? I honest to God feel that a weight has been lifted from my shoulders. We really weren't right for each other. I'm glad this happened. In fact, I passed up a date tonight just to bring this money to you."

She blinked. "You work fast. We broke up only two hours ago."

Harvey laughed his small business chuckle. "Yes, that's me. Zena Ballanger was sitting in my office with me when you called. She's been working on the story every minute since you disappeared. She's interviewed everyone, including your assistant and me, since you met her at lunch."

Amanda felt a little better. Perhaps Zena would console him. "You didn't tell her anything, did you?"

"I told her I had to decline her invitation to go out for a drink or two because I was meeting you in Tampico." Harvey chuckled again. "You're a pill, Amanda. I'm quite put out with you."

He didn't sound very angry, but he was right on all counts. "I'd better be going."

"I understand." Harvey was polite to the end. "Oh, by the way." He motioned in Brad's direction. "Your French representative there—what does he have to do with the American Embassy and Margaret Cullen?"

A chill of fear shot through Amanda. "Nothing."

"Nothing, eh?"

"No, he said he's not with the government."

"Well, he may not be, but that slick Jaguar he was driving is registered to Margaret Cullen."

Amanda didn't like this news but took it philosophically. She had always known Brad was an agent. Presumably, his denials were just an obligatory part of the game.

"How did you find that out?"

Harvey preened a little. "I took the liberty of checking the number on the plates. I wrote it down the other day when I saw you."

"Oh." Of course, Harvey was very efficient.

"And one last thing, Amanda. Since we'll be seeing less of each other, I have a word of advice."

"Yes?"

"I'd watch my flank if I were you. Your assistant is a very ambitious man. He may have sold you out to Congressman Slater. Slater was all ears when I saw them talking at the embassy."

What was Chris doing at the embassy? "How could he sell me out? I have nothing to hide."

"It's only a thought." Harvey checked his watch. "Now I must run. I may give Zena a call when I get back to the city. After all, I'm a free man now." He smiled paternally.

"Thank you, Harvey. You're a very special person, even though we weren't meant to marry. I'm glad you're recovering from your—broken heart so quickly." She kissed him lightly on the cheek, and he returned the kiss, just as usual.

Then Amanda turned and walked away. Dear Harvey, always cautioning and always advising. He never had cared for Chris; that was obvious.

Yes, Harvey said to himself, admiring the dignity with which he'd handled the situation. He was recovering. Amazing. He watched Amanda rejoin her friends with the briefcase filled with money and stared after her until she was out of sight. Then he shook his head and walked back through the gate toward the next plane to Mexico City.

His mind taunted him as he walked. *I can't believe I lent Tri-Cola millions because of her. It would serve her right if I called in every loan she has. Oh, no, no, that would be such a petty thing to do. Petty, hell! Business is business. I might have real trouble over those loans. Must give this some serious thought.*

"We'd better get out of sight fast," Amanda warned. "An acquaintance of mine and Harvey's has found out where we are. There's no telling who she may have told by now. I have a feeling we may have more trouble soon." She slammed the bus door and locked it behind her.

"We're gone," Brad acknowledged as he hit the starter. Enrique wedged himself between the cylinders.

"Good!"

Amanda's eyes brimmed with tears. She was quiet for a long while, lost in her thoughts. Strange, how much could be learned about yourself when you broke out of your rut.

"I'm sorry you had to do that," Brad sympathized, misunderstanding her silence.

"You have nothing to be sorry for," she responded truthfully. "The breakup was long overdue. You were just a—a catalyst. And don't kid yourself. Harvey's a good guy, but he's no fool. He'll probably call in my plant-expansion loans first thing Monday morning."

"That rat! Just because you wouldn't marry him?"

"More likely he thinks I've lost my marbles. Business comes first with him. Just forget it; it's complicated."

"Oh, I think I understand. But don't be too hard on him. He considers you a poor risk now because you've done something erratic with your own life and your own money. And because no banker's allowed an error in today's business lending climate, he's probably sweating it, blaming himself for your anticipated failure."

Amanda looked at Brad with admiration. "Very good. A-plus!"

Enrique stuck his head through the curtain. "We're getting close. Get ready to turn onto the beach road and have the money ready. I hope this works."

"You said all we needed was a ton of money," Amanda reminded him.

"I know, but I always worry that maybe I'm not as smart as I think I am. The guy with the barge is my second step-cousin's brother-in-law on my father's side. But he's a sucker for a lady with a sad story, too."

"It'll work. I have confidence in you," Amanda assured him. "We've come too far to fail now."

"Right!" Brad added, his confidence not all that high. "Just remember that money talks—I hope!"

"You sound like Harvey when you say that."

Brad shook his head and gave a lusty laugh. "I assure you, that wasn't my intention. But don't worry; we'll be in the States before you know it, off-loading those cylinders at Padre. No sweat, love."

It was a starless night. Following Enrique's instructions, Brad eased the bus through a forest of dunes to a stop by a small shack in a dark and deserted-looking beachfront area. A single light high on a pole gave the place a ghostly appearance. Pinioned in the dim headlights, an ancient landing barge of World War II vintage was beached, yawning wide, next to the shack.

"That's not—it, is it?" Brad asked, knowing the answer.

"Not too good, huh?" Enrique admitted.

Amanda's courage vanished instantly. "We could never go out into the Gulf in that thing. It's older than the bus."

An ominous-looking shadow separated itself from the darker shadows and approached the bus. Brad tensed.

"It's okay," Enrique whispered. "That's him. *Holà, Juan.*"

"*Buenas noches, Enrique. ¿Cómo está usted?*" Juan answered.

"*Muy bien. ¿Y usted?*"

"*Así mismo. Nada de nuevo.*" Juan lifted his shoulders and shifted his weight, then fell silent, waiting.

The preliminaries were only small talk. The moment for decision had arrived. Amanda took a deep breath and began speaking in animated Spanish as though her life depended on it.

# Chapter Fifteen

The monotonous drone of high-speed twin diesels intruded upon Amanda's troubled slumber. For a moment, nestled comfortably in the warm circle of Brad's arms, she was disoriented. Brad slept on. Groggily, she recognized the interior of the bus, but its movement and the sound of its engine were different. Then everything tumbled back into her mind.

They were aboard Juan Carillo's barge, *El Albatros*. No wonder Brad was still sleeping; he was exhausted from a night of Gulf winds and waves pounding the barge as it fought its way northward toward a landing on a South Padre beach, northeast of Brownsville, Texas. Texas! Never had a word sounded so good, so comforting. U.S. soil at last. No one would dare follow them there.

Enrique's fears had been groundless. Amanda smiled as she recalled how Juan, looking like a twentieth-century pirate—which he very well might be—had agreed to the voyage without comment, as though he made a clandestine run to the U.S. regularly. He had simply nodded and accepted the briefcase filled with money without so much as checking the amount in their presence. No story was necessary. No scuba gear for the tourist trips Enrique had mentioned was visible. Juan was bound to be a smuggler.

In any case, the deal was struck quickly.

Amanda closed her eyes at the awful memory of loading the bus onto the barge; it had nearly scuttled the operation. Three times they had tried to get it up the hastily fabricated ramp, and each time they had failed. The fourth time was successful. The bus was squeezed aboard, and the barge put out to sea with the vehicle lashed securely—or so they had thought.

A squally storm had sneaked up, turning the small seas into mountains but threatening no immediate danger. Then, at midnight, Juan's radar revealed a vessel approaching rapidly. He changed course and brought the *Albatros* to full throttle. It hit the waves crosswise. The rising wind and powerful seas began to break over the sides of the barge.

One of the lashings snapped, and the bus had charged aft and crashed into the improvised wheelhouse from which Juan steered the vessel. When the barge dipped into the next heavy swell, the bus slammed forward. Without hesitation, risking his life, Brad had grabbed a line and snubbed the bitter end around the front bumper, while all hands had pulled together to bring the lashing tight.

Later, the seas had moderated. Enrique reported no sign of any other vessel on the radar screen. The sea wind had turned and pushed. Juan kept the engines at full power, and the barge skimmed forward at a remarkable speed. At last they could relax for a while. Brad had spread a pallet in the bus's cozy, dry, hay-filled interior, and Amanda had joined him there.

"Hey, you guys," Enrique shouted from the chart house. "We're almost there."

Brad groaned and opened his eyes. "What a night. Some romantic cruise on the Gulf." He rubbed his bearded chin. "Will I ever shave again?" Amanda's jaw snapped open in a yawn, and then she stretched like a cat all the way to her toes. He ran his hand all the way from her thigh to her breast and added, "After we land, let's find a great motel in Brownsville. We can shower and get a few hours of rest. Or whatever comes first."

She pulled him down for a quick hug before they made their way out of the bus. She loathed sleeping in her clothes but was glad she'd packed her sweat suit. Though hardly fresh, it was at least comfortable. Salt spray didn't count as a shower, either.

The distant beach looked dark and desolate in the murky light before dawn. Dark clouds scudded furtively overhead; occasional lightning sizzled across the sky. Fleetingly, Amanda wondered what Nathan Perry had felt like poised to assault a beach under fire. At least this was a friendly beach inside her own country. She was safe now. She could breathe easily. The dangerous journey was nearly over, the fare paid to second step-cousin Juan.

"Have some fish," Enrique urged. "Just caught and cooked by the captain." He handed them two steaming plates of tortillas and fried fillets of white fish. "The captain always runs a drag line off the stern," he explained as Amanda and Brad attacked the food ravenously.

"I wouldn't say we were hungry," Amanda joked, licking her fingers.

"More like starved," Brad said, handing the empty plates back to Enrique. "Now that was a breakfast. Our compliments to the chef."

"Looks like rain," Enrique pointed out as he headed aft with the plates.

"I hope not. Who's steering the barge?" Brad asked.

"Nobody," Enrique shouted. "Juan lashed the helm."

A stream of loud Spanish erupted from the chart house, followed by Juan's head. The engine changed pitch, and the barge leaped forward. Approaching from the south, perhaps from Tampico, a helicopter swept low over the water, then circled them slowly. After jagged lightning had flashed perilously near it, the helicopter turned and streaked away into the darkening Gulf.

The *Albatros* raced straight toward the deserted shore. "I don't like that a bit!" Brad growled as he watched the helicopter fade into the distance.

"Who was it?" Amanda shouted, more concerned about the weather than the unwelcome visitor.

"I have no idea, but look way out there in the Gulf." Amanda followed Brad's pointing hand. A fishing boat was ploughing through the seas in a straight line directly toward them.

Juan lowered a pair of powerful binoculars. "The *Grand Finale*," he roared above the sound of his straining diesels.

"Oh, no, the boat from Tampico. Guando's men!" Amanda cried out, her heart beginning its breathless tattoo.

"We'll make it!" Brad assured her automatically. The fishing boat was less than a mile away and bearing down on the hapless barge, but the *Albatros* had reached shallow water and was charging toward the sand. Juan knew exactly where he was going.

That was more than Amanda knew. "Brad," she snapped, "ask Juan where we are. And get Enrique ready to release the lashings. I'll start the bus. Prepare to go the second Juan opens the ramp." Tensed to perform her best, she slid behind the wheel and wrestled with the starter. The engine wheezed and coughed, then sparked hoarsely to life just as the barge reached the desolate beach.

"Please don't fail me now," Amanda pleaded as the barge grounded. Juan dropped the forward ramp with a swift jerk, and soft, wet, uninviting sand lay before her. Would the tires get traction?

Enrique, followed by Brad, jumped into the bus, and Amanda floored the accelerator. The engine roared to full power. She let out the clutch carefully. The bus charged forward over the ramp, hit the shallow water with a tumultuous splash, then sloughed through the soupy sand, threatening to bog down at any moment.

"Don't let it bog down," Enrique hollered.

Amanda fought to keep the bus moving. The engine, though laboring, was undauntable.

Home at last. The cylinders settled down to their familiar din.

Juan closed the barge's exit ramp and backed off the beach. The fishing boat, frustrated by the shallow water, turned and raced at full speed in the direction of Brownsville.

"Maybe the coast guard will get those guys if they try to land," Amanda said wistfully. "Where do I go now?"

A weak sun at the horizon was all but obscured by a veil of charcoal clouds. Thunder rumbled, but as yet there was no rain fall.

"We're somewhere up the coast from Brownsville," Brad said, scanning the area for a trace of the roadway Juan had promised they would find. The tires fought the pull of the sand as the bus topped each hillock, weaving drunkenly inland.

"There's the road," Enrique called.

"That's not a road; it's a path," Brad scoffed. "We're lost."

"No, we're not. The road's over there." Amanda nodded to her left at a road, narrow to be sure but leading straight inland.

It was rutted and bumpy, and it led immediately to another hillock. Amanda gripped the wheel like death, for the road threatened to drop away and disappear at any second. The Gulf was lost from view.

First a single drop of heavy rain splattered ominously onto the windshield. Then came the deluge. An old concrete structure partially hidden in the sand came looming through the curtain of rain. Amanda stopped the bus.

"I can't see to drive," she admitted wearily. "Maybe we should wait until it stops raining."

Brad nodded agreement. Hail was beginning to fall, tiny pellets that sounded like machine-gun fire. He shouted over the racket, "We'll be okay here."

"What is this place?"

"It's an old bunker, I think. The government erected a bunch of them back in the forties. They've been deserted for years."

"Thank goodness. I've had enough trauma to last a lifetime."

"We're safe now. That helicopter couldn't stay to track us. They'd be foolish to try anything here in the States." The hail had stopped, but the rain was still a steady downpour. Brad moved closer to Amanda. "It's kind of relaxing, isn't it?"

"I guess," she agreed tentatively. She glanced back at Enrique, who waved from his nest, already stretched out to nap as though he had not a care in the world. "Without him, we'd never have made it."

"He's got the right idea." Brad yawned. "I'm going into the back to catch some sleep myself."

Amanda was left alone in the cab. The bus was cozy and warm, but she also felt very much in need of a shower. The rain was falling in blinding sheets outside. She had an idea. Why not take advantage of this rain?

From her overnight case she retrieved a pair of clean sweatpants, her last T-shirt, and lacy bikinis. Her soap was still good, but her towel was stiff and none too fresh. She would improvise. She stripped and wrapped her dirty sweatshirt around her to use as a towel, making herself a promise—never to take any kind of trip without a full bedroll and two suitcases filled with linens.

Quietly she stepped out into the rain. The chilly downpour made her gasp and her teeth chatter, but in back of the ancient bunker, its sting was less shocking and more invigorating. Lathering up, she felt as solitary as in her own bathroom. The shower she'd taken with Brad the other night had been much more fun. She soaped her short hair, eyes closed, then let the rain rinse it.

Her old shirt wrapped around her, Amanda ducked her head and started back to the bus, now intent on getting out of the blinding rain. Suddenly she bumped into a pair of blue jeaned legs. Her heart thumped once, but slowed when Brad slipped his arms about her and kissed her rosy wet lips.

"Enrique's not right behind you, I hope."

"No. As a matter of fact, he woke me up and said I'd better make sure nothing happened to you. He's guarding the bus."

"He's a very intelligent person," she murmured, and slipped her arms around Brad's warm, rain-soaked waist. "We have to stop meeting like this."

His whisper near her ear sent a shower of heat radiating through her veins. "On the contrary, we need to do this regularly, but in slightly more comfortable circumstances." His lips found hers again, igniting latent fires below.

The blinding rain, intensely unifying, bound them in a sheltered embrace. Amanda pulled back a bit to catch a breath. Brad murmured, his breath on her cheek, "I want to count every freckle on your body and trace every curve."

She took his hand and started reluctantly back to the bus.

"Tonight," she whispered.

"And tomorrow, and tomorrow."

Amanda hurried into the bus, calling, "I'm warning you, Enrique. Stay behind that curtain until I say all is clear." There was no answer. He was asleep again.

Brad stayed outside to shower while Amanda dressed in the cab.

Afterward, wearing a new, white Guayabera shirt, embroidered and tucked, and new jeans from Tampico, he huddled close to Amanda and declared, "I don't care what happens. That's the last outdoor shower I'm taking."

They held each other like two naughty children cuddling in the front seat. Luckily, Enrique slept on, lulled to slumber by the pelting rain on the roof. Between kisses, Amanda and Brad studied the area map supplied by Margaret Cullen.

The storm continued all morning. Enrique awakened rested and hungry. While he ate and handed snacks from their picnic supply to Amanda and Brad, they all worried about their plight.

"Although the desalinization plant is not shown on the map," Amanda murmured, "it has to be close by."

The trio waited impatiently for the weather to clear enough to let them be on their way. Finally, just after one in the afternoon, the rain began to slacken.

"We probably should wait for dark to move out," Amanda said. "No use in tempting fate."

"Nobody in their right mind would try to attack us now," Brad countered. "We're too close to a government installation." He checked the map. "It can't be more than a mile or two north of this miserable excuse for a road to Corpus Christi. They'll be plenty surprised when we dump these cylinders on them. Besides, I'd like to sleep in a warm bed tonight. If we wait, this rain may come back at double strength and flood us out." He put the map aside and climbed into the driver's seat. "Okay?" He started the bus.

Amanda shrugged. "Might as well." As they pulled around to the other side of the bunker, she glanced back nostalgically at the dune where she and Brad had kissed that morning. It was their own private island.

"After we unload our cargo, we'll head back and find a place to stay overnight in Brownsville," Brad said happily. "That suit you, Enrique?"

"Oh, sure. You know, I've got relatives in Austin and San Antonio. I may visit them for a while."

"I guess the first thing I have to do tonight is have a long talk with my assistant, Chris Hubbard," Amanda said listlessly. "There are a few problems with him, apparently. Then, tomorrow, I'll have to fly back to Mexico City—if I still have a business to run."

"And a fiancé?"

"You better know the answer to that. Harvey's otherwise occupied, and I'm glad of it."

"Good! I'm glad you have no regrets." Brad checked the odometer and frowned. They had traveled north just over three miles. Nothing but empty space and sand lay in their path. "I'm surprised you're not going to ride back to Mexico City with me and my bus. This is my only transportation now, if you recall."

"I was only going to be gone a couple of days. We'll see."

"This love stuff is getting too deep for me," Enrique grumbled. "You guys are no fun anymore. I'll be glad to get back to work, too. Where is this salt plant, anyway? I thought it was supposed to be right here."

"That's what I thought," Brad said. They rode in silence as more miles ticked off. Brad was growing increasingly agitated. Suddenly, he brought the bus to a halt. "That's it," he growled.

"Where?" Empty sand stretched for miles, and the Gulf to their right.

"We're here." Brad stabbed Ms. Cullen's map. "Something is very wrong."

"What are you talking about?"

"There is no desalination plant. We should have come across it long ago."

"But Brad, that's not logical. The Padre Island plant has to be here somewhere."

"Where? Do you see anything? I don't. We're wandering around with highly explosive cylinders, and there is no place to get rid of them." He squinted into the distance ahead. Several specks were approaching rapidly. "In fact, we're in worse trouble than that. I think we'd better get out of here fast." He shoved the stick into gear, managed a U-turn on the pathway and sent the old bus roaring back in the direction from which they had come. The rain had lightened to a mist, but now a new front was rolling in from the Gulf. Its full fury descended a few moments later.

"Where are we going?" Amanda screamed. Why were they still running, and from whom?

"We've played this game long enough. We're going to the police, and Brownsville is the closest city."

"But Brad, who's chasing us?"

"I don't know, and I don't care to find out. Something is wrong with this whole situation." They were closing in on the bunker, and the bus was laboring. Brad glanced at the outside mirror. The pursuing vehicles were hidden by the rain. "We'll hole up here," he shouted as he whipped the bus around to the other side of the bunker. It came to a stop directly in front of the seaward entrance.

They waited with pulse rates soaring. Minutes ticked by, but nothing happened; no cars passed the old fortress.

"I'll go take a look over the top." Brad opened the door and braved the howling storm.

"Wait a minute; I'll go with you," Amanada called out.

The climb was a fight for footing every inch of the way. At the top, they crouched low and raised their heads only high enough to peer over the parapet without being seen.

Three large black limousines were parked about a hundred fifty yards away.

As they watched, the door to one of the cars opened, and from it stepped a familiar figure dressed in dark clothes and hat. He glanced toward the bunker.

"Guando," Amanda murmured, despairing.

Guando braced himself against the blowing rain, then, disdaining the elements, walked unhurriedly to a limousine both larger and slightly closer to the bunker than the others. As he approached the car, a darkened window slid down like the blade of a guillotine.

Guando huddled close to the window.

He started to gesture violently toward the bunker and argued with someone inside the car. Then he threw his hands in the air, defeated, and listened, hunched and dripping, to the shadowy figure in the limousine. He slunk back to his own car.

The window of the bigger car remained open; the figure inside raised a pair of binoculars, which seemed to Amanda to be pointed directly at her. She shrank back involuntarily as a bolt of lightning briefly illuminated the scene and the identity of the person inside the car. "Duck!" she whispered sharply.

"Damn! What the hell are we going to do now?"

A crack of thunder punctuated his words.

# Chapter Sixteen

"I don't know what to do," Amanda whispered, working hard to control her breathing. Though she shuddered with cold chills, stark hot fear shot through her. "Let's get back to the bus." They slid back down the slippery bunker to find the bus sitting at an odd angle. A rear tire was rapidly going flat.

"Oh, Brad," Amanda muttered as an icy trembling gripped her. "What next?"

"Get in," he ordered. "I'll fix it later."

"If there is a l-l-later!" she stuttered, teeth chattering.

"Just get in where it's dry, at least." They tumbled back aboard the bus. Brad looked into Amanda's distressed face, framed by dark, wet tendrils of curls. He wanted to comfort her. "We're safe here for the moment. If they were going to move in on us, they would have done so by now. Apparently they feel we're trapped and they can afford to wait for the storm to clear. Did you recognize that woman with Guando?"

Now she was not only cold; she was humiliated, as well. "I certainly did. Her name is Zena Ballanger."

Enrique, wide-eyed and listening closely, interrupted. "The newspaper lady?"

"Yes. She owns a number of newspapers in several countries, including Mexico and the United States. She's the one who wanted to do the story on me that day I met Harvey for lunch." Amanda felt sick. "That's why she must have questioned me so fully. I practically told her what I was doing."

Brad gave her a sympathetic hug.

"What is going on?" Amanda pleaded. "Why is there no desalination plant? What are we doing here? What do you suspect?"

"I told you—" Brad said, keeping his voice calm, though he was on edge himself. "I don't know where the plant is or if there ever was one. And we're here because you insisted we follow through. I'm as baffled as you are."

"Oh, I feel so stupid," Amanda moaned. "I had no idea Zena was one of them."

"It's not your fault. You're an amateur. The State Department should have left you alone. You were suckered in," Brad said with real bitterness in his voice. "I warned you not to trust my patriotic mother. Her job at the embassy means everything to her. She'd sacrifice anything for her country—just as she sacrificed me."

Amanda jerked back as though he had slapped her face. "Your mother? What? Margaret Cullen is your—"

Brad doubled up his fist and slammed it into the dashboard. "Damn!"

The relationship was news to Enrique, too. He was clearly impressed. "Your mother is with the American embassy?"

Finally, Brad spoke again. "Yes, Margaret—is my mother." The words didn't come easily. "Look, it's her big secret. Oh, I can see why you didn't guess. She's eighteen years older than I am, and she's a very handsome woman. I didn't really know how handsome until I found out you were jealous of her the other day when the bus broke down. Margaret would be very flattered if she knew.''

''Jealous! I wasn't jealous.'' Amanda lifted her chin defiantly.

''Oh, Amanda, you certainly were,'' Brad continued.

''Don't Amanda me!''

''I was about to tell you the facts the day the bus broke down, but we got into an argument.''

''How despicable! You let me think she was your mistress all that time.''

''No! I thought she had told you when you called me from the airport. You told me you had to send me home to Mama. I should have known you were just taunting me. She never tells anyone. I'm her one big mistake. Her illegitimate, teenage pregnancy. She's been in the diplomatic service for years.''

''But you talk so badly about her, you talk as though she's deceitful and devious.''

''She is. When it comes to her patriotic duty, nothing stops her. She didn't want me involved in this for any number of reasons. All I was supposed to do was pick you up at the Palacio, deposit you at the meeting place, then take you home. I've told you repeatedly I'm not connected with the government. I'm just staying at her home while I'm in Mexico on vacation with a business conference thrown in.''

''So you're Bradford Cullen.''

He winced. ''Technically, I guess I am. But I was never supposed to admit the Cullen part. Since you want details, years ago I legally changed my name to Forrest C. Bradford.''

"God, why didn't you tell me?"

"It was none of your business at first. How did I know I was going to fall in love with you?"

"That's—no excuse," Amanda stammered. "You should have told me."

"I just have. I would have told you sooner, but the timing has been wrong. And still is." He looked toward the enemy encampment, then deep into her eyes so that she could see the truth in his. "I meant to tell you when I realized what you thought after the bus broke down. But then we got—close—and you seemed to like me better when you could throw Margaret at me. Honestly, she doesn't want anyone to know she has a son, especially one the same age she pretends to be."

"What business are you in?" Amanda demanded flatly.

Brad flushed and exhaled raggedly. "Amanda, this is no good. We have big problems. There are people out there who want to kill us. We may not live to—uh, we mustn't waste time raking me over the coals. My business—is my business."

Her immediate anger with him momentarily drowned her fear. "I want to know. It's important to our lives. No more secrets!"

"All right." He shrugged dejectedly. "It doesn't matter, anyway. I'm with World Banking Systems— first vice-president."

Enrique stared in awe. "You're a banker?"

"No! Not a banker." Amanda could not believe her fate.

With a wry twist to his lips, Brad said, "Yes. On vacation. And to drop in on the O.I.B. Conference if I felt like it." He paused. "When I left my office in D.C., I didn't contemplate a trip like this."

Yet another blow hit her. "Brad! You mean you're really not an agent? You really don't know what you're doing!"

He raked his hand through his hair several times. "If you mean this chase stuff, you're right. I'm along to help you drive."

"To drive—" she echoed, defeated. Then her eyes widened and glazed over. "Then we've made it all this way on nothing but luck." Her voice weakened. "We are in serious trouble."

"Amanda," he reasoned, "calm down. You told me luck was the secret of the universe."

She was reeling from one shock after another. "Dammit, you don't have to rub it in or say I told you so. I know I was a fool to listen to your mother, but I wanted to do this to prove something to my— I still want to complete the job."

"Correction," Brad said dispassionately. "I've known all along what you want to prove. I've read all about your father. You're just like him. Gung ho to the end. You wanted to win your own Medal of Honor to go along with his. Another hero."

Enrique wished to clarify this newest astonishing revelation. "Your father won a Medal of Honor?"

Brad turned to Enrique and answered for Amanda. "Yes. He was a war hero. He was as much a super-patriot as my mother. And Amanda's as bad as both of them. You can't play with people's lives without someone getting hurt."

He shouldn't have said that. It was one thing for her to criticize her father, but she didn't like Brad doing it. And he'd neatly taken the spotlight off himself. "You're not being fair. He saved lives. And I'm nothing like him. He even got himself killed in a stupid accident just to protect me." The words slipped out before she knew it.

But Brad only continued, unheeding of her pain, unhearing. "I may not be fair, lady, but he was a crowd pleaser. You said it yourself." Tears sprang to her eyes, but Brad went on ruthlessly. "And you may as well face it. You want to prove that you're tougher than he was, even though you won't admit it."

How could she have ever thought she loved this stranger? She could no longer even stand to look at him and his mean, arrogant face. She turned away and stared at the rain.

She grew bitterly calm. "Okay, fine, think what you like. What did I expect from a—" she spat out the word and snapped her head back "—a banker. You're more interested in your balance sheets than human love and affection. I love my father. And I know now they don't make men like him anymore. But by God, I'm going to figure a way to get out of here alive if it kills me!" Her words echoed in her ears, and she realized they were exactly what her father would have said.

"I rest my case." Brad somberly turned away.

Enrique tried to clear the air and introduce a note of optimism. "We'll make it, I hope."

"Which reminds me," Brad said grimly. "We have a flat I have to change. Would you dig out the jack, Enrique?"

"Sure." Enrique scurried to get the tools.

"I may be just a banker, but I haven't given up yet, either. They're still going to have a fight on their hands sooner or later." He nodded toward the back. "Maybe we should just give them the cylinders. We might be able to walk away."

"No!" Amanda said firmly. "I'm not against negotiation, but I don't trust them. I'd rather make a run for it in the bus."

Brad winced. "Good point." A forgiving smile tugged at the corner of his mouth. "You and I can fight out other matters later. Now, I'll see what I can do about that tire. I didn't need this scene."

"Who did?" She took a breath. "Need any help?"

"No. Just be ready to drive like hell—right through the middle of that bunch out there, if we have to."

"Yeah, right through the middle." As she began to imagine driving the bus right through her tormentors, she perked up and faced the situation with renewed determination.

Enrique came forward lugging a monstrous jack, assorted tools and a tarpaulin. "We can rig a tent. I don't know if we can get a solid footing to put this jack on. It might just sink into all that sand. What we need now is some pretty good luck."

"Or for the cavalry to show up." Brad hunched his shoulders and headed back into the rain to repair the tire.

"I'll go for that," Enrique agreed. "Armored cavalry." He followed Brad out the door.

Amanda marveled at their cheerfulness. She sat near the back window, straining to hear their banter as they scooped out sand and hammered and swore and scooped and shoveled some more. They sounded as though they were having fun. Was their good humor real or faked? Did it make any difference?

She slumped on her cylinder. Why had Ms. Cullen sent her on a mission to a nonexistent place? Certainly when she found her path blocked in Tampico, she had extended it further than she had been asked. But if she had in fact been able to turn over the cylinders to the operative on the *Grand Finale*, would he have brought them here, to this deserted place? Or would he have known their true destination?

However, that was all water over the dam. She still had the cylinders, and the enemy was poised to wrest them from her. She couldn't, wouldn't, let them get the catalyst.

*I'll figure out something. Anything other than capitulation, anything but failure.*

Another cold wave of understanding broke over her. Brad was right. She'd heard her father use words very much like those many times when she was young, when she had had to listen to him talking about all the battle plans he had made and actions he had led.

Too bad she hadn't learned something. She might sound like her father when she expressed her determination, but obviously she had absorbed none of his ability. She hated war and guns and fighting of any kind. Why had she ever agreed to deliver the catalyst? She was no heroine. She was nothing but an empty shell that had run out of luck.

Amanda glared at the cylinders. They looked enough like Tri-Cola containers to be real. A sudden paralyzing thought touched her mind. No! Impossible! But Ms. Cullen was just devious enough to have done that, too.

Amanda, heart pounding, edged among the cylinders. They didn't look dangerous to her. She reached over into the tool box from which the tire tools had been removed and found a pair of pliers. Then she took hold of the cylinder closest to her, tipped it onto its side and slowly, nervously, tried to turn the square yellow relief valve on the top. It was stuck. "Damn!" she muttered in frustration. "I'm not going to ask him to open this for me." Sweat beaded on her forehead. She stopped and rummaged through the tool box again. A crescent wrench. That should do it.

With each moment her anxiety grew. If Brad came back, he would try to stop her. She heaved mightily on the valve. Damn him! And his mother! It moved slightly. Then it moved a fraction more. A tiny bubble rose, then another dark brown bubble, and then more. She closed the valve. Her hands were shaking, and she could barely move. She'd been holding her breath and breathed out sharply. What if she were wrong? She put her finger to the sticky brown ooze, then shakily raised it to her tongue.

"Amanda!" Brad's voice cut like a knife through the sound of the rain. She jerked her hand away as if his voice had burned it. "Come here quick and see what we've found," he shouted. "Hurry!"

# Chapter Seventeen

Once more Amanda stepped out of the bus into the cold rain and howling wind. She edged alongside the bus toward the source of Brad's voice, eyes smarting, pummeled by the driving rain and sand, but her greatest problem by far was her inner storm. Her mind, battered by her new discovery, groped helplessly for a logical explanation.

"Back here," he yelled. She could see him now, holding the tarpaulin up for her. One side had been tied securely to the bus and the other to the entrance of the old bunker to make a shelter.

Brad's strong hand grasped her arm and helped her under the tarpaulin, his touch only accentuating her feeling of confusion. She scurried to the center of the shelter, her arms wrapped around her ribs.

They had a small lantern burning that Enrique's uncle had donated to the tool box. A pungent tang of kerosene permeated the air. She looked all around and wondered why Brad had called her.

"Pretty good, huh?" he enthused.

Perhaps she had been secretly hoping he had called her out to show her a miracle, but everything looked as miserable as ever. He and Enrique appeared to be about through with their work on the tire.

"Bradford," she replied. "You scared the wits out of me. I thought Guando had attacked. Do you need me to help you?"

"No, I want you to see something. Look."

Amanda had noticed only that the bus was jacked up, the offending tire removed and the spare in place, but now she saw Enrique hauling a dark green box out of a deep hole in the sand to the rear of the bus.

"We had to dig a little," Brad explained, "to get the jack stabilized. That's when we found it."

"Found what? What is it?" She was curious now.

"Pirate treasure," Enrique supplied, his dark eyes snapping with excitement.

"Let me get a hand on it," Brad said. "It looks like a military shipping container."

"Military?" Amanda's eyes widened. "Be careful. It could be dangerous."

"I will be." While he wiped the sand from the lid with his elbow, his glance jumped from the box back to her. His eyes twinkled. "The only dangerous thing this banker ever did was get mixed up with one Amanda Perry." This she ignored. His attention went back to the lid. He read, "Department of the Army, Washington D.C. 1-M14A2-42266. What does that mean?" He fingered the sealed latches. "It's been here awhile. The box is in poor condition."

Amanda knew what the numbers meant the moment Brad read them out. The implication stunned her. Her ears rang, and she felt as if a thousand crickets were creeping up her spine. The bitter taste of spent cordite began to overpower her. Her mind slammed closed the doors of remembrance.

She grew less shaky, even though her hands still trembled when she reached out and tentatively touched the box. The government seals were still in place. She took a much-needed breath.

"When you open it," she said huskily, "you may find an old automatic rifle in there."

"You're kidding!" Brad scoffed. He broke the seals and lifted the lid easily. Before him lay a number of long metal pieces, a jumble of disassembled parts wrapped in disintegrating oiled paper.

"Looks pretty good," Enrique said, awed by the meaning of their find. "But how did it get here?"

"It was probably stolen and somebody tried to smuggle it out of the country," Brad surmised. He was already unwrapping the corroded parts. "Let's get this into the bus and assemble it."

Amanda stood back, her hands flattened against her thighs, repelled by the sight of the ugly weapon.

"But why would somebody leave it here?" Enrique asked as he and Brad gathered the pieces.

"They might have been scared off or caught or planning to come back and get it sometime. It's illegal to have one of these babies without a permit. It's like a fully automatic machine gun. Here, Amanda," Brad said, "would you carry these clips?"

She recoiled from his touch when he tried to hand her the ammunition clips. "Put it back where you found it," she said, her voice quaking. "I hate guns. And especially that thing."

Brad laughed, exhilarated by hope, so filled with the joy of discovery that he barely heard her. "Don't be a nut. This is a miracle. This gun is our ticket out of here. We can blast our way through that bunch."

"I doubt that," Amanda said, trying to steady her voice and emotions. "That weapon is probably useless. Look at the corrosion. I doubt that it would fire, and if it did, the ammunition is old and corroded, too. It would be dangerous to try and fire it, in any case."

"You certainly seem to know a lot about it. Why are you so pessimistic?"

"I ought to know about weapons. I lived with them long enough as a child. That's nothing but a piece of fieldstripped junk. I wouldn't touch it if I were you. I don't even want to see it. It smells of death."

"Good Lord, Amanda, what do you want?" Brad exploded. "This is a chance, even if it can't be fired. Maybe we can use it to bluff our way out rather than blow up the catalyst to keep it out of their hands. You're not against getting out of here alive, are you?"

"Of course not! But you don't know a damn thing about that weapon. It's a piece of false security. I'm not blaming you, Brad. You're as much of a fool as I am. I've been suckered into something that's even worse than I knew."

"What do you mean?"

"I mean that not only is there no desalinization plant; there is no catalyst, either."

"What? What the hell are you raving about? What's in those cylinders if it isn't catalyst?"

Amanda could have sworn that Brad was being sincere. "You really don't know? Brad, there's nothing but Tri-Cola syrup in them."

His mouth opened. "That can't be true. Why do you say that?"

"Because I just opened one of the containers and checked the contents. Nothing but pure, perfect Tri-Cola syrup. Believe me. I've been around it for years."

IT WAS A FACT. Brad believed her now. So did a wide-eyed Enrique. She had reopened the container and proved her point.

Why fight Guando for useless booty? They calmly pushed the entire load of cylinders out the back of the bus and onto the sand.

Now Brad, slumped against the side of the bus, his exhausted body anchored to the hay-covered floor, was a man plagued with an enormous number of questions.

Let Guando and Ballanger have the cylinders was Brad's plan. But Amanda objected. Even if they surrendered the cylinders, why should Guando and Ballanger let them go? No, a better plan had to be invented. They couldn't let the cylinders go that easily.

Darkness came, and there was no movement from the people waiting less than two hundred yards away. They could afford to wait. The trio in the bus, their backs to the wall, could not move in the storm, which seemed intent on lasting forever. Twice Brad had climbed to the top of the bunker. The cars were still waiting.

"We're safe here until this storm lets up," Brad surmised. He had peeled off his soaked clothes and put on the slightly drier pants and shirt he'd worn on his previous expedition to the top of the bunker. With a fatalistic sigh, he sat down and went back to work on the disabled gun for lack of anything better to do. Enrique was sound asleep in the front of the bus but dressed and ready to leave whenever Brad and Amanda said so.

Amanda nodded woodenly. A wall of silence had overtaken them. She was wrapped in guilt for attempting the venture and stubbornly wanting to continue. She wanted to be held by Brad, soothed, comforted. She gravitated to his side and sat down. He didn't look up, but she felt better from being near him. She watched absently. He was stuck. He didn't really know how to assemble the rifle correctly. How could he? He was only a silly banker. No! That was unfair.

"I'm sorry," she murmured. "I've not been very cooperative."

"Forget it." Brad trained a woeful grin on her. "If we get out of here alive, you can make it up to me."

She brightened. "Buy your dinner?"

"I had something else in mind."

"You're not angry?"

"At you? No! Waste of time. You know I love you, lady, hang-ups and all."

She kissed him tenderly on his scratchy, unshaved cheek, then sat back and watched him struggle with the gun.

"Uh, you've done a wonderful job assembling it."

"Thanks. But I've got a problem."

"I know. I used to have to fieldstrip rifles like this."

"You did?"

"It was Dad's idea of fun, but he'd rap my knuckles if I didn't do it fast enough to suit him."

"Well, that's one for Dad!" He offered the gun to her. "Can you tell me what's the matter with it?"

Amanda braced herself against her feelings and took hold of the heavy automatic rifle. Surprisingly, her mind busied itself only with the problem of assembly. "I don't know for sure, but I'll try to put it together, if you want me to."

"Want you to?" Brad smiled. "I'd love it. You know I've struggled with that stupid thing for hours."

"You've cleaned it up beautifully." She looked down the barrel against the dim glow of the lantern, checking the bore. "The barrel is in better shape than I thought." She flipped the weapon around, then began to fit the various parts with slow deliberation. Her spirits began to rise. "The trouble was with the operating rod spring and guide. Here's your connector lock. Hand me that firing mechanism." She stripped it in. "Now the connector assembly." Once she had the pieces together, she checked the fit. "Okay, now you put your finger on the rear release bracket and your second finger inside the rear of the receiver—"

"You won't cut off my fingers, will you?"

"Hope not. Just do as I say."

"Okay." He shrugged and followed her directions faithfully.

She was performing magic in front of Brad's eyes. She finished with the barrel assembly and stock group, popped in an empty twenty-cartridge magazine, turned the spindle valve and handed him the assembled piece.

He shook his head. "That's amazing. What did you do there at the last?"

"Oh, that. I moved the spindle valve away from the grenade firing position, which was on horizontal, and put it on vertical for automatic fire."

"Incredible. A woman doing that."

"Chauvinist," she said, smiling. "Nothing to it."

"Hey, that's talent. I couldn't figure out how to put it together correctly. I fieldstripped an M16 when I was in the army a number of years ago, but this old weapon baffled me."

"You'd have figured it out; it's similar. But you're right. This is an old weapon, obsolete, based on the old M1 Garand patent and modified for automatic fire with a bipod attached. It's in dangerously poor condition.''

"I'm impressed."

"Don't be. I still hate firearms," Amanda said grimly.

"So I gathered. Could I ask a question without offending you?"

Amanda knew what the question was; she should have remained silent, but she had opened the door to it. "Yes." She crossed her legs, feeling uncomfortable.

"What was the accident that killed your father?"

Even the question brought back a flood of suppressed memories. They were painful, but they had been threatening to surface more and more during the journey. Once again she could hear the wild firing, smell the spent powder, taste the fear and agony, touch the warm blood. She fought back hot tears.

"You don't have to tell me." Brad was filled with compassion at her obvious pain.

She swallowed down a jagged lump lodged in her throat. "No, It's all right." She cleared her throat again. "It was a fluke accident. I swore I'd never tell anyone, but I must have wanted to tell you, or I wouldn't have mentioned it in the first place. I've got to tell you now for my own peace of mind." She paused, then rushed on, determined to see it through and tell all.

"You see, right or wrong, we always had guns around. I grew up with them. My father was always supercautious. He taught me to do everything his way, the right way." Her voice grew dull and slowed as she strove for distance from the memory. Her eyes were unseeing, she stared out at the raging weather. "We were on the rifle range at the base, in off hours, a Saturday practice—not exactly according to regulations, but my dad did things in the army that no one else could get away with. Anyway, I'd gone along for the fun of it. I adored him, went everywhere with him. I was a military brat. My dad had been training several guys in automatic weapons' use and safety. It started to get late. I was in a hurry and wanted him to take me home. I yelled for him to hurry and finish practice. I guess I was bouncing up and down, doing gymnastic runs, somersaults, back flips." She sighed. "Showing off," she admitted with difficulty. "Distracting his men."

She drew her knees up to her chest and gripped them tightly. "One of his inexperienced men got flustered, and as my dad turned away, the guy looked at me strutting around—a teenager in shorts and halter—and accidentally tripped the trigger on an M14 automatic rifle. I know this sounds ludicrous. But it happened. I caused it to happen. It was horrifying."

"Good Lord." Brad grimaced at the image.

"The guy froze on the trigger. The weapon had been pointed at the ground, but it rode up and kept firing. My father was the only one hit. He wouldn't have been if he hadn't thrown himself at the weapon and deflected it from all the other men—and from me. He saved my life. But seeing that happen shattered my little bubble of invincibility. It was—just—horrible." She hid her head on her knees.

Brad was silent for a few moments, then gently took her in his arms and held her close, wanting to comfort her. "I can see why. I'm glad you told me. I apologize for riding you about your dad."

She clung to him, her arms tight about his neck, head digging into his warm chest.

Finally, she muttered against his shirt, "Don't worry about it. I guess it's all too late now. I know I have a lot of mental hang-ups." One tear escaped down her cheek. She cleared her throat and continued in a muffled voice, "I virtually withdrew from the world for a while, but I recovered eventually. I'm glad I told you." She issued a long, weighted sigh and ached with emptiness.

Brad hugged her closer, one hand cupped against the back of her head, the tousled dark curls against his palm. "So am I. But you're not going to give up, are you? I think we can get out of here well and healthy." His deep voice resonated in her mind.

"I wish I thought that."

He held her away from him, hands on her shoulders, and smiled directly into her face, beautiful to him even though tear-stained and forlorn. "Well, I'm no gunman. I'm just a stodgy banker. I don't really know why I'm here, but I have a plan."

That brought a gleam to her eyes. "You're not stodgy. In fact, for a banker, you're positively a superman. What's your plan?"

"It's nothing but a bluff. I say we should mount this machine gun on the hood of the bus, pretend it works and drive right past them. Intimidate them."

Amanda thought for a moment. "To tell the truth, I think we have to be bolder than that." She brightened and stood up, then began to pace the small area, trying to come up with an answer. She stopped and with a purposeful look braced her arms on her hips. "One thing my father taught me. Don't bluff unless you are forced to, and then if you do, prepare to do it in style. Charge right into the middle of them, all barrels blazing.''

"Oh, you have more guts than I think I have. What do you have in mind?" Brad held up the automatic rifle. "Remember, this barrel won't blaze."

"I know. We don't even dare test it for fear it either blows itself apart or just goes klunk. But I have an idea, too—a suicide mission—if you approve," she said with a solemn wink.

"Oh, oh. I can hardly wait to hear the details."

# Chapter Eighteen

Just before daylight the rain began to diminish. The storm had run its course. When Amanda climbed the bunker to reconnoiter, daybreak was chasing the cloudy remnants inland. The black cars were still waiting to flush out their quarry. Amanda scurried down to tell Brad.

They had worked the better part of the night. She was dirty and bruised, her elbow skinned and her fingernails broken. Stress and exhaustion and the damp salt air were making her skin itch all over. All the food was gone, and they were on their last bit of drinking water.

Timing was everything.

"Are we ready?" Amanda whispered hoarsely.

Brad's pant legs were rolled to his knees, and he was barefoot. His shirt was torn and marked with rust and grime. Enrique looked jolly. He had donned his red-and-gold devil's costume, which added carnival color to the scene. Off and on he would burst out with a mariachi melody.

"Sure are," Enrique sang out as he tied the last knot.

He stood back to admire the new look of the bus, the exterior of which was completely draped with cylinders strategically placed and lashed securely with the rope that had formerly bound them together. "Looks like armor," he judged approvingly. "Do I get to man the machine gun?" His devil's tail dragged on the ground as he strutted a couple of steps toward the automatic rifle, which was set upon its bipod on the hood of the bus.

"No!" Brad said abruptly, his nerves tensed to the breaking point. "You stay down and out of sight in the back. Amanda drives, and I'll be on the rifle."

"Then I should negotiate," Enrique pouted. "I'm a good negotiator."

"I know that." Amanda gave him a quick hug. "You're the best. But Brad looks meaner. Just look at that beard and his hair all plastered and wild. He looks really crazy." Her jaw set grimly. "He has to convince them he means to blow us all up if they try to move on us."

"I don't know," Enrique said doubtfully. "He doesn't look like he's got that killer instinct."

"The hell I don't," Brad growled. "For your information, I'm scared to death. But it's either bluff our way out or maybe get killed."

"At least if they fire at us, we'll be protected by all that Tri-Cola syrup. What a mess that'll be." Enrique chuckled. "Why didn't they trust you with the real stuff?"

Amanda's face fell. She shook her head. "I don't know why they risked our lives to carry Tri-Cola to Tampico. But they'd better have a damn good reason when I see Ms. Cullen again."

"Amen!" Brad grinned. "Let's go. Sun's coming up fast. Let's do this before I chicken out." He took his position on the hood, and Amanda tied cylinders in place to the right and left of him. She was ready to tie the last cylinder.

"Before I do this," she offered, "do you want a last sip of pure Tri-Cola energy?" Since she'd first opened the cylinder last night, they'd all taken an occasional taste of its contents. The syrup gave them energy, though the concentrated sugar burned up fast.

"No," Brad said. "Just tie it on." He settled down behind the rifle and leaned back against the middle of the windshield.

Amanda roped the last cylinder directly in front of the automatic rifle. "That okay?" she asked. "I think that one is enough."

"Right, let's go. Looks good to me." Nervously, Brad inserted a full clip of ammunition into the rifle and once more checked the automatic firing position. He said softly to the clip, "I only wish you could fire." The weapon looked surprisingly lethal; only a close inspection disclosed the corrosion and flaws.

Amanda climbed into the driver's seat. The old engine came to life at the first try. She shifted, and the bus edged forward, clanking like a thousand knights in rusty armor. The engine faltered and Amanda pumped the clutch and accelerator frantically. The bus backfired like a cannon, but its engine smoothed out, and the vehicle crept forward.

Guando, angry at the wait imposed on him by Zena Ballanger and stiff from spending the night in the limousine, heard what sounded like a shot from a heavy weapon at the bunker. His hand reached for the pistol next to him. So the Americans were finally going to make a break for it. He leaned on the horn, alerting his troops. Heavily armed and ready, his six trusted, reliable henchmen piled out of their car.

Zena Ballanger stepped from the adjoining limousine.

Guando both feared and grudgingly admired the beautiful, vibrant woman with the fiery temper who went by the masculine name of El Tigre. And woe to anyone who objected to the name or feminized it. It was rumored to have been given by her terrorist father when she was young. He had ordered her to kill a man, and she had done so immediately and without remorse. Since those days, she had killed only when forced to by circumstance. But if she had to kill, she would do so with deadly accuracy and efficiency. El Tigre was a tiger indeed.

She had masterminded this operation perfectly. She had correctly deduced that the Americans were the ones who really were carrying the entire supply of the secret catalyst. What a bonanza to obtain from a bureaucratic mistake. Now El Tigre would get not only a small amount to test but the entire supply. Her organization would reap great profit from the highest bidder. Brilliant!

And how perfect that El Tigre had extracted the information about the *Grand Finale* from the congressman Slater only minutes after he'd learned it from the American ambassador. She had passed the word to Guando, who had found the fishing boat and it was only bad luck that he had not trapped the Americans there. Guando stepped from his limousine.

"Stand by to block them," El Tigre ordered. "Under no circumstances let that bus go by us. But no firing. One bullet in those cylinders would blow us all away. Be cautious."

"But of course!" Guando assured her smoothly. "I'm not a fool."

"No, Guando. You've done quite well. Now, how long will it take to transfer all of the cylinders to the boat?"

Before he could answer, the hood of the bus appeared at the corner of the bunker. The entire vehicle came into full view, cylinders clanking and swaying and bouncing dangerously. El Tigre flinched involuntarily.

Guando replied in a hurried monotone, "The vessel will be at the beach twenty minutes after we have the catalyst."

"Excellent. You will transfer to the submarine as soon as contact is made. Everything is arranged at the island. Deploy your men. Now!" El Tigre snapped.

Guando jerked away. He hastily signaled his men to follow his lead, but as the bus continued toward his position, he muttered warily, "What is going on? What is that crazy gringo doing?"

Brad, looking like a madman, was yelling at the six gunmen. Guando would have liked to pick him off, silence him, but the man was sitting behind a machine gun aimed directly at one of the cylinders.

"Where in the world did that machine gun come from?" Ballanger hissed, glancing nervously at Guando. "She told me she hated guns. Don't make any sudden moves. Let me talk to them. Their position is hopeless, but they may be dangerous."

Zena looked more like a vivacious fashion plate out for a day at the beach than a deadly terrorist as she strode confidently to meet her foe. The long, full sleeves of her crimson silk jump suit billowed in the breeze. She waved cheerily with both hands and smiled to show she carried nothing to harm them. Guando and his men hung back menacingly.

Amanda brought the bus to a halt and trained her eyes on her enemy.

"Good morning, Amanda," Zena said lightly, ignoring Brad and the rifle. "I'm glad you've finally come to your senses."

Amanda felt hopelessly inferior. Nothing about her even hinted at glamour. She and her sweat suit were grimy, and her hair was stiff from sand and rain. It was days since she had even thought of makeup. How could Zena look so terrific and be so friendly? Zena's expensive perfume wafted toward the bus.

An urge to give up and hand over the cylinders edged into Amanda's mind. They could flee. But she knew, Zena of course, couldn't be trusted.

"I've nothing to say." Amanda's chin shot up in defiance.

"Just stay where you are, Ms. Ballanger," Brad interrupted. "I don't want any trouble out of you people or I'll blow this load to hell and wipe out that bunch with you at the same time."

"Now, there's no need to be hostile," Zena said smoothly, without looking at Brad. "You can walk away from this. We only want your cargo. I don't want anyone hurt. It's not worth it." Zena's clear green eyes held no menace; she radiated confidence, truth and warmth. "Amanda, I know you have no reason to be here."

That was certainly the truth. "But I am here." Amanda motioned toward Guando. "He's been trying to kill us since before we left Mexico City."

Zena frowned. "I'm sorry about the way he's treated you," she replied earnestly. "He's an animal. It was only yesterday that I found out how badly he'd dealt with you. He was determined to attack then, but

I stopped him. I detest violence. There are civilized ways to gain our ends.''

"And what are those ends?''

"I want only the catalyst. The American government doesn't deserve to have it. Neither do their opponents. I intend simply to let one side or the other ransom it. It's only a matter of money. I promise you, I want no one hurt. Guando will not touch you. I swear it. Please believe me.''

"How can I believe you?'' Amanda wished to God she could trust the sincere face in front of her.

Brad fidgeted, nervously keeping his hand in place on the gun. Why was Amanda listening to that woman? He wanted her to just bluff and go, to get the hell out of there.

Zena Ballanger held Amanda's eyes. "Because I'm telling the truth. Politicians have plunged this world into a terrible mess. There's no use in any of us dying to enrich international bankers and governments that don't care. You know the United States cares nothing for you, or you would already have received help. That ass Slater told me you were to be cut adrift. What are you fighting for? A country that won't back you up?''

Zena's words rang with truth. Amanda recalled what Ms. Cullen had said. Once the cylinders were in her care, she was on her own and could expect no help. Amanda wanted to believe Zena. If only Guando weren't there with the guns.

As though Zena had read her mind, she exclaimed, "I'll prove what I say is true.'' She turned to her men. "Guando,'' she ordered, "put down your guns. All of you.'' When Guando looked as though he was going to protest, she ordered sharply, "Now!'' All the men hastily laid their weapons on the ground. "Now all of you, go back to the cars. We will let these people go.''

The men began to retreat sulkily. Zena turned back to Amanda. "I despise that man. He won't dare harm you." There were tears of sincerity in her eyes.

"You'll let us go?" Amanda queried. "With the cylinders?"

Zena nodded. "I will. To save bloodshed—though I wish you would leave them. It'll be difficult to control those animals after you leave."

Amanda began to hope. Why shouldn't they leave the cylinders?

"I hate this confrontation with you. We could be friends. Think about Enrique. He's only a child. He has his whole life ahead of him."

Amanda felt that everything about the situation was her fault.

"Hey, lady, don't you worry about me," Enrique piped up. "I'm doing fine."

Brad grimaced. Zena had confirmed that Enrique was present. He could see her mind at work. Divide and conquer. "Just keep those guys away and let us leave the beach," he yelled angrily.

Zena was unruffled. "Fine. Fine," she agreed reasonably. "Just leave one of the cylinders. That will keep them busy. They've been promised a lot of money, but I'll force them to let you go. I promise. I'll protect you from these people."

Zena sounded so rational. Amanda wanted to shout to Brad, change the plan, give her a cylinder. Surely a cylinder would win their freedom. The woman wanted no bloodshed. What could it hurt to give the woman a container of Tri-Cola?

Brad's eyes darted to Amanda. She was weakening. He knew it; she knew it.

Zena was crying. "Oh, please, Amanda, I can't stand the pressure of this confrontation any longer.

Let's end this futility,'' she pleaded, now looking beyond Amanda to the brightening sky. "We are so much alike we could have been sisters. Please?"

Amanda could no longer resist. She glanced at Brad. He, too, knew it was over.

Amanda turned back to Zena. For a moment she hesitated, mesmerized by the woman's jade-green eyes staring dazedly out to sea. Zena had won; Amanda knew the meaning of luck, and Zena was born with it. She turned her eyes away and saw what Zena was watching. Four black specks were approaching in the distance. It was too late. Zena must have been stalling until her henchmen were reinforced.

"All right," Amanda said dejectedly, "you've won—"

Zena had backed away. She turned and ran rapidly back to her limousine, attempting to put distance between herself and the bus.

They were going to blow up the bus! Amanda was confused but angry. "Not without a fight, you won't," she screamed, shifting the bus into gear. She stomped the accelerator to the floor. Why wait around to be blasted by helicopters?

The move caught Brad unaware, and he nearly fell off. He held on for his life as Amanda turned the bus in a tight, backfiring turn. The entire group of men, clustered at the cars without their weapons, flung themselves to the ground.

Brad clung to the hood, his feet dragging the ground like a bulldogging cowboy. "Get the hell out of here, Amanda," he shouted.

The bus responded with a wheeze and a puff of smoke, then ground to a halt.

The thunder of the landing helicopters blanketed the beach. Amanda's head spun, her ears ached, her heart pounded her breath away; still she fought to start the recalcitrant engine.

Suddenly her concentration was snapped. Brad was at her side, shouting something she couldn't hear.

"Leave me alone," she yelled, wrestling with the obstinate bus.

"It's okay. It's okay," Brad kept saying. "Look!"

Amanda's anger and tears gave away to the realization that the situation had changed. Guando, Ballanger and the other six were being rounded up by men wearing green fatigues and carrying automatic weapons.

Her hands dropped from the wheel. Margaret Cullen stepped from one of the helicopters. She ran forward, arms outstretched, and hugged Brad. What was Ms. Cullen doing here?

"Hey," a voice came from the rear of the bus. "Can I come out now? I think something's wrong with the bus."

"Come on out." Amanda's voice was dazed. "I think the marines have just landed." She watched the soldiers efficiently herd together Zena Ballanger and her men and move them closer to the bus.

"Amanda," Ms. Cullen enthused, "I'm so happy and grateful that everything has worked out so well. I thought the storm would never clear. That was a magnificent move to draw them all together for us as soon as the storm ended. Perfect timing."

"That was pure luck," Amanda stated grimly. Her mind rioted with bitterness and angry questions.

But Margaret Cullen was talking fast. "Amanda, because of your ability, we've cracked a very difficult ring. We've caught the leader herself." Ms. Cullen glanced over at Zena Ballanger, who glared back at her, haughtily ignoring the guards busily shackling her men. "I think we'll be able to make a multitude of charges stick and put that woman away for many years. She's had access to untold secrets, and she's one of the most dangerous criminals in the world, the infamous person known as El Tigre."

Amanda remembered Zena's tears. She doubted the charge. Zena wanted no harm to come to anyone. Ms. Cullen was the more dangerous, Amanda thought secretly. Why had she sent them on this chase to nowhere? Why not find out right now? Amanda turned to Ms. Cullen, ready to demand why she had risked their lives to deliver worthless cylinders? But suddenly her attention was diverted. The scene before her slipped into horrifying slow motion.

Zena Ballanger moved with the swiftness of a cat. Effortlessly, she eluded her guards and leaped onto the hood of the bus. Before anyone could react, she had control of the automatic rifle, and worse, she knew what she was doing. She slipped the weapon off safety and chambered a round. Aimed directly at the cylinder in front of it, the weapon was now armed and ready to fire. Everyone froze in anguish. Ms. Cullen turned pale.

"I'll blow up this bus and all of you to hell if anyone moves. Now, release Guando," Ballanger snapped.

"Don't anyone move," Ms. Cullen warned. "She means it."

Amanda walked calmly forward. If the rifle was fired, it would blow up in Zena's face. Amanda had to stop her.

"Zena," Amanda called out as she approached, "you didn't want anyone hurt. I saw those tears. Don't try to fire that weapon. You can't do it. It won't work. I know you care about people, about lives."

"And you're a sentimental fool, Amanda Perry," Zena Ballanger spat. "Just stay where you are. And don't try any of your famous father's tactics, because you'll fail. You may have bought my story, but I'll wipe out all of you rather than fail myself."

Amanda was concerned only about the danger to Zena; the cylinders were harmless. She knew she could stop the woman if she could move fast enough and with no hesitation. She tried to remember a trick her father had taught her years ago, a standing back flip that could remove a person from danger when executed properly. It was almost like one of her gymnastic moves.

Amanda turned away as though to leave, instead, she gathered her strength and neatly executed the difficult flip. She felt her feet connect with Zena's shoulder as everything spun about her. She was vaguely aware of someone screaming, of people diving out of the way, of the M14 firing. It was firing on and on and on. Impossible! Amanda felt herself overbalance and she took Zena with her to the ground. Then she was back on the rifle range at the base and screaming, "No! No, Daddy! No!"

IT WAS OVER. Zena lay on the ground, stunned and unhurt but shackled. Amanda came to her senses slowly. Brad was hovering over her.

"I'm sorry," Amanda babbled. "Is she okay?"

"Yes, she's fine, but you hurt your arm when you hit the ground."

Amanda's arm felt numb, but she was more interested in the rifle. It had fired all twenty rounds into the cylinder in front of it, which was oozing Tri-Cola syrup everywhere.

"That was a very foolhardy move," Ms. Cullen scolded. "You might have killed yourself and everyone here."

Amanda saw red. "I suppose risking our lives for fifty worthless cylinders and a nonexistent desalination plant was your warped idea of patriotism."

"What are you raving about?" Ms. Cullen demanded.

Brad leaped into the fray. "You know perfectly well what she means. What is leaking from that cylinder?"

Margaret Cullen flipped her head impatiently. "It's syrup, of course. You're an extremely lucky young woman, Amanda. I admit you made a very daring and spectacular move to stop Ballanger, but if those bullets had hit any cylinder other than that one, we'd all be dead."

Amanda had grown faint and sick at her stomach. The pain in her arm had increased. On his knees beside her, Brad supported her in his arms. "What are you saying?" she said weakly.

"I'm saying that it was lucky you had the machine gun aimed at that one cylinder. The one with the yellow relief valve is the only cylinder with syrup in it. It was our decoy in case it was needed. The others—the ones with red valves—contain the catalyst."

Her words hit with full force. "You mean they're all real?" Amanda nearly blacked out. Brad quickly stretched her out on the sand, stroked her forehead and watched her silently as his mother spoke on.

"Of course they're all real. You don't think we went through this for nothing, do you?" Ms. Cullen snorted.

"But where's the Padre plant?" Brad demanded. "This beach is a wasteland."

Margaret pointed toward the Gulf. "Do you see that oil platform a couple of miles off the beach? That's the Padre plant. It's disguised to look like a drilling rig. There was no need to inform you of all that. When you landed here, one of our helicopters spotted you, but then the storm closed in and grounded us temporarily. You both went beyond what I thought was possible. You're to be congratulated. I believe you've performed the greatest service your country could ever ask—even though you went too far and almost ruined everything."

"Just drop it!" Brad said. "Can't you see this isn't the time for a patriotic pep talk?"

Amanda moaned. Brad settled her head on his shoulder and cuddled her tenderly. Enrique sat anxiously beside them.

Amanda was tired and in pain. The mission was over. She had completed it, but at a fearful price.

A tide of regret washed over her. She had nearly killed them all through ignorance and vanity and bravado. She could never face any of them again, especially Brad. He couldn't possibly respect her after all that had happened.

Time was what she needed, time to sort out the bitter lessons she had learned.

# Chapter Nineteen

Sweat streamed from Amanda's shiny flushed face and all the way down her legs. Her hot-pink leotards were soaked. Slippery with perspiration, her hands made the balance beam slick as she repeated her intricate routines time and again, forcing herself toward perfection. She'd been working out for over two hours and was determined to get the routines right. She repeated the final movements one last time, swung into the dismount position, then followed through with a fair landing, marred only by a quick step backward to keep her balance.

"Terrific, perfect," said Chris Hubbard. He clapped his hands appreciatively. The sound made a hollow echo through the empty gym.

"Not even close," Amanda said. "Next time." Automatically she started to scrub her hands dry in preparation for another try, then winced. Once she was into the workout, pain-deadening endorphins made her forget her strained left arm. It was healing slowly. Meanwhile, she concentrated on routines in which she used her right arm exclusively. Nursing the damaged arm was tricky and required even greater concentration than usual.

"If I could only do that," her assistant said wistfully.

"Ready for the somersault again?" she prodded.

"A forward dive only. I did ten sets, and the rollovers. Ugh!" He rubbed his side. Crouched by an exercise mat, clad in ancient gym shorts and a heavy sweatshirt with "Harvard" across the front, he looked like an overweight bear. He wasn't a bad student, just not very well coordinated. "I've really enjoyed what you've shown me, really," he groaned, and sat down in his warm-up position.

"Don't overdo it. Just take your time learning. No need to go fast."

Chris went back to work on the simple basic tumbling Amanda had taught him, and while he grumbled and groaned, he kept an eye on Amanda, wishing she would follow her own advice.

This early Saturday morning, with only Chris working on the routines she had promised to teach him, the health club gymnasium was deserted. That was what Amanda needed. Since returning to Mexico City a month ago, she had preferred solitude. As long as she put in ten-hour days at the Tri-Cola plant and lost herself in strenuous workouts for two or three hours early in the morning or late at night, her isolation was assured.

With her mind focused on business or on perfect physical coordination, she strove to block out all thought of those days with Brad and what might have been. She sought an inner balance in her life. She was still trying to reconcile the Amanda she thought she was with the Amanda who had so closely imitated her father. All those years she had struggled to be his antithesis, only to discover that she had failed. Where in all this was the real Amanda?

She was awakened every night by nightmares replaying the terrors of her mission, and during the day the last hours at Padre returned incessantly to her mind.

In her exhaustion she had been desperate to escape from everything and everyone that was pressing in on her, even Brad.

In spite of her efforts, she could not block memories of Brad and their wrenching goodbye. She was haunted by the memory of his agonized face as they stood in the wind made by a helicopter ready to whisk her off to the Brownsville airport. He had intended to go with her, but she'd made it clear that she wanted to be alone. Her life had been changed forcefully. She needed time.

*Your mind's wandering! Shape up, Amanda. You're only wasting time this morning,* she remonstrated with herself.

Tiredly, she picked up her towel from the exercise mat and wiped the back of her neck and the dark, wet tendrils that fell from her absorbent terry headband. As she dabbed at her temples, a lone silhouetted male figure in the doorway of the gym captured her attention. Amanda's breath caught; her heart skipped and thudded raggedly.

Brad! He'd come to get her.

She was overwhelmed with relief. No more analysis—only joy remained. She was his, yes, yes! He had come to her. Perhaps he had forgiven all the pain she'd caused him. She turned away and dabbed her towel at her eyes and forehead, then brushed her hair with her fingers. How did he find her here? Harvey was the only person other than Chris who knew where she was this morning. Chris, twenty feet away, was absorbed in his practice.

Amanda turned back and looked closely at the approaching figure. It wasn't Brad; it was Harvey. He'd come to pick her up for their tennis game. Her heart sank to her stomach.

She mustn't let her disappointment show. He'd been so patient.

"Amanda," Harvey called. "Good morning. How's it going?" He glanced briefly in the direction of Chris Hubbard and nodded stiffly. Chris self-consciously rose to his feet, unable to work with others present, especially someone as critical as Harvey.

"I'm doing fine," Amanda responded dully. Impulsively sublimating her disappointment, she threw down her towel and made one final, blistering run across the mat, dove into a double flip, tucked her legs under herself and somersaulted twice in the air, then nailed her landing rock steady at the far edge of the mat. Chris applauded.

"Beautiful!" Harvey congratulated. He came up and gave her a peck on the cheek. She didn't withdraw; she felt safe with Harvey. Not happy but safe. He looked at her soulfully.

She returned his look. "What is it, Harvey?"

He motioned toward Chris. "May we go somewhere to talk? I have something to say to you."

"I have no secrets from Chris."

"I was just leaving," Chris said, taking the hint.

"You really should treat him better," Amanda said when Chris was gone. "He's trying hard. He's loyal to me, and he wasn't responsible for the information leak. That was Congressman Slater's doing."

"Oh, I know that," Harvey responded. "Hubbard's not a bad sort. But how was I to know he was just trying to get an autograph from that fool Slater that day I saw him at the embassy?"

"He was at the embassy checking out information for me. And fool or not, Chris happens to admire the congressman. He was embarrassed when you caught him getting Slater's autograph. That's why he looked so guilty."

"Yes, yes. So you've said." Harvey shook his head. "Enough of your assistant. It's good you're shaping him up, but I'm concerned about you."

"Me?"

"Amanda, dear, you don't make this easy."

"What? What are you trying to say?"

"I'm trying to say that I can't stand any more of this martyrdom of yours. You're so damned unhappy, so miserable. I can't bear it any longer."

"Harvey, I'm trying to do everything right now. I'm back. I'm straightened out. Strictly business from now on. I'm getting my life in order."

"Said the condemned woman."

"What do you mean?" Amanda demanded.

"Simple. You're so in love with that man Bradford that you can't see anything else in the world. Breaking our engagement was the right thing to do. But now you seem determined to act like an automaton in my presence, a robot, because— I believe, you feel you're a failure at obtaining perfection."

"Perfection? I thought we talked this all out when I came back. I explained my failures. I thought you understood."

"Exactly. You were an emotionally stressed person when you returned. Yes, I was angry with you for about twenty minutes after I left you at the airport in Tampico, but I got over it. I know we are not suited for each other. But you, Amanda, are human, not a machine. You may not be able to face the love you have for Bradford, but you cannot continue working yourself to death because you think I might call in your loans or because you think I disapprove of him or wish you to come back to me. I do not wish to become involved with you or anyone else for the moment. Do you understand?''

She blinked and nodded, nervously twisting her towel.

Harvey explained, ''I'm a bachelor and likely to remain one. But I, too, have feelings. You do understand, don't you? We are business associates. I don't want to walk on eggs in your presence.''

She knew he was right. ''All right, Harvey,'' she said with a defeated sigh, ''I admit it. I do love Brad.'' Unwelcome tears sprang to her eyes. She brushed them away with the back of her hand. ''But I've made so many mistakes. I've made so many wrong judgments. I nearly got everyone killed by doing the very same thing I condemned my dad for doing. I've lost respect for my own judgment.''

''Oh, horse briquettes!'' he snorted vehemently.

She had to smile in spite of her tears. That was extremely undignified, very un-Harvey, yet he was proper to the end. She winced away from his stare. ''Brad has no faith in me.''

''You're just feeling sorry for yourself. You want someone to baby you. Grow up, Amanda! Don't lose him.'' Harvey looked a little shaken by his own forthrightness. ''I hate to talk to you like a father, but someone has to; you're so stubborn. Show a little backbone. Go after him.''

Her spine straightened. A burden had been lifted. Harvey was right except in one thing—she'd already lost Brad. Brad had gone back to the States. He hadn't come back to Mexico City. Harvey had found that out.

"I don't know where he is, but I think you're right." She absently massaged her tender arm. "I don't think he still cares, but I'll try to find him."

"Thank goodness you're talking sense at last." Harvey exhaled heavily and crossed his arms over his clean white knit polo shirt. "As a reward, I shall even attempt to trust your assistant in the future."

"Now shall we go play tennis?"

He glanced at his watch. "That depends. I'm going over to the courts right now. I have to meet someone there in ten minutes, but I left the car out front. I'll get Hubbard to drop me off at the court, so drive over when you're ready." He cheerfully kissed Amanda on the cheek and walked out.

She picked up her towel, slung it around her neck, then stood alone in the solitary gymnasium, hypnotized by the shafts of light that slanted across the gleaming hardwood floor. Her mood plummeted again; she wasn't exactly sorry for herself but terribly aware that she was the root of her own problem. She'd held Brad at bay, loving him but not ready to commit herself to him fully—too much shadowboxing with fears and doubts. She should have phoned him the very day he sent that truckload of flowers—roses, tulips, lilies, daffodils, iris and even ranunculus. He must have emptied every flower shop in Mexico City. His card had read simply, "Please know I love you." She should have returned his calls. She should have had her act together when they met. But she should have come to terms with her fears much sooner, and not lost herself in her own misery.

She was sick of shoulds!

Only just a few minutes ago, when she thought Harvey was Brad, she had responded freely and eagerly. She was obviously ready for Brad but once again had failed to know her own true feelings.

She snapped her towel angrily and started for the dressing room. The front door of the club opened, then closed. She glanced up. Harvey had come back. He stood in the shadowed doorway once more. Again, Amanda had the haunting feeling that it was Brad she was seeing. This time she didn't turn away. She stood her ground and watched him cross the room into a patch of sunlight that revealed him fully. She caught her breath with a gasp. It *was* Brad. He approached her now, looking gaunt, as if he'd lost weight.

"Hello, Amanda."

She felt naked, as self-conscious as a twelve-year-old. She didn't know what to say. "B-Brad. Good morning." Oh, how formal, how wrong. He nodded, his hands me face serious. Amanda had never felt more awk ard. She fought for something to say. "Uh, how's the us?" Why did she say that? Her voice came out inordinately stiff.

"Oh, yes, the bus. My mother's not thrilled, but it's completely overhauled and redone. Enrique saw to that." Brad's breath was ragged; he attempted a chuckle. "You should see it. My bank and my bank account may never recover from this last month." He became silent.

Guilt and sympathy played across her embarrassed face. "Uh, how's Enrique doing?"

"He's fine. What else?" Brad seemed more comfortable with this subject. "Did you know his relatives own half of San Antonio and he's a personal friend of the mayor? He stayed in San Antonio with the bus while the mechanics restored it, and then he and some cousin drove it back down here. He's hoping to get back to San Antonio and became an aide to the mayor. I guess you haven't talked to him.''

Amanda had to smile at the thought of Enrique. ''No, I haven't talked to him—or anyone—other than Harvey.'' She wanted to feel Brad's arms around her but didn't want to make the wrong move. It was so great to see him. He looked wonderful—if thinner—in his white tennis outfit, just like the first day they had met. If only—

He seemed uneasy. ''Well, you certainly look good. Back to normal. Life here agrees with you.''

No, she wanted to say, I've been miserable and lonely, but she nodded instead.

He took the nod for dismissal.

''I guess I shouldn't have—come—umm—bothered your workout.'' He cut his eyes away and looked over her head.

''No, it's all right. I'm finished.'' She fell silent, unable to think of anything else to say. They stood facing each other, yet averted their eyes.

''Okay.'' He put his hands in his pockets, then withdrew them. He was obviously as nervous as she, afraid of saying the wrong thing. Why? He had everything going for him. He cleared his throat, seemed about to speak, but didn't.

Amanda fumbled for words to cover her anxiety. Anything to keep him talking, hold him with her a minute or two longer. ''And your mother?'' she asked hurriedly.

He gave a faint chuckle then he raised his hands in exasperation but began to talk more freely. ''Still as tricky as ever.'' He shook his head. ''We had a terrible row over the ethics of my trading her Jaguar for a bus. I'm still working that out. However, she recommended you for a couple of dozen presidential citations, of course.''

"I didn't want any glory. I still don't.''

"I know. But her mind works that way. She and I had a few pitched battles and a standoff on executive orders and the ethics of her patriotic badgering of you. You're aware that she sent dummy cylinders out in two other directions. At the president's request, she was determined to catch the ringleaders and the person known as El Tigre.'' He still kept a discreet distance.

"No, I didn't know any of that. But it doesn't surprise me. I was so sure that our cylinders were dummies. Now I know I was the dummy.'' She was filled with scorn at her own poor judgment. "I didn't believe there was a desalinization plant. And I actually believed Zena Ballanger was going to let us go. That was an error, too.''

"Not an error at all. I talked to Zena Ballanger later. I believe she may have been sincere when she said she would let us go. Later, when cornered, she changed her tactics. She was doing her job as she saw it. She'd restrained Guando from violence before. He disdained working for a woman even if he was afraid of her. I didn't know—in the international conspiracy business there's a fine line between bad guys and the good guys. Margaret and Slater being cases in point. Sometimes there's a little good and a little bad in everyone. The thing is, Amanda, try to keep from losing faith in yourself just because heroes, people, even situations, don't turn out as you thought they would. It's just the nature of life. And we all have clay feet. We're all human.''

Very slowly he extended his hand to her. Shyly, she took hold of it. Then she looked up, and their eyes locked in mutual love.

"I guess you're right," she murmured, suspended in the deep blue depths of eyes that were as full of yearning as she felt. Her hand in his seemed electric with messages. It was hard to concentrate. "My wild swings of mood, my raving—"

"Wasn't raving, it was interesting. Hope you won't accuse me of raving. I'm not too good at this." He shifted his weight and held her hand tenderly, wanting her in his arms. He hardly knew what he was saying. He simply lingered in the yielding warmth of her gaze. Was he welcome, or was he kidding himself?

"I—I want—uh, thanks for the flowers. I apologize for the way I've acted. I'm sorry I couldn't—didn't call." She swallowed for courage. "I thought about it and thought, and then it seemed too much time had passed and it was too late to call. I guess I was feeling sorry for myself." She lowered her head, her voice but a whisper. "I've gone through hell without you, Brad. I've relived the whole thing, every minute. I—I was a terrible leader."

Tentatively, he took her other hand, all the while gazing at her with a dreamy smile. He gently placed both her hands behind his waist and encircled her with his arms.

She lifted her face to his and loved the strength of his body against hers. She molded herself to him.

He sighed with immense pleasure. "Don't you believe it. You're a great leader. I wasn't so hot myself. I swear to God, I never thought that rifle would fire."

She cuddled her head on his chest. "I didn't think it would, either. Thank goodness we only put that one safe container in front of it." She tightened her arms about him, and he pressed his palms against her back reassuringly.

"Right! Which you did on purpose. Perhaps, somewhere in the back of your mind, you were taking no chances."

"I don't know."

Holding her, he felt reassured. Coming back had been the right thing. "Forget all that for the moment. This is what's important."

Brad reached into the pocket of his shorts and brought out a small black box. Nervously, he held out an exquisite ring that sparkled with square-cut rubies, emeralds and diamonds. "Amanda, my love. I'm not good at speeches," he said huskily. "But I think the universe was made for love. I believe that we, you and I, female and male, are what makes this planet go round. And I want you to marry me—immediately— for richer, for poorer. We'll work everything out."

Brad took Amanda's unresisting hand and slipped the glittering ring on her finger. It fit perfectly. Amanda's smile competed with the brilliance of the gems. She found enough breath to whisper, "Yes! Oh, yes."

His head dropped down, his lips quivering as they tenderly found hers, wonderfully salty and sweet. She slipped her arms around his neck and hugged him as if never to let him go.

Their kiss deepened in a rush of commitment. His arms surrounded her body, and his hands roamed across her hips. Already exhilarated, now afire with longing, Amanda clung to his kiss, losing herself in his arms. His head moved away a fraction, his dark eyes intense with longing. "I love you madly, Amanda Perry, till the day after forever."

Her head spun. "Oh, I truly love you, Brad. God, it feels great to say that! I love Forrest Cullen Bradford, or whatever your name is! In any case, it's a much better name than Harvey Bannon.''

Harvey—Harvey was waiting at the tennis court.

"Brad," she said, embarrassed, "I'm supposed to meet Harvey over at—''

"The tennis courts," Brad finished for her. "Don't worry. He's well taken care of." Brad grinned. "I don't want to hear any more protests. I don't want you to have any more guilt feelings. We're quite a team. We'll make it just fine."

"But," Amanda protested weakly, "he left his car for me. He's expecting me."

"No, dear. The bus is out front, parked and waiting. I'm the one who must apologize this time. I set you up for this. I asked Harvey to help me win you back. When I walked in here with Harvey this morning, I had to let you two talk first. I chickened out when I saw you doing your routines, so confident, so perfect and so complete within yourself."

"I wasn't confident. I was lonesome."

"Me, too. I almost walked away. But Harvey stopped me. He came in to talk to you and smooth the way. I didn't know if you'd accept me or not. Anyway, Harvey and my mother are over at the courts playing tennis. He's become quite fond of her, and she is just tricky enough to make him my new father."

Amanda gasped. "I had no idea. But I doubt she's that tricky. Harvey's a confirmed bachelor. He told me so only today."

"Just speculation. You're probably right. Both have their rigid ways. In any case, I don't think they expect us to come over unless we can't think of anything better to do with our time together." He began to lead her across the gymnasium toward the front door. "The bus is waiting out front for us to take us on our honeymoon wherever we wish. It's completely rigged out for that one purpose. Just you and I alone this time. How about it?''

''Sounds wonderful. But we still have so much to work out. My job. Your job. We're worlds apart on some things.''

''It'll make life all that much more interesting. We'll work it all out even if I spend the rest of my life commuting.''

''You won't,'' she promised. She relaxed back into his arms holding her hand to admire the fire glancing from her ring. ''The colors of Mexico. Pretty confident, weren't you?''

Confidence was catching. As long as she and Brad were together, she could do anything, stand any pressure. She could let Nathan Perry's ghost rest and forget the past. The future was all-important. Amanda knew with certainty that everything was as it should be.

Harlequin Intrigue
Because romance can be quite an adventure.
Available wherever paperbacks are sold or through
Harlequin Reader Service
In the U.S.
901 Fuhrmann Blvd.
P.O. Box 1325
Buffalo, N.Y. 14269
In Canada
P.O. Box 2800, Station "A"
5170 Yonge Street
Willowdale, Ontario M2N 6J3
INT-6R